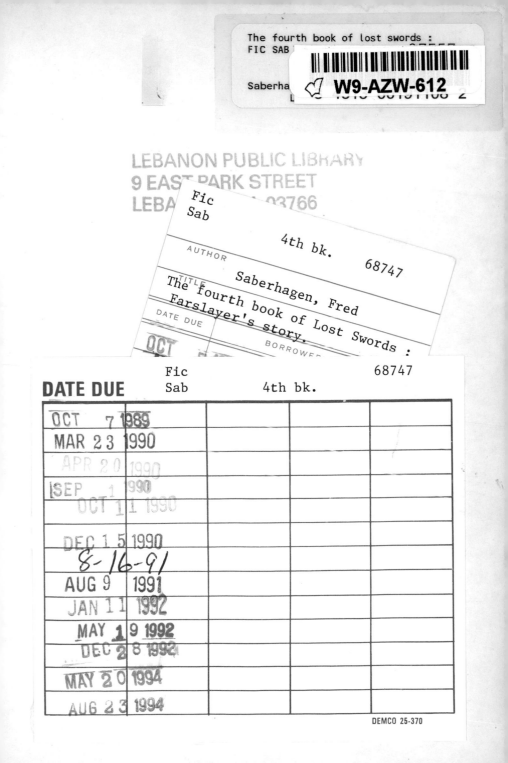

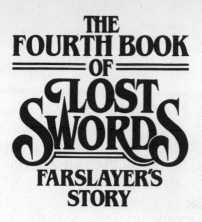

THE FOURTH BOOK OF LOST SWORDS
FARSLAYER'S STORY

Tor Books by Fred Saberhagen

BERSERKER BASE (with Anderson, Bryant,
  Donaldson, Niven, Willis, and Zelazny)
BERSERKER: BLUE DEATH
THE BERSERKER THRONE
THE BERSERKER WARS
A CENTURY OF PROGRESS
COILS (with Roger Zelazny)
THE DRACULA TAPE
EARTH DESCENDED
THE HOLMES–DRACULA FILE
THE FIRST BOOK OF SWORDS
THE SECOND BOOK OF SWORDS
THE THIRD BOOK OF SWORDS
THE FIRST BOOK OF LOST SWORDS:
  Woundhealer's Story
THE SECOND BOOK OF LOST SWORDS:
  Sightblinder's Story
THE THIRD BOOK OF LOST SWORDS: Stonecutter's
  Story
THE FOURTH BOOK OF LOST SWORDS: Farslayer's
  Story
THE VEILS OF AZLAROC

THE FOURTH BOOK OF LOST SWORDS

FARSLAYER'S STORY

FRED SABERHAGEN

TOR
fantasy

A TOM DOHERTY ASSOCIATES BOOK
NEW YORK

068717

THE FOURTH BOOK OF LOST SWORDS:
FARSLAYER'S STORY

Copyright © 1989 by Fred Saberhagen

A TOR BOOK
Published by Tom Doherty Associates, Inc.
49 West 24 Street
New York, NY 10010

First edition: July 1989
0 9 8 7 6 5 4 3 2 1

PROLOGUE

IN the middle of the day the black-haired mermaid was drifting carelessly in a summery river, letting herself be carried slowly through the first calm pool in the Tungri below the thunder of the cataract. It was a pool that was almost big enough to be called a lake, surrounded by the greenery and bitter memories of the shores.

Her name was Black Pearl, and she had been a mermaid now for something like six years, even though she had been born with two good legs and no tail at all, into a family of fisherfolk seemingly as far removed as anyone could be from magic.

Black Pearl's pale face, now framed by the water, held an expression of intent listening, as if she might be trying to read some information from the open sky. Her black hair swirled in the water around her head, her small breasts poked above the surface. Drifting immobile now, holding her tail perfectly still, she was allowing the current to carry her out of the broad pool which was almost a lake, on a course that would take her between the two islands that were the most prominent features of this portion of the river.

To judge by the expression on Black Pearl's face, if the

sky was indeed trying to tell her anything, she did not care for the message it conveyed.

Mermaids' Island, overgrown now with summer's own green magic, slid by to the mermaid's north, on her left hand as she floated on her back. Magicians' Island, somewhat smaller and stranger and somewhat less green, with a certain aura of the forbidden about it, would soon be passing to her south.

According to her own best calculation, Black Pearl had recently turned eighteen years of age, at the beginning of the summer. She knew, therefore, that she had not very many years of life remaining. Mermaids, fishgirls, of her age never did. Black Pearl's mother would be able to remember her age with accuracy, she supposed. But for years now her mother had no longer wanted to come to the shore and talk with her. If, indeed, her mother was still alive. A long time had passed since Black Pearl had tried to see any of her relatives.

As for the bitter memories—

Somewhere to the south and west of where she drifted now, no more than a few kilometers over the water, was Black Pearl's home village—though it was home to her no longer. Now, the only semblance of a home she knew was Mermaids' Island. Her only family were the two dozen or so other fishgirls inhabiting this stretch of the Tungri, and with many of them Black Pearl did not get on at all.

If she made the effort, and sent her mind groping under a cloud of black and evil magic for the appropriate memories, Black Pearl could vaguely recall being caught, lured ashore from these waters three or four years ago. Caught in a net, and sold, and carried upstream riding in a tank of water carried in a wagon driven by strangers. Upstream, she had first become part of some small traveling show. And then—

And then, somehow, she had been with that relatively innocent traveling show no more. But still she had been upstream, somewhere, so far that there the Tungri bore a different name. There she had been under the domination of a terrible and evil magician, whose face she could recall but not his name. A magician who had used her—

There were certain gates of memory beyond which she was always afraid to go.

Outside those ominous gates, memory produced another face, this one with a clear name attached, that she had known briefly in those strange days. It was the face of a young man with curly hair, and who walked upon two legs of course—as far as Black Pearl knew, nowhere in the world did there exist any young men who were equipped with tails and scales instead of legs—that fate was reserved for females. The name of this young man with curly hair and two strong legs was Zoltan, and though she still sometimes dreamed of him, in recent months such dreams were becoming rare.

Now, at the pace of the river's flow, here about that of a walking man, Magicians' Island was drawing near. With mild surprise the mermaid observed that she might actually be about to drift ashore on it, where only moments ago she had expected to pass at a good distance.

Drifting still, Black Pearl raised her head slightly from the water, looking down almost the full length of her body, white skin above the hips and silver scales below. Skin and scales alike were as magically immune to summer's sun as they were to winter's watery cold. As she raised her head, the ends of her long black hair floated about her delicate white breasts.

Once Zoltan's hand had touched her there.

Thoughts of Zoltan abruptly vanished. Only now did Black Pearl realize that there was a kind of music, Pan music, pipe music, in the air, and that for the last several minutes she had not been drifting in such perfect freedom as she had imagined. Rather the music had been drawing her unawares, influencing her ever so slowly, and gently inducing her to steer herself by subtle movements of her tail toward the island.

The music was coming—had been coming, for now it ceased—from somewhere among the greenery and rocks that made up the irregular shoreline, all strange projections and hidden coves, of Magicians' Island.

And now abruptly the musician became visible. A young man, one Black Pearl had never seen before, a well-dressed youth, stood staring at her from behind some of the tall reeds of that unpredictable shoreline. One of the young man's hands was holding the panpipe, letting it hang loosely as if it had been forgotten. Though the instrument was silent, the subtly entrancing music it had produced seemed still to be hanging in the air.

This young man was nothing at all like Zoltan. She had a good look at this one now, and his intense dark eyes returned her stare as she came drifting past him at a distance of no more than ten meters.

"I have been trying to summon up the spirits of sunlight," he called to the drifting mermaid in a rich tenor voice, at the same time holding up the panpipe carelessly for her to see. "Trying to call into being an elemental, composed of summer and the river. And, lo and behold! Success, beyond my fondest hopes! What a vision of rare beauty have I evoked to gaze upon!"

"Even in summer," Black Pearl said—and with her tail moving underwater she stopped her drifting motion gracefully—"even now the depths of the river are dark and cold, and full of hidden, ugly things. Are you sure you really wanted to raise an elemental of that kind?"

A careless wave of the panpipe in the young man's hand dismissed the idea altogether. Judging by the animated expression on his face, a busy mind was rushing forward.

"Will you sit near me for a few moments?" The question was asked of the mermaid in tones of the gravest courtesy, even though he who asked it did not bother to wait for a reply. Instead he came stepping toward her through the muddy shallows, with little concern for his fine boots or clothing. At the very edge of the current he sat himself down cross-legged on a flat rock whose top was no more than a few centimeters above the restless surface of the river, and once he was seated there gave trial of a few more notes upon the pipes of Pan.

This time, thought Black Pearl, if it was indeed a magical net that had drawn her to this island, it was a very subtle one. Not like that other time, when she had been sold upstream like so many kilograms of fish.

Curiosity overcame caution. With a surge of her body and a spray of droplets, Black Pearl came sliding lithely out of the water to sit, mermaid fashion, upon another rock, a little bigger but very similarly situated, about three meters from the one where the young piper had settled. She thought he was a few years older than herself, and now that she looked at him closely she could see by his jewelry and clothing that he possessed at least some of the outward trappings of the magician. It was a subject in which she had firsthand experience.

But if this youth was indeed a wizard, still somehow she found nothing about him frightening. "Now that you have caught me," she asked saucily, "what do you mean to do? Sell me up the river to live in a tank, for country folk to goggle at in fairs?"

"I? Sell you? No, not I." And the young man seemed not so much scornful of that idea as hardly able to comprehend it. It was as if the ideas of capturing and selling lay so far from the place where his thoughts were occupied that he could not accept them as entirely real. "And you have gray eyes," he murmured, looking at her closely.

And he raised the panpipe to his lips again and tooted on it, displaying moderate skill. He sat there on the rock wearing his ill-fitting wizard's paraphernalia, which somehow looked as if it did not truly belong to him at all. He was very handsome, and though he was almost as young as she, somehow Black Pearl had already caught the flavor or image of something tragic about him.

She said challengingly: "I've been sold up the river, you know, once already."

The dark eyes fixed on her again. "Really? I didn't know that. But I did think from my first look at you that there was something . . ." He put the silent panpipe away, letting it fall into his pocket, and made a polite gesture toward rising, which was hard to accomplish neatly on his slippery rock. He said, as if introducing himself to an equal: "My name is Cosmo Malolo."

Malolo. He was a member, then, of one of the valley's two contending clans, whose domain included her home village among others. But it had been people from the other clan, or so thought Black Pearl, who had sold her up the river before.

"My name is Black Pearl," she said in turn, remembering the manners of her childhood, those ten or twelve years in which she had been wholly human. But she stared at the young man levelly, being as ready to assume equality as he was. Mermaids were beyond, or beneath, the usual rules of social intercourse, as their families of fisherfolk were not.

She saw the young magician's gaze pass, hungrily for a moment, across her breasts, and she made no move to try to cover them with her hair. Mermaids had nothing to hide, very little to lose, and little to fear in the way of rape. Or so Black Pearl thought. She was as far beyond fear as she was beyond courtesy.

He looked away from her at last, and once more seated himself on his rock, this time settling squarely, knees up, elbows outside knees, staring at the linked fingers of his two hands, on which certain rings of power flashed in the sun.

"Let me speak to you plainly, Black Pearl," Cosmo said in a level voice, not looking directly at her. "It was not the spirits of sunlight that I sought to call with my music today, or any elemental of the river. I set out to call up a mermaid, and I have done so. But please believe that my purpose was not to capture you or sell you."

There was a pause, long enough so that at last the mermaid felt compelled to ask: "Why, then?"

"It may be no accident that you, out of all the fishgirls in the Tungri, were the one my little spell attracted. Oh, it's only a very little spell indeed. Quite gentle. You can break it at any moment, if you wish. Plunge off that rock and swim away."

"I know that. I can feel my freedom. But I am still here."

"Good. Black Pearl"—and here his dark eyes turned full upon her once again—"are you happy to be a mermaid? Or would you like to walk the land on two good legs once more?"

"That is a madman's question. What woman could ever be happy like this?" And the flatness of her tailfins smacked at the water, with a violence worthy of some much larger creature.

He looked a question at her.

Her anger quivered in her voice now. "Don't you understand? We lived on land, all of us, until we were ten or twelve years old, not knowing that this was going to happen to us, but knowing that it might. All because of some curse pronounced a hundred years ago, in that damned stupid feud between your family and those others. And then one day, like a bad dream really coming true, the curse struck me. And when that happens it is really the end of life. Because what is there for a mermaid to live for? We can never be women. We can never walk, never be away from the smell of the river and of fish. And in a few more years the curse strikes its final blow, and we die, and float down the river like so many dead fish for the turtles to eat. Have you ever seen an old mermaid? One who lived long enough to have gray hair?"

Halfway through this tirade the young man, Cosmo as he had named himself, had begun shaking his head soberly. When Black Pearl was finished he said quietly: "I believe your answer. Believe me, in turn, that I did not ask the question lightly."

"Why then do you ask it at all?"

"Because I think I may be able to help you."

"Help me how?"

"Help you to cease to be a mermaid." With a swirl of the short wizard's cape that hung from his shoulders he stood up on the rock. "How willing and able are you to keep a secret?"

Before the day was over Black Pearl had learned from the young magician of the existence of a grotto on Magicians' Island. In the island rather; it was a strange cave of a place carved out at some time in the dim past for some purpose of magic or ritual that no one any longer understood or believed in. A daring mermaid could reach this grotto easily by swimming underwater for only a few meters, from an entrance almost un-findable amid the outer limestone rocks of the island's upstream end, and emerging at last into a pool in the bottom of a roofed cave near the island's center. Here on this island, as Cosmo said in welcoming her to the grotto, the influences were favorable for good magic.

But mermaids as a rule kept clear of this small isle entirely, for there were certain frightening things, creatures of magic, who dwelt here. Black Pearl became fully aware of those powers for the first time only when, at the young magician's insistence, she was swimming through the tunnel. When the powers came buzzing invisibly around her ears, considerable determination was required for her to go on. Had she not already begun to believe Cosmo's promises to her, she would have managed to turn around somehow—no matter that the underwater tunnel was barely wide enough for her to pass straight through—and would have hurried back to the open river.

As it was, she clenched her teeth and swam on, meanwhile hearing and feeling the magic powers as they swarmed about her head and body. They were small, no more intelligent than insects, and like certain insects indifferent as to whether they moved in air or water.

But the tunnel was really very short, and the guardian powers did not sting, at least in the case of this invited visitor. Black Pearl was intrigued by what she found at the inner end of the tunnel. The small pool and its enclosing cave had rough walls of stone and appeared to be partly a natural formation. Higher up there were a couple of ways into the cave for people who breathed only air, and walked on land. Through those openings enough daylight was coming in now, on a bright day, to make the place almost cheerful.

Still Cosmo had a small oil lamp burning, at least partly for magical purposes, as Black Pearl supposed.

There was an easy, sloping ledge on each side of the little pool in which the tunnel terminated, and at the magician's invitation Black Pearl sat on one of these flanges of rock. She and the young magician talked for a while, and as the minutes passed she gradually came to feel at ease.

They discussed, among other things, her history. In general it was rare for any mermaid to come back to this valley after having been sold away. Rare, but not unheard of. And in Black Pearl's case, at least, no complaining purchaser had so far come looking for her. That had been known to happen in other cases in the past.

Cosmo expressed his own quiet outrage over the whole situation, his own quiet determination to find a way by which the mermaid curse could be ended for good and all.

Only then, when the mermaid had begun to feel fully at ease with him, did Cosmo's magical tests begin.

Words were chanted, incense was burned. By the power of the young wizard invisible forces were gathered in the air of the grotto and then dispersed again. Black Pearl's tail remained firmly in place, and she gave no sign of growing legs. The problem, said Cosmo, as he had expected from the beginning, was proving to be a difficult one, and a single session of course was not enough to develop a proper counterspell.

Again and again, on that day of their first meeting, before Black Pearl swam away through the narrow tunnel, Cosmo pleaded and threatened and urged absolute secrecy upon her. He assured her again and again that his magical investigations, her hope of ever being cured, depended entirely upon that.

Black Pearl kept the secret until their next session on the following day. Even her friendship with the mermaid Soft Ripple was not enough to induce her to talk about this, though she had the impression that Soft Ripple sensed that something in her had changed, and was trying to puzzle out what it was.

And on the following day, during Black Pearl's second

visit to the secret grotto, in a pause for rest, Cosmo said to her: "You are a strange girl, I think, even for a mermaid. Perhaps it is because of the unhappy experience you had with that magician upstream."

"He was a much stronger magician than you are."

Cosmo did not appear to be upset by the comparison. "I don't doubt it. I know that there are some whose powers exceed mine."

"But he was wicked, and I hated him from the start. And yes, I think that you are right, there has always been something out of the ordinary about me."

"Why do you say that?"

The mermaid shrugged her ivory shoulders. "I don't think my parents were even surprised when I became a mermaid. It happens only to about one of four girls, you know, in the villages. No one knows in advance which girls the curse will strike, but I don't think anyone was surprised when it struck me."

"I admit that I have been intrigued by you, since I first saw you." Suddenly the eyes of Cosmo blazed, so that it seemed remarkable that his voice could remain steady. "Have you kept the secret of our meetings? Even from the other mermaids who sometimes swim about with you?"

"I have kept our secret," she said softly.

"See that you do. We have already progressed too far, much too dangerously far, for the secret to be revealed to anyone else."

Another day, another meeting.

Cosmo had been stroking with his fingers, making magical passes, across her shoulders and her hair. Then suddenly he let her go. "The aura, the touch, of his powers—I mean that one upstream—still clings about you."

Black Pearl shuddered slightly, through her whole

body down to the tip of her scaly tail, as she lay exposed on the flat ledge of rock. "Then cleanse me of it, if you can."

"I will. I will, as much as possible. But still . . ."

"Still what?"

"I find it intriguing."

Her pink lips snarled at him. "You've said that before. His touch was evil!"

"Oh, I agree, his was an evil magic, to be sure. But now it is gone. Only the flavor, the aura, the smell of it remains. Weak enough to be attractive. Like a pungent seasoning in food."

"If you can't wash it away, don't speak of it."

"Oh, I can wash some of it away at least. I am not totally incompetent, and there is much that I can do. But let us thank all the gods that the power of that evil wizard is gone. And I am sure that it was evil. I can sense the impression that it left on you—as if you had been clamped tightly in some great, iron fist."

"Sometimes I think that I can still feel the pressure of that fist around me."

"No, the power of it is gone. But what I would learn of it are the shaping, the ingredients, that made it so powerful. So that my own magic, which is intended to do good, may be strengthened."

The mermaid, lying beside the little pool that was not much bigger than a bathtub, looked up at him doubtfully.

Cosmo asked, almost pleading: "Does it seem to you that I am a bad man?"

Despite the feelings she had begun to have for the magician, it took Black Pearl a long time to answer that. "No," she said at last.

"Then trust me. Will you trust me? It will be very hard for me to help you otherwise."

*   *   *

It was during that same meeting, only their third magical session in the hidden grotto, that Cosmo first slipped over Black Pearl's head the fine chain that held the amulet. She held it up before her eyes and looked at it. The amulet was plain, almost crude, a little knot of glazed clay with symbols on it.

Having put the little chain over her head, he hesitated. Then he said: "We are almost ready to make a serious attempt now; still I fear you are not ready." But even as he spoke his great dark eyes were glowing their message of compassion, of love, into her eyes, into her heart.

Cosmo moved a little closer, and with his right hand he brushed back Black Pearl's long, black hair so that he could see more clearly into her eyes. Again he repeated another warning he had already given her several times.

It was this: that the cure, even if against all odds it could be achieved this early in the course of treatment, could be no more than temporary at first.

"However successful we are at this stage, you will revert to being a mermaid again, in less than a quarter of an hour—quite possibly much less. Such a temporary alleviation of the curse would be a first step only. But it would also be proof that eventually other steps are going to be possible. Strong evidence that in time we will find a way to cure you completely, permanently. You and all the mermaid sisterhood."

The mermaid nodded.

His hand took her hand as she lay floating in the shallow water. And then, as he muttered incantations, his fingers began to stroke her hand, her arm, her shoulder.

And it was during that very treatment, what Cosmo had said would be the first serious attempt, that the miracle occurred for the first time.

Black Pearl's body, already awakened sensually by the

magician's caresses even before the change he wrought
had come fully upon it—her body found itself suddenly,
entirely human. Completely and wholly that of a woman. Utterly female.

And Cosmo, responding to her sobs of joy with certain
rather similiar sounds of his own, was right at her side
when the change came. Right there to draw Black Pearl
from the water, cradling her two lithe, gently kicking legs
in his left arm, his right arm under her shoulders. There
to swing her round with a swift motion of strong arms to
the soft bed only two meters distant, where, as he said,
he sometimes slept.

A quarter of an hour later, when the expected return
change overtook Black Pearl, her new lover, despite all
of his cautions that such a relapse was bound to happen,
looked disappointed. But not for long. And she, absorbed in her new happiness, accepted the situation, too.

The sessions of magic, lovemaking, and magic again,
went on. There were many such sessions, one every few
days, extending over several months. Sometimes the
periods of two-legged normalcy were a little prolonged
—once almost to half an hour—but still the final,
permanent cure eluded the researcher and his patient
lover.

Each time Black Pearl swam into the grotto to meet
him, Cosmo questioned her sternly as to whether she
was continuing to keep their secret.

"We are not so deeply into this that everything—your
own fate as well as mine—depends upon your sharing
the knowledge of what we do with no one. If you fail, the
powers of magic will, I fear, doom you forever to keep
your mermaid shape. Indeed—I have no wish to frighten you, my darling, but I must say this—they might
warp you into something truly hideous."

So Black Pearl continued to keep the secret faithfully.

She would have done anything, that the burning joy of her meetings with her lover might be made permanent.

Autumn was yielding to the onset of this land's brief winter when a night came that changed everyone's life. A riverboat, whose origin Black Pearl was never to discover, came plunging down the Tungri from upstream, hurtling through the series of rapids and cascades known as the Second Cataract. The passage was extremely difficult even in bright daylight, even for an experienced crew. In wind and rain and clouds and fading daylight, the crew of this ship probably never had a chance. The bits and pieces of their upriver craft that later washed ashore were of no familiar make.

The riverboat might well have been in precipitous flight from someone or something. In any case it failed to make the passage, which only experienced boatmen who were favored by a measure of luck could ever hope to complete successfully. The craft was knocked to pieces upon the rocks within the gorge, with the loss of all hands so far as could be told.

Most of the inhabitants of the valley, the many who lived on land and the few who dwelt in water, were not aware of the wreck until hours or days later. Black Pearl, because she had just left a secret rendezvous on Magicians' Island, happened to be first to reach the scene of the disaster.

And so it was she who discovered Farslayer, one of the Twelve Swords of power and legend, lying undamaged and uncorroded on the river bottom, where the smashing of the boat had dropped it, among the deep cold boiling wells of current just below the cataract. Only a mermaid or a dolphin could have reached it swimming.

Whenever a wreck similar to this one occurred, which was not often, the mermaids as a rule came swarming round, trying to help the injured and save the drowning if they could, trying also to see what treasure and trinkets they might be able to salvage from the victims' cargo.

But here were no survivors or victims, living or dead, immediately visible. When Black Pearl first saw the Sword lying in the twilight of the river bottom, her first thought was for almost-forgotten Zoltan, because this impressive weapon so closely resembled one she'd seen him wear. She'd seen him use it too in her defense.

Much additional memory that had been almost lost came rushing back. If Zoltan had indeed been in the wrecked boat, she'd save him if she could.

Swimming and looking amid the watery thunder at the bottom of the falls, Black Pearl searched as only a mermaid could. She did indeed find one dead body, caught on the rocks nearby, but to her relief it was not Zoltan's. One other man, who was still breathing when she found him, died even as Black Pearl was trying to decide how best to carry him to shore, died without saying a word in answer to her questions.

No other survivors or casualties were discoverable at the site of the wreck. The mermaid thought to herself that there was no point in searching anymore, trying to look downriver for Zoltan; bodies and wreckage would be scattered for kilometers downstream already, and scattering farther every moment. Not even a mermaid would be able to find a single man, especially with nightfall coming on.

Black Pearl gave up thoughts of rescue, and dove back to the Sword, which lay just where she had seen it last. There was barely enough daylight still penetrating the depths to let her mermaid's vision find it once again.

When she had brought the marvelous weapon to the surface, she could see that it was not, after all, the same Sword that Zoltan had carried. His, as she remembered, had borne the symbol of a small white dragon on its black hilt, where this one showed instead the concentric rings of a small white target.

The young mermaid knew only a few fragments of the history of the Twelve Swords of Power. But she could see that this Sword, whatever its true nature, must be quite valuable.

Zoltan dropped from her mind. Black Pearl's next thought on having discovered this treasure was to take it straight to the man she loved.

Cosmo would know what to do with her find. And if there were any benefits to be had from it, Cosmo, her true love, would see that those benefits were shared with her.

Fortunately for her plan Cosmo had not yet left the grotto on Magicians' Island; there was some magical tidying-up that had had to be attended to. He was surprised to see Black Pearl back so soon, and more than surprised to see what she was carrying.

Balancing the naked Sword thoughtfully and carefully in both his hands—all magic aside, those edges, as he had already proved, were ready to cut tough leather as easily as water lilies—he agreed with her that it was probably hopeless to seek any further for survivors of the wreck tonight; tomorrow he would see to it that a party of fishermen went out from the villages on the Malolo side, to see if any might have been washed ashore alive.

But his attention had never really left the Sword. "No, Pearl, I have never seen its like before." He held the weapon in his hands up higher, the better to catch the light of his little lamp, and marveled at it. "But yes, I know what it is. Once there were eleven others like it in the world, and still there are probably nine."

"But what *is* it? Magic, surely."

"What is this one specifically? Magic such as you and I are never likely to see again. This one is Farslayer, as I can tell from the symbol on the hilt. Farslayer kills, at any distance and with absolute certainty. Hold it in your hands, and chant the name of your enemy, and swing the weapon round, and let it go—and lo! The Sword is gone to find your enemy, and he is dead. Even that evil one who once held you bound would not be able to stand against one of these. No power on earth could save him, I think—except perhaps one of the other Swords."

Black Pearl's eyes were wide with wonder. "What are you going to do with it, then?"

"Put it away in a place of safety, for now. Then I must think." And the magician opened a small locker or safe, cut right into the stone beside their couch, a safe that Black Pearl had never known was there. And Cosmo put the Sword in there, and with a word of sealing magic closed it up.

He frowned down at her as she lay in the water. "Not a word to anyone else, of course. Now there are two secrets you must keep, and this one is every bit—or almost—as big as the first."

"Of course. Not a word to anyone." And joyously she saw in Cosmo's eyes renewed evidence that she was trusted by him.

Then another thought occurred to the mermaid. "When I was swimming back here just now, I thought I saw another boat, smaller than yours, coming toward the island."

"Oh? And from which shore?"

"The north."

"That probably means Senones. Don't worry. Even if they should dare to touch shore here, I've made this ground my home, and I can make myself invisible to enemies whilst I am on it."

"Are you sure?" The Senones clan and that to which Cosmo belonged were ancient enemies.

"I'm sure. And now, besides, I have the Sword for my defense." He smiled. "The wonderful Sword that you have brought me, and for which I am very grateful. And you must be very tired. Go and rest on the other island. Or back to the wreck and look for other trinkets if you like." He seemed very loving and very confident. He added at last: "I love you, Pearl."

Black Pearl, delighted to the depths of her heart that she had been able to bring her lover such a prize, plunged obediently into the narrow tunnel and swam away.

ONE

Heavy wind filled the bleak and rugged gorge of the Tungri, dragging heavy clouds through dark night. The short winter of this land was not yet over, and the freezing rain that had been falling at sundown had turned to snow some hours ago. The hermit Gelimer was snug under blankets and skins in his lonely bed, and when the half-intelligent watchbeast came to wake him he turned over with a faint groan and tried to pull the furs up over his head. Even before the hermit was fully awake, he knew what an awakening at this hour of such a night implied.

But of course Gelimer's conscience would not have allowed him to go back to sleep when he was needed on such a night, even had the anxious beast allowed it. Three breaths after he had tried to pull the covers up, the man was sitting on the edge of his simple cot, groping for the boots that ought to be just under the foot end.

He had both of his eyes open now. "All right, what is it, Geelong?"

The speechless animal, with melting sleet dripping from its fur, moved on four feet toward the single door of the one-room house, and back again. Its movement and the whole shape of its body suggested something between a large dog and a miniature bear. Geelong's front paws, capable of clumsy gripping, came up in the air as the beast sat back on its haunches, and spread their digits as much as possible in the sign that the watchbeast usually employed to mean "man."

"All right, all right. I'm coming. So be it. I'm on my way."

The animal whined as if to urge the man to greater speed.

As soon as his boots were on, Gelimer rose from his cot, a strongly built man of middle size and middle age. Only a fringe of once-luxuriant dark hair remained around a pate of shiny baldness. His bearded face in the fading firelight of his hut was shedding the last traces of sleep, putting on a look of innocent determination. "Ardneh willing, I'm on my way." Now the hermit was groping his way into his outer garments, and then his heavy coat.

He hooked a stubby battle hatchet to his belt—there were dangerous beasts to be encountered on the mountainside sometimes—and grabbed up the backpack, kept always in readiness, filled with items likely to be useful in the rescuing of stranded travelers.

Then, before Gelimer went out the door, he paused momentarily to build up the fire. Warmth and light were both likely to be needed when he got back.

The small house from which Gelimer presently emerged, with torch in hand, had been carved out of the interior of the stump of an enormous tree, easily five meters in diameter at head height above ground level. From just in front of the house, the tremendous fallen trunk was still partially in view, lying with what had been its crown downslope. So that log had lain since it was felled decades ago by a great storm, and so it would probably lie, the splintered remnants of its upper branches sticking out over the gorge of the Tungri itself, until another windstorm came strong enough to send it crashing the rest of the way down.

What he had last seen as freezing rain, a few hours ago, was now definitely snow, and had already produced a heavy accumulation. Gelimer grimaced under the hood of his anorak, and turned to a small lean-to shed built against the outer surface of the huge stump. From this shelter he pulled out a sled about the size of a bathtub. After lighting ready torches that were affixed one on each side of this vehicle, he harnessed Geelong to it. All this was quickly accomplished despite the wind and snow. A moment later the powerful watchbeast sprang away, and the hermit clinging to the rear of the sled by its handgrips had to run to keep up.

The beast ignored the thin path by which the rare intentional visitor ordinarily reached the dwelling of the hermit. Instead it struck off climbing across the rock-strewn slope above the house. Here and there along the slope grew more big trees, dimly visible now through swirling snow, rooted in pockets of soil on one broad ledge or another. Some of these trees were of the same species as that which formed the hermit's house, though none of these still-living specimens had attained the same size.

The vigorous watchbeast, anxious to do the duty it had been trained for, lumbered on, snow flying from its splayed paws.

In this direction, very nearly directly south of the hermitage, one seldom-used trail came over the mountains. It was on this slope that travelers were most likely to encounter difficulties, particularly when the weather and visibility were poor.

A few hundred meters above the hermit's dwelling, the path from the south split into two routes, one going

east and the other descending in a treacherous fashion to
the west. The eastern path rejoined the riverside one a
few kilometers east of and above the gorge, the two paths
uniting at that point to form a better-defined way that
could almost be called a road. Meanwhile the western
fork came down eventually to a village on the shore of
Lake Abzu, where the Tungri calmed itself after the
turmoil of the gorge.

The reality of the trails was much more complex than
their simple goals would indicate, for in conformity with
the rugged mountainside they all wound back and forth,
up small slopes and down, around many boulders and
the occasional tree or grove. And all of the trails were
poorly marked, if marked at all, steep and treacherous at
best. At night, and in a snowstorm—

The hermit's feet, accustomed better than anyone
else's to these particular rocks, slipped out from under
him, and he would have fallen painfully but for his tight
grip on the handles of the sled. Muttering a prayer to
Ardneh to grant him speed, he pressed on, crossing a
small stream upon a newly formed bridge of ice and
snow.

Without the aid of his beast, Gelimer could never have
found the fallen man, nor, perhaps, would he have had
much chance of saving him when found. But with
Geelong to show the way the search, at least, was soon
successful.

The body lay motionless under a new coat of snow, in
moonless, starless darkness. Gelimer turned it over with
a mittened hand. The fallen stranger was of slight build,
his handsome face smooth-shaven, pale in the night. His
forehead was marked by a little dried—if not absolutely
frozen—blood. Even in the wind the hermit could hear
that the man was still breathing, but he was not conscious at the moment. His fine coat, trimmed in light fur,
and his well-made boots indicated that he was no

peasant. Whoever he was, having fallen on a night like tonight, he was lucky to be still alive.

Another and larger mound of snow, a little way downslope, stirred when the light of the sled's torches fell upon it. That illumination, faint at the distance, now revealed the head and upraised neck of a fallen riding-beast, and a faint whinny came through the wind. Most likely a slip on ice, thought Gelimer, and a broken leg. Well, it was too bad, but beasts were only beasts, whereas men were men, and freezing to death would doubtless be as kind a death for a beast as having its throat slit in mercy. The hermit was going to have all he could handle trying to save one human life tonight.

The fallen man lay surrounded by sizable rocks, and it was impossible to maneuver the sled any closer to him than three or four meters. When Gelimer lifted the hurt one, he woke up. He was still too weak to stand unaided, or even to talk to any purpose. His mouth seemed to be forming stray syllables, but the wind whipped them away, whether there was any sense in them or not.

The man's eyes were open, and as soon as he realized that he was in a stranger's grip they widened briefly as if in terror. As if, thought the hermit, he had more fear of being caught than expectation of being rescued. But now, of course, was not the time to worry about that.

Weak and confused as the fellow was, still he was able to cling with a terrible strength to a strange pack or bundle, long as a man's leg, that he must have been carrying with him when he fell. It came up out of the snow with him, clamped in the crook of his right arm, and when Gelimer would have put the bundle aside, if only for a moment, to get the man into the sled, the object of his charity snarled weakly and gripped his treasure all the harder.

"All right, all right, we'll bring it along." And Gelimer somehow bundled the package along with its owner into the sled, and pulled up furs around them both. "Any other treasures that are worth your life to save? Evidently not. Geelong, take us home!"

In a moment the sled was moving again, first back to what with normal footing would have been a trail, and then taking a generally downhill direction, switchbacking through the altered and darkened landscape toward the hermit's house. On the return trip Geelong moved less frantically, testing with his forefeet for treacherous drifts, nosing out the limits of the trail.

Once during the ride back to the house, the man who was bundled into the sled began to thrash about. He moved his arms wildly until he again managed to locate his package, which had somehow slipped momentarily from his grip.

"Poor fellow! That bang on the head may have made you crazy. But take it easy now, you're in good hands." It was doubtful at best that the man would be able to hear him in the wind, but Gelimer talked to him anyway. He hated to miss a chance to talk when one presented itself. "We'll see you through. You're going to make it now."

Even with Geelong guiding the sled and pulling it, regaining the house was a tough struggle into the wind. The firelight within offered some guidance to the seeker, shining out in feeble chinks around the edges of the single shuttered and curtained window.

Hardly a routine night's work for Gelimer, but not an unheard-of adventure, either. This was far from being the first time he had taken in a fallen or stranded traveler, and a good many of those he'd tried to save had lived to bless him for his aid.

When they reached the hut, Geelong remained outside at first—the watchbeast was capable of unharnessing himself from the sled. Gelimer hoisted and wrestled his client, and of course the omnipresent package, out of the sled and through the small entry hall, doored and curtained at both ends for winter, that pierced the thickness of his house's circular wooden wall. Once safely inside, Gelimer let his new patient down upon the single bed, and moved quickly to build up the fire again. Indeed, both light and heat were wanted now.

Apart from the head wound, which did not look likely to be fatal, and some bruised and probably cracked ribs, there were no wounds to be discovered upon the patient's body, which was lean but still looked well nourished. The rings on his fingers suggested that he might be a magician, or at least had aspirations along that line. That crack upon the head, and exposure, would seem to be the problems here, and Gelimer thought them well within his range of competence. Despite his white robe he was no physician, but the experience of years had taught him something of the art.

Once the stranger had been undressed, examined, and tucked into a warm bed, the next step was to try him on swallowing a little water, and this was soon managed successfully. When the patient was laid flat again, his blank eyes stared up at the rough-hewn wooden ceiling of the tree-stump hut, and his limbs shivered. Then suddenly he started up convulsively, and would not lie back again until Gelimer had brought him his long package and let him hold it.

In intervals between other necessary chores, Gelimer started the soup kettle heating. Presently the patient was swallowing soup as the hermit spooned it out to him.

After he had taken nourishment, the fellow slid into what looked like a normal sleep, still without having uttered a coherent word.

Gelimer, looking at his patient carefully, decided it was now certain that he was going to live.

By this time the hermit was more than ready to go back to sleep himself, but before doing so he wished to satisfy his curiosity about something.

"Well now, and just what is this treasure of yours, that you are so reluctant to give it up? And will it perhaps provide me with some clue as to just who you are and whence you come?"

The shabby package, a bundle of coarse fabric, appeared to have been hastily made, then tied shut with tough twine. The knots in the twine were somewhere between wet and frozen, and when one of them stubbornly resisted the hermit's fingernails he went for one of his kitchen knives. The wet twine yielded to a keen edge.

When Gelimer had the package lying open on his largest table, he took one look at the leather scabbard and the black hilt he had uncovered, and turned his head to glance at his mysterious visitor once again. It was a different kind of glance this time, and he who delivered it breathed two words: "No wonder."

What had been revealed was a sword, and something about it strongly suggested that it was no ordinary weapon. The hermit, intermittently sensitive to such things, caught the unmistakable aura of strong magic in the air.

When the hermit—who had less experience than Black Pearl had had with this particular magic—had drawn the blade from the plain sheath, he turned his head again for yet another look, this one of wordless wonder, at the man who had been carrying it. The blade was a full meter long, and had been formed with supernal skill from the finest steel that Gelimer had ever seen. The polished surface of the steel was finely mottled in a way that suggested impossible depths within.

Even the plain black hilt was somehow very rich; and the hermit, turning the weapon over in his hands, noticed now that the hilt bore a small white marking, two rings concentric on a dot, making a symbolic target.

Now, for a few moments, Gelimer reveled in the sheer

beauty of the thing he had discovered. But within the space of a few more heartbeats he had begun to frown again. He had a vague, only a very vague, idea of what he was holding in his hands.

In the next instant, he was rewrapping the Sword in its old covering, and wishing heartily that he could immediately put it out of his house and away from himself completely. But suppose the stranger should awaken, and find his treasure gone from his side?

He left the wrapped Sword on the table.

"I must sleep while I can," said Gelimer then to Geelong, who had come in by now and was curled on his own blanket on the far side of the room. Presently the hermit too was dozing off, a blanket over him, his body nested among extra pillows, his back against the wooden wall where it was quite warm near the tiled fireplace.

An hour passed, an hour of near silence in the house, while the storm still howled with fading energy outside. Then a piece of wood, eroded by slow fire, broke and tumbled suddenly on the hearth, making a small, abrupt noise. Gelimer, frowning, slept on. The watchbeast, sleeping, moved his ears but not his eyelids. But the eyes of the man in the bed opened suddenly, and he sat up and looked about him with something of the expression of a trapped animal, not knowing where he found himself. He looked with relief—or was it resignation?— at the package on the table beside him, then at the other human occupant of the room, and then at the dozing animal.

Then he swung his feet out of the bed, and paused, raising his hands to his face as a surge of pain swept through his skull.

The animal opened one eye, gazed at the houseguest quizzically.

Another moment and the visitor was standing, moving swiftly and stealthily, hastily pulling on such of his garments as lay within easy reach, including his damp boots that someone had left to dry at a prudent distance from the fire.

The animal had both eyes open now, but still it only looked at the stranger dumbly. To get up and dress was something that humans did all the time.

The hermit, still sleeping in exhaustion, was lying now at full length on the warm wooden floor, with his head fallen back between a pillow and a piece of firewood. The firelight gleamed on Gelimer's bald head, and he snored vigorously.

The visitor unwrapped his package, not noticing, or perhaps not caring, that the ties had earlier been cut. Then he pulled the Sword from its sheath, and shot another glance in the direction of the sleeping hermit.

The hindquarters of the watchbeast moved in a swift surge, straightening its body in a line aimed at the stranger. The animal crouched, a very low growl issuing from its throat.

But the stranger failed even to notice. His dazed mind was elsewhere, and he had no designs on his rescuer's life. Instead, he was already making for the door, the drawn blade still in his hand. With his free hand he lifted the latch silently.

Geelong subsided on his old blanket. Humans went out of doors all the time, in all kinds of weather. It was a permissible activity.

The inner door was pulled shut, very softly, behind the stranger. The small tunnel penetrating the thickness of what had been a great tree's bark was long enough to muffle the entering cold wind, muffle it enough so that Gelimer in his warm place by the fire was not awakened.

Now all was silent again inside the house except for

the furtive small noises of the fire itself. A stable warmth reestablished itself in the atmosphere. Faintly, as if at a great distance, the wind howled across the upper end of the carven passage of charred wood that served as chimney.

Only a short time passed before cold air moved in again, faintly, under the inner door; and then that door opened once more. It had been left unlatched. The watchbeast raised his head again, alertly.

The stranger entered, empty-handed. His face had a newly drained and empty look, paler even than before. Mechanically, unthinkingly, he latched the door behind him. Then he moved, very wearily but still quickly, to stand over the wrappings that had once held the Sword but now lay empty and discarded on the bed.

He moved his hands over the emptiness before him, in what might have been either an abortive attempt at magic, or only a gesture of futility. His lips murmured a word, a word that might have been a name. Then he raised his eyes from the bed, and stood, swaying slightly on his feet, staring hopelessly at the curve of wooden wall little more than arm's length in front of him.

Again his lips moved, silently, as if he might be seeking the help of some divinity in prayer.

Except for that he appeared to be simply waiting.

The sound that at last awakened Gelimer impressed the hermit as enormous, and yet he could not really have said that it was loud. It was as if the human ear, sleeping or waking, could catch only the delayed afterrush of that vast howling as it faded. As if mere human sense was inevitably a heartbeat too late in its perception to receive the full screaming intensity of the thing itself.

The hermit woke up, to find himself lying in a strained position by the fire, with the strange remnants of that unearthly sound still hanging in the air. Upon the hearth the weakening fire still snapped and hissed. Across the room his watchbeast was standing up and whining softly, looking toward the bed.

Even before he looked, Gelimer knew that whatever event had awakened him was already over.

Sitting up, he turned his eyes toward the bed. And then he sprang to his feet.

His visitor, once more fully clothed or very nearly so, was now sprawled facedown and diagonally crosswise upon the narrow bed, with the toes of his wet boots still resting on the floor. Above the stranger's inert back protruded half a meter and more of beautiful steel blade, broad and mottled and glinting faintly in the firelight, beneath that black hilt with its god-chosen symbol. The blade was as motionless as the shaft of a monument; the body it had struck down was no longer breathing.

A great disconsolate whine came from the crouching watchbeast, and Gelimer without thinking could interpret the outcry: This was bad, this was very bad indeed, but there had been no way for the animal to prevent this bad thing happening.

There would have been no way for a human being to stop it either, perhaps. Gelimer glanced toward the door, and saw that it was securely latched.

The wet boots, still delicately puddling the wooden floor, would seem to mean that the man had got up, had gone outside for whatever purpose, and had come back in before he met his death.

The hermit approached the bed. There was no doubt at all that his late patient was now certainly dead. Still the hermit turned him partway over, and saw a hand-breadth or more of pointed Swordblade protruding through what must be a neatly split breastbone. Death, of course, must have been instantaneous; there was only a very moderate amount of blood, staining the cloth that had wrapped this deadly weapon and was now lying crumpled beneath the body.

With the door latched on the inside, it seemed an impossible situation.

Not knowing what else to do, and moving in something of a state of shock, Gelimer wrenched the Sword out of the stranger's body—that task wasn't easy, for the blade seemed to be held in a vise of bone—and stood for a few moments with that black hilt in hand, looking about him suspiciously, ready to meet some further attack, an attack that never came.

"Geelong, I don't suppose that you—? But of course not. You don't have any real hands, to grip a hilt, and . . . and of course you wouldn't, anyway."

The watchbeast looked at its master, trying to understand.

And certainly no man would ever be able to stab himself in such a way.

Eventually the hermit wiped the blade on the coarse cloth that had been its wrapping—the steel came clean with magical ease—and put it back into the sheath that he found lying discarded on the floor in the middle of the room. Then he went to arrange the body more neatly and decently on the bed, wadding the Sword-wrapping cloth underneath in an effort to save his own blankets. There was not going to be that much more bleeding now.

Then he decided that the only practical thing to do was to go back to sleep again, after satisfying himself that his door and his window were indeed closed tightly, and latched as securely as he could latch them. Geelong continued his whimpering, until Gelimer spoke sharply to the beast, enjoining silence.

A few moments after that the hermit was asleep by the fireside as before. The silent presence of the occupant of the bed did not disturb his slumbers. All his life Gelimer had known that it was the living against whom one must always be on guard.

In the morning, before the sun was really up, the hermit went out to dig a grave, and to see to one or two other related matters. The snow had stopped an hour ago, and by now the sky was clear. He left the sled in its shed, but he took Geelong with him.

The fallen riding-beast, as Gelimer had expected, was dead by now, already stiffened. The saddle it bore was well made, and the beast itself had been well fed, he thought, before it had started out on its last journey. There were no saddlebags; most likely the journey had been short.

With considerable effort, and with the aid of his dumb companion, Gelimer tugged the dead animal to the edge of the next cliff down, and put it over the drop, and looked after it to see where it had landed. Not all the way into the river, unfortunately; that would certainly have been best. Instead the carcass was now wedged in a crevice between rocks on the lip of the next precipice. Good enough, thought Gelimer, quite good enough. In that place, the hermit thought, the carcass should be well exposed to flying scavengers, and at the same time out of sight and smell of any human travelers who might be taking the usual trails.

Having disposed of the dead beast, the hermit now went to dig a grave for the dead man.

He dug it in the stand of trees nearest his house, where many centuries of organic growth and deposit had built up a deep soil, supported by one of the largest ledges on this side of the mountain. As soon as the sun was well up, in a brilliant sky, last night's snow began melting rapidly, and thus caused very little interference with his digging. Here the air never remained cold enough for long enough to freeze the ground solidly or to any considerable depth. Black dirt piled up swiftly atop melting snow as Gelimer plied his shovel.

When the grave had grown to be something more than a meter deep, Gelimer called it deep enough, and hiked back to his dwelling to evict its patient tenant. He noted hopefully as he walked that there was still enough snow on the ground in most places to allow him to use the sled for transport.

The trip back to the grave, with mournful Geelong pulling the burdened sled, was uneventful. Into the earth after the stranger went the bloodstained cloth that had once wrapped the Sword.

Gelimer said a devout prayer to Ardneh over the new grave just as soon as he had finished filling it in. When he opened his eyes afterward, he could see, at no great distance among the massive trunks, a place where some years ago he had laid another unlucky traveler to rest. And if he turned his head he could see, just over there, another. That grave, representing the saddest failure of all, held a young woman with her newborn babe.

After the passage of a few years these modest mounds had become all but indistinguishable from the surrounding floor of the grove, covered with dead leaves and fallen twigs under the melting snow. In a few years this new grave too would totally disappear. That is, if it was allowed to do so. That was something Gelimer was going to have to think about intensively. He still had no real clue to the identity of the man he had just buried.

Frowning, the hermit put his shovel into the sled and urged Geelong back to the hut. The Sword that awaited him there, he was beginning to think, might well pose a more difficult problem than any mere dead or dying traveler.

Now even in the shade the snow was melting rapidly, and in another hour or so all tracks made in it would be gone. That was all to the good.

Secure inside his dwelling place once more, the hermit drew the Sword out of its sheath, and looked at it even more carefully than he had before. Perhaps he should have put this treasure into the grave too, and tried his best to forget about it; he had come very near to doing just that. He foresaw that no good was likely to come of this acquisition. Yet there was no doubt that the thing was immensely valuable, and he supposed it must be the rightful property of someone. He had no right to lose the wealth of someone else.

Gelimer was still troubled by the face of the Sword's last possessor—handsome, haunted, but now finally at peace.

TWO

ALMOST a month passed after the stranger's burial before the hermit looked upon another human face, living or dead. Then one day he was standing inside his house, almost lost in meditation, when Geelong suddenly lumbered to the door, sniffing and whining. A moment later a completely unexpected voice called from outside, hailing whoever might be in the house.

Awaiting the hermit in his front yard, regarding him when he came out with a look of fresh and youthful confidence, was a young man of about eighteen. Curly brown hair framed a broad and honest-looking face, above a strong and blocky body, not particularly tall. The youth was clad in the gray boots and tunic of a religious pilgrim, but he still wore a short sword belted to his side—a reasonable and common precaution for any traveler in these parts.

It struck Gelimer as odd, though, that this visitor was carrying nothing at all besides the weapon, no pack or canteen.

"Good morning to you, Sir Hermit. Or do I read your white robes wrongly?" The young man's voice was as cheerful and confident as were his face and bearing.

"No, you read them properly. I have lived here alone

for some twenty years, trying to serve Ardneh as best I
can. My name is Gelimer." He stroked the watchbeast's
ears as it crouched beside him, trying to quell the
excitement inevitably produced by any visitor.

"And I am Zoltan. I come from the land of Tasavalta,
which as you must know lies far to the north and east of
here. My companion and I find ourselves somewhat
inconveniently stranded at the moment. There was a
little wind and rain last night, which confused the
captain of our riverboat completely, and he succeeded in
running us aground on some of the many rocks below."
And the youth nodded carelessly toward the gorge, from
which the faint voice of the Tungri could be heard as
always.

"Ah, then no doubt you are embarked upon some
pilgrimage downstream? But I am forgetting to be
hospitable. You are doubtless hungry and thirsty. Come
in, come in, and—"

"Thank you no, Hermit Gelimer. So far we've not
lacked for food or drink."

"You mentioned a companion?"

"Yes, a lady. Being somewhat older than I am, she
preferred to stay below with the boat rather than climb
the cliff. But she too is well provisioned."

Still Gelimer continued to press his offer of hospitality. Presently Zoltan, who seemed at least willing to
continue the conversation, accepted.

No traces of last month's visitor now remained inside
the dwelling. Zoltan chose one of the two chairs and sat
down, crossing his legs and making himself at ease.

"From Tasavalta, you say?" The hermit was heating
water on the hearth now, starting to brew tea. Meanwhile Geelong had lain down with head on forepaws on
his mat, still perturbed by the fact of another visitor in
the house. The last one had not worked out at all to the
watchbeast's liking.

Gelimer continued: "That is the country, is it not, where the king has so many magic Swords stocked in his treasury?"

The visitor shook his head. "The rulers of my homeland are a prince and princess, rather than a king. Prince Mark and Princess Kristin. They do possess a few of the Twelve Swords—so it is said. But I think they keep them in the armory."

"Ah yes. Of course." And Gelimer, carefully spooning out tea—a treasured gift from another traveler—took thought as to just how to proceed with his questioning. He wanted to gain knowledge without giving any of his own away.

He already knew what almost everyone else knew about the Twelve Swords, those mighty weapons that had been so mysteriously forged, more than thirty years ago, by some of the now-vanished gods. And the hermit had heard some of the stories to the effect that the Swords themselves had had more than a little to do with the strange disappearance of their powerful creators.

Each of the Twelve Blades was burdened with its own distinctive power, and according to all the testimony of witnesses there was no other force anywhere under the sun capable of standing against the power of any one of them.

"I know that there are twelve of them, or were," Gelimer went on, talking to his newest guest. "But I forget what their names are." He blinked, trying to look as holy and unworldly as he could. Sometimes he could be successful at it.

His young guest, thus encouraged and apparently finding no reason to be suspicious, was soon rattling off the names and attributes of the various magic weapons, as if he indeed might be something of an expert on the subject. From the few blades that were generally admitted to be kept in the Tasavaltan vaults, his cataloguing soon moved on to others. Presently it arrived at the one in which Gelimer had reason to be particularly interested.

"—and then there's Farslayer, which is sometimes also called the Sword of Vengeance. Though of course it can be more than that."

Gelimer blinked. "It sounds truly terrible."

"Oh, it is, believe me. You whirl it around your head, and chant—I forget just what words you're supposed to use, though my uncle did tell me once."

"Your uncle is a magician, perhaps?"

"No." Then young Zoltan for just a moment put on a look of wary intelligence, like one who realizes that he has almost said too much. Gelimer pricked up his ears. Then the youth went smoothly on: "Anyway, I'm not really sure that any of those trimmings, the whirling and chanting and so on, are really necessary. The point is, when you throw Farslayer with deadly intent, it will go on to bury itself in the heart of your chosen target, whether man, god, or demon. Even if that target is halfway around the world and you don't know where, surrounded by defenses."

"Magical or material? I mean, what if your target was enclosed by material walls?"

"Walls of stone or wood or magic, it would make no difference. Farslayer would come through 'em like so much smoke."

"Oh." And perhaps Gelimer's expression of careful vacuity changed now; but if so, the change was quickly smoothed back into blankness.

"Oh yes. There's no defense, of steel armor or of sorcery, that can save the intended victim, once Farslayer is thrown against him—or her. Two of the gods, Mars and Hermes, have died of that very blade."

"Now *that* I find hard to believe." The hermit was trying to provoke more details.

Young Zoltan was quite ready for a little good-humored argument. "I know someone who with his own eyes saw Hermes lying dead, with the wound made by Farslayer still in his back."

"That someone must have led a very adventurous life."

The young man glanced up when he heard the deliberate tone of disbelief, then calmly disregarded it. Suddenly Gelimer found the youth's implied claim of expertise considerably more convincing.

The hermit asked innocently: "And is there no possibility of defense at all?"

"None at all, I should say, apart from the other Swords. If you had Shieldbreaker in your possession, for example, you'd be able to laugh at anyone who threw Farslayer against you. Shieldbreaker's already destroyed two other Swords, Doomgiver and Townsaver, when people were foolish enough to bring them into combat directly against it."

"I see. I suppose your adventurous friend saw them destroyed also?"

"No."

The hermit saw that now he had gone too far. "Please, I did not mean to imply that I doubted your word. I only thought that perhaps some friend of yours had somewhat embellished his stories. There are many good folk who like to do that from time to time."

"But that's not what happened in this case."

"I believe you, and I am sorry. Please, go on. I find the subject of the Swords intensely interesting."

"Well—where was I?"

"You mentioned Shieldbreaker."

"Yes. Then there's Woundhealer, which can cure any wound, even a thrust of magic through the heart, if it's brought into play promptly enough. And then, maybe, Sightblinder—I don't know if Sightblinder would offer any protection against Farslayer or not. It's an interesting thought, though."

And with that the youth, his good humor apparently restored, suddenly threw back his head and began to recite:

> *Farslayer howls across the world*
> *For thy heart, for thy heart, who hast wronged*
> *me!*
> *Vengeance is his who casts the blade*
> *Yet he will in the end no triumph see.*

The youth made a good job of the recitation, putting a fair amount of feeling into it. Gelimer made himself smile in appreciation. He had heard some of the old verses about Swords before, decades ago, and over the past days those rhymes had been slowly coming back into his memory, as he continued to think and fret about the subject.

Young Zoltan cheerfully continued his cataloguing of the remaining Swords. The hermit made sure to seem to be paying equal attention to the verses and anecdotes about Coinspinner and Soulcutter and the other Swords that followed, that his interest in the subject might not seem too particular. Meanwhile, in his concealed thoughts, he was increasingly aghast. His worst fears about the treasure he had hidden had now been confirmed, and he still had no hint as to who ought now to be considered its rightful owner.

The hermit had not been keeping count of verses, but he was just thinking that the catalogue of Swords must be nearing its end, when it was interrupted. Geelong the watchbeast sprang up suddenly on all four legs and whined loudly, facing the door. Someone else must be approaching the house.

When Gelimer went out into the front yard this time he stopped short, blinking in mild surprise.

A white-haired lady, whose age at a second look was hard to guess, was standing confronting him on the north side of his little yard, as if she had perhaps just climbed up from the river. Her erect body, clad like Zoltan's in pilgrim gray, might have belonged to a vigorous woman of forty, but her lined face looked twenty years older than that. The pilgrim gray she wore confirmed some connection with the youth, who now had followed Gelimer out of the house into the bright day of sunlight melting the last spring snow.

Zoltan quickly performed introductions.

"Lady, this is the hermit Gelimer, who has kindly offered us food and shelter should we be in need of either. Gelimer, this is the Lady Yambu, whom I serve."

"Say rather, with whom you travel." The lady's voice, like her bearing, had something regal in it. She smiled at Gelimer and stepped forward to grip him heartily by the hand.

When Zoltan had earlier informed him that his companion was a lady somewhat older than himself, several possibilities had suggested themselves to Gelimer. This lady did not appear to fit any of them very neatly.

"Yambu," repeated Gelimer aloud, and frowned in thought. "Some years ago there reigned, far to the east of here, a queen who was called the Silver Queen, and that was her name, too."

"That queen is no more," the lady said. "Or she might as well be no more. Only a pilgrim stands before you."

Smiling slightly, she shifted the direction of her gaze to Zoltan. "The captain has informed me that the *Maid of Lakes and Rivers* has now been permanently disabled," she reported. "Therefore, from here we must proceed for a time on foot. There is no need for us to return to the boat, as I have brought along all that was essential of our baggage." So saying, the lady slipped a pack of moderate size from her back and dropped it on the ground in front of Zoltan; it would be his to carry now.

Gelimer took a moment to reflect that the lady must be far from decrepit with age, to have made the steep climb up out of the gorge while carrying the pack. Then he courteously invited both of his visitors back into his humble house.

Half an hour later, the hermit was serving both the travelers some hot tea and simple food, meanwhile pausing frequently in his own mind to wonder what further questions he ought to ask them. They repre- sented his first contact with the outside world since the Sword had come into his possession, and he thought that his next such contact might be months away.

But it would not do to stick too doggedly to the subject of Swords. When Gelimer asked the Lady Yambu polite- ly about the object of her pilgrimage, she smiled at him lightly and told him that she was seeking truth.

"And Truth, then, is to be found somewhere down- river?"

She sipped her tea regally from its earthen cup. "I have had certain intimations that it might be."

"It might not be easy to find another boat to carry you on from here. The fishermen have boats, of course, but as a rule they don't want to go far."

The lady was unperturbed. "Then we shall walk."

Gelimer switched his attention to his other guest. "And you, young man? Do you seek Truth as well?"

"Yes," said Zoltan, and paused. "But not only that. Tell me, good hermit, do you know anything of a race of merpeople living in or near these waters? I have seen several of their kind far upstream, but no one there seems to know where they come from."

Gelimer looked at him, and thought carefully again. "Aye," he said at last. "There are mermaids in these waters. Hardly a race of them. But there have been a few such folk, whose homes are not all that far from where we sit. All maids, fish from the waist down. Their fate is a result of magic directed at certain fishing villages, by enemies."

Zoltan's eyes lit up at the discovery.

"Whose magic, and why?" Yambu asked at once. Suddenly she seemed almost as interested as the young man.

Gelimer heaved a sigh. "It is a long story," he said at last. "But if you are interested—I suppose you should hear the main points of it anyway, if you are going on downstream from here by foot—the journey, you must realize, will not be without its dangers."

"Few journeys are," said Yambu calmly. "At least among those which are worthwhile."

"When you have finished eating and enjoying your tea," said the hermit, "you must come outside, and we will climb up on a rock. From there we will be able to look downstream for many kilometers, and see the land on either side of the river; and there I will tell you something of the situation."

Presently, when their modest meal had been consumed, they were outside again. Gelimer took them to a promontory a little above his house, a place from which they could look to the south and west and see where the Tungri eventually lost itself among distant hills.

Gelimer waved his right hand to the north. "The land on the right bank is, for as far as you can see from here, under the domination of a clan called the Senones. The land on the left bank, whereon we are standing, is ruled by the Malolo clan. The two clans are bitter enemies, and have been so for many generations. The mermaids you have seen upstream were girls from one of a handful of small villages on the Malolo side, down there beyond the place where the river widens—you can barely see it from here.

"Their strange, unnatural form is a result of Senones magic, a bitter and destructive curse that was inflicted upon people in the Malolo territory several generations ago. Sometimes the girls deformed by the curse are sold into slavery as curiosities. I have heard that traveling shows and the like buy them. An evil business."

"Yes. I see," said young Zoltan. He was shading his eyes, and staring very intently and thoughtfully at the village barely visible in the distance. "And has no one ever found a cure for this particular curse?"

"It would seem that the Malolo at least have never been able to find any."

Zoltan was silent, gazing off toward the horizon. It was left to the Lady Yambu to ask their host some practical questions about the trails.

Shortly after he had imparted that information, Gelimer was again left without human companionship. His guests were on their way—long hours of sunny daylight still remained, and both pilgrims, the young man and the older woman, were eager to be gone.

The hermit, looking after them when they had vanished down the trail, still could not quite decide what was the relationship between them. The young man seemed more true companion than servant. And if that woman had really at one time been the Silver Queen . . . having talked to her now, Gelimer found he could believe she had.

Eventually the hermit, frowning, turned back to his hermitage. Hiding the Sword had really done nothing to relieve him of its burden. He still had matters of very great importance to decide.

THREE

THE sun had nearly disappeared from sight behind the tall trees of the valley's forest before the two pilgrims again came in sight of the small fishing village they had glimpsed from the crag above the hermit's house. Now they were walking close beside the river, and were almost on the point of entering the settlement.

At the point where the trail they had been following emerged from the forest, on the south bank, Zoltan paused and turned to look over his shoulder to the northeast. He thought that he could see that crag again, still clearly visible in the light of the lowering sun. Now, of course, those heights were much too far away for him to be able to make out whether the hermit or anyone else was standing there.

He faced forward again, and with the Lady Yambu at his side approached the village. The pair of them advanced slowly, wanting to give the inhabitants plenty of time to become aware of their arrival. Three or four of the fisherfolk were visible, garbed in heavy trousers and jackets. The place seemed quite ordinary for a settlement beside a river. It consisted of twelve or fifteen bark-roofed houses, some of them raised on stilts along the shoreline, and actually extending over the water.

Thin columns of smoke from several fires ascended into the air. Just behind the village the forest rose up dense and tall, beginning to be clothed in the new growth of spring. One or two of the trees loomed impressively, being of the same gigantic species as the one that had formed the hermit's house.

The hermit Gelimer had told the travelers that this was one of the handful of villages, all within a few kilometers of each other along the Tungri, whose inhabitants lived under the mermaid curse. Those few who were now visible to the slowly approaching travelers had nothing out of the ordinary in their appearance—not, Zoltan supposed, that there was any reason to think they would. Three or four fishing boats were tied up at a dock, and only a few patches of ice were visible along the shore. At this lower altitude the ground was completely barren of snow.

"Remember, Zoltan, how the hermit warned us," admonished Yambu, watching her companion closely. "In my opinion he advised us well. You should say nothing at all about mermaids while we are among these village people, at least not until we have gained some understanding of their attitude on the subject. It must be a matter that they are not inclined to treat lightly."

"I understand. I agree," Zoltan answered shortly. He was having a difficult time trying to control his impatience, and he supposed the difficulty showed.

During their long day's hike down the mountain and through the forest he had talked at some length with Yambu about his continuing determination to seek out one particular mermaid.

"You say, my lady, that you are making this pilgrimage to seek the Truth. Well, so am I, in my own way. My goal is to find that girl—I cannot forget her. She has come to represent Truth to me."

Since leaving their native lands months ago, the two

pilgrims had had this same conversation, or one very much like it, several times. By now Yambu knew almost as much as Zoltan did about the particular mermaid he was seeking. And she had learned better than to argue directly against the youth's objective. Instead she now asked him: "Exactly how many times did you really see her, in all?"

"Three times, at least. Oh, there were other occasions on the upper river when she was only a shadow, or a ripple in the water, or a movement in the leaves along the shore. But three times, later, I saw her solidly, and talked with her and even touched her."

"Given the other things that happened, we must consider that those earlier appearances were a result of evil magic."

The young man shook his head violently. "Not *her* evil. Not her magic, either."

The woman remained perfectly calm. "No. Or at least not hers primarily. But the attraction you felt and still feel for her had its root in that same evil magic."

"She was enslaved then by that ghastly wizard Wood, or one of his lieutenants!"

"True. But it seems to me that what we still do not know is to what degree, how willingly, the girl, the mermaid, went along with what the Ancient One wanted her to do."

"She did not help him willingly at all, I tell you!"

Yambu only looked sympathetically at her young companion.

Zoltan got himself under control as well as he was able. "I tell you that I saw this girl, talked to her, several times as I moved farther down the Sanzu. She was—she truly wanted to help me. She did her best to help me against the dragon at the end."

"Ah well, you were there and I was not." Yambu

conceded the point. "Even so, that was three years ago. Even if you do succeed in finding her now, you ought to remember that much can change in three years, in the life of any person. Particularly in a young woman's life, whether she's half fish or not." To herself Lady Yambu was thinking how hopeless it always was to try to shield the young against their own enthusiasms.

But now, before Zoltan was required to answer, the two travelers had to put their debate behind them. Raising open hands in gestures of peace, Zoltan and Yambu were approaching the fishing village. Children came running to look at them, and then some of the adults.

As they met the inhabitants they took care to observe the little hints, given them by the hermit, as to what was locally considered proper conduct. The people spoke a variation of the common tongue, not difficult to cope with. The greetings the two travelers received from the adult villagers were tinged at first with obvious suspicion. Zoltan was not surprised by this, considering that if all the stories of the clan feud and its consequences were true, these people had every reason to be wary.

Still, Gelimer's coaching paid off. An elder appeared at last, and the two travelers were invited in and offered food and shelter for the night. The local hospitality was somewhat more cheerfully displayed when Yambu demonstrated her readiness to pay a small amount of coin.

As soon as the sun had departed from the sky the air grew chill, and mist rose from the river, which here below the rapids of the gorge widened to such an extent that it might almost have been called a lake. Both shores were heavily forested, and after sundown the cries of exotic animals, strange to Zoltan's ears, began to issue from the darkness within the nearby forest.

Against the sunset sky fairly large building, of an

ominously dark color, could be seen perched atop a denuded hill at a distance of two or three kilometers from the village.

In answer to the visitors' questions, the villagers informed them that this structure was the stronghold of the Malolo clan, and in it dwelt the overlords of this and half a dozen other settlements upon the southern shore.

After the two pilgrims had enjoyed a good supper, largely of fish and bread, Yambu turned in for the night in the House of Women, and Zoltan went to the Dormitory of Unattached Men, which was one of the houses built out over the water on stilts. Tonight, for whatever reason, it seemed that he was going to have no more than a couple of roommates, two tired-looking village youths who had already stretched out their sleeping mats at the far end of the large room.

So far, although Zoltan had been looking and listening alertly since entering the village for anything that might suggest mermaids, he had seen and heard nothing to suggest that this place was home to them. Indeed, there was no indication that anyone here had ever heard of such creatures. Zoltan had followed Yambu's counsel, though with some difficulty, and had refrained from mentioning the subject. Now as he lay wrapped in his blanket, looking out at the misty, wintry lake and listening to the dark water lap the slender pilings below him, the thought of having to live in that water was enough to chill him to his bones. Of course real fish lived in it and prospered the year round . . . but she, the girl he sought, was not a fish. With his own hands Zoltan had touched her cool smooth shoulders, and her long black hair. Damn it, by all the gods, she was a human being like himself, even if she was burdened with a terrible curse . . . even if he did not yet know her name . . .

*   *   *

Zoltan slept. And then, in the middle of the night, he came awake, softly and suddenly. In the cold moonlight that fell in through a nearby window he beheld the very girl he had so long pursued. She was sitting close beside him and leaning over him, so that an amulet of some kind that she wore around her neck swung free. Her black hair fell in wet strands past her white shoulders and around her pale breasts. Below her slender, human waist, her body continued undivided and tapering, legless and silvery, scaly and graceful and terrible, down to the broad fins of her tail. In this dream—as Zoltan first believed it was—the young girl was just as he remembered her, and the three years that had passed since their last meeting might never have existed.

"Who are you?" he breathed, still more than half convinced that he was dreaming.

Her voice too was unchanged from what he remembered. "My name is Black Pearl. This is my friend, Soft Ripple. And you are Zoltan. Do you remember me?"

Only now did Zoltan realize that there was another mermaid sitting a little behind the first. The one immediately in front of him, who had called herself Black Pearl, had her silvery tail bent up gracefully beneath her, allowing her to sit in an almost completely human posture. Behind and around her, moonlight mottled empty sleeping mats, and the shadowy figure of her companion in the background. Water was dripping slowly, irregularly, from both the mermaids' hair.

"Do I—"

Suddenly the conviction was borne in up Zoltan that this was no dream. He sat up abruptly. "Do I *remember* you? I never knew your name, but I've done nothing for the past months but look for you. I've come down the river all the way from Tasavalta . . ."

He reached out suddenly to take Black Pearl by the

hand. She made an effort to pull away at first, but his grip was too swift and, once anchored on her wrist, too strong. "Tell me," he pleaded. "Tell me what I can do to help you."

Down at the far end of the room one of the two bachelor youths snored, loudly and abruptly. Zoltan glanced in that direction, but as far as he could tell both of the young men were really still fast asleep.

In the stillness of the night Black Pearl's shadowy mermaid companion murmured something that Zoltan could not quite make out. Black Pearl understood what had been said, though, and ceased trying to pull free. Instead she took Zoltan's wrist in her own grip.

"We've come to bring a warning to the village. Men from the other side of the river, where the Senones live, are coming across in two boats tonight. They must be intending some hostile action."

"Men from the other side? What should I—"

"As soon as we two are gone, raise the alarm. But you must not say that my friend and I were here and told you. Otherwise the elders might ignore your warning. So please, forget we were here!"

"Very well. This place is dangerous for you, then?"

The mermaid shook her head, as if to say there was no time to explain now. "Meet me—Zoltan, meet me tomorrow night at midnight, at the edge of the lake near the mouth of the creek that flows past the Malolo stronghold. Come out in a boat if you can. If not, then watch for me from shore. Will you do that?"

"I will, I swear I will!"

Black Pearl flashed Zoltan a last look, a look that held a kind of desperation. Then in the next moments she and her silent companion were gone, as softly and swiftly as diving otters, disappearing at once through an aperture in the floor. It was the same entrance commonly used by people who arrived at the dormitory in boats. But there was no boat below the entrance now.

Only a small stain of water upon an empty sleeping mat remained to show that the visitors had not been a dream after all.

Rising silently from his blanket, Zoltan moved quickly to one of the windows on the lake side of the house and looked out. Out on the misty lake at least two large floating objects were dimly visible, holding place against the current. They had to be boats, moving silently in the moonlight, creeping in toward the village docks.

Zoltan drew in breath and shouted, as loudly as he could.

The two youths at the far end of the dormitory sprang up instantly, as if they had been prodded with sharp spears. Zoltan pointed through the window toward the boats, and shouted some more. His two roommates looked where he was pointing, and a moment later added their voices to his at full volume.

Next, drawing his short sword, Zoltan rushed outside, onto a deck built above the water. Already the uproar he had started was spreading to the other houses. Within a matter of a few moments more, it seemed that everyone in the village was awake, and all the men had sprung to arms; the small docks were swarming with defenders.

Three large boats, full of would-be attackers, could now be seen quite close to shore. The craft of this flotilla turned briefly broadside to the bank, from which position their shadowy crews launched a light volley of missiles, stones and arrows. Then the intruders dropped their weapons and plied their paddles vigorously, heading out into the concealing mists again. They were pursued by a scattered response in the form of arrows and slung stones.

In the space of half a dozen breaths the skirmish, if it

could even be called that, was over. No one on shore appeared to have been injured, and there was no damage done.

Within a few minutes after the attackers had disappeared, the village leaders, gathering in torchlight among their armed and assembled people, wanted to know who had first raised the alarm. Zoltan raised his hand. He explained that he had just happened to be wakeful, and had seen the enemy approaching.

The people of the village accepted this explanation, and were quick to praise the stranger for his alertness. But Yambu, listening, looked at Zoltan strangely. Her gaze said that later, when the two of them were again alone, she would insist on being told the truth.

FOUR

IN the hours following the departure from the hermitage of the pilgrim pair, Gelimer, feeling himself
unable to make headway on profound problems, decided
to concentrate for the time being on simple ones. He
began to take an interest in his garden, to see how the
various herbs had passed through the winter, and to
make somewhat belated preparations for the busy season of spring. It was a peaceful interlude. There were
moments when he could almost have been convinced
that the man who had brought the Sword, as well as his
two most recent visitors, and all their problems including the Sword itself, were nothing but creations of his
imagination.

The hermit's respite from the problem of Farslayer
was brief. About noon on the day after the two pilgrims'
visit, his fourth visitor of this extraordinary spring
showed up.

This latest arrival was a man in his mid-thirties,
dark-skinned and lean, and with a fierce, competitive
eye. He had come a long way, and he had seen hard
traveling, as could be told by the state of his mount and
his equipment. Still he was well dressed, his riding-beast
was a noble animal, and the way he wore his weapons at

his belt suggested that they had most likely seen hard use at some time or other.

With an unconscious groan Gelimer straightened his back from garden chores, and calmly made this latest traveler welcome. Last night what must finally have been the last storm of the season had dusted three or four more centimeters of snow over his garden and everything else in sight, including the new grave in the grove, and the fast-disappearing carcass of the last riding-beast to have carried its master along these trails. Here in the sun the snow had already melted, but in the woods its white veil would still endure.

Since the day after the death of its last owner, the Sword itself had been hidden as well as the hermit knew how to hide anything. Gelimer doubted very much that anyone was going to find it, barring interference by some major wizard.

"Thank you for the invitation to dismount, good hermit . . . ahh!" And the formidable-looking rider, in turn, groaned with relief as he swung himself down from his saddle.

The visitor introduced himself as Chilperic. No second name. And Gelimer still did not allow his suspicions to be aroused, when, almost as soon as he had settled himself upon a chair inside the house, this newest visitor inquired: "I suppose that a fair number of travelers are fortunate enough to enjoy your hospitality, good hermit? You occupy a somewhat strategic situation here."

"This site where I live?" Gelimer looked around him, as if he could see out through his wooden walls. "It is important only in potential. Ah, 'twould be strategic indeed if there were any measurable amount of traffic up and down the river here, but the water's almost always too rough for that. Or if armies were often marching through this pass . . . but for twenty years at least that hasn't happened, either. The war-makers both upstream and down all have enough to do in their own territories without tackling more. So this is only a lonely mountain-side, left to me. Often months go by without a soul appearing at my door."

"I see. Interesting. And has this past month been entirely devoid of visitors?"

Now, Gelimer was unable to accept this innocent-sounding question at face value. Indeed, he was almost convinced already that the serious search for the Sword, which he had been more than half expecting for many days, had finally arrived. For some reason it surprised the hermit at first that the searcher, if such he was, did not appear to be a local man at all. But on second thought, that was really no surprise.

Gelimer answered: "On the contrary, sir, the past month has been comparatively busy. There have actually been three other travelers before yourself." Here the hermit paused to sip his mead. Then he went on, trying to give the impression of a man who did not need to be prodded to talk to one random visitor about another, who in fact was even eager to talk on the subject, because he had something mildly unusual to tell.

"The first one who stopped here gave me the impression of a man fleeing something, or someone." And here the hermit, who had been granted time to think what he should do, went on to give a rough description of the man who had died with the Sword run through him, and of the strangely shaped bundle that man had been carrying. It was Gelimer's idea, right or wrong, that an honest owner looking for his lost treasure would come out honestly and say what he was trying to find.

Chilperic sipped at his mead, too. If the shape of the stranger's bundle had suggested anything to him, he did not say so. When he spoke again his tone indicated no more than a polite interest, though indeed the question he asked was pertinent enough: "Ah, and how long ago was this?"

The hermit allowed himself an equally polite effort to recall. "Let me see now. Was it before this past full moon, or after? But lately most of the nights have been cloudy anyway. I really cannot say with any certainty."

The other leaned forward, and spoke with evident sincerity. "I will be glad to make it worth your while to try to remember. The fact is that I have been searching for this man."

"I see. And what will happen when you find him?"

"Oh, I am not a manhunter. Nothing like that." The visitor, smiling, leaned back in his chair again. "I seek him only to satisfy my own curiosity. Nor do I really travel in search of this fellow you describe. It is only that in the course of my travels I keep encountering him— and his strange story. As an interested observer, I would like to know the ending of that tale. No, if you are kindly disposed toward the fellow, you need have no fear that he is going to suffer harm because of anything I do."

"You intrigue me."

"I should not. His story is not mine to tell."

Gelimer shrugged, doing his best to revert to an attitude of indifference. "Ardneh enjoins us to be kind to everyone. But I have no particular reason to wish this fellow well—or to wish him ill, for that matter. If you told me he was a thief, though, and that you were trying to bring him to justice, I would be inclined to believe you."

"Why so?" asked Chilperic.

"Because of the strange and jealous way he treated the peculiar bundle that he carried. As if—perhaps it had been stolen. Because of—well, because of a certain furtiveness in the fellow's manner."

"Ah, yes, you mentioned a peculiar bundle. And you said it was of an unusual size and shape?"

"Yes. Well . . ." And Gelimer gestured vaguely, measuring the air with his two hands. "A package wrapped in rough cloth. A weighty thing. It might have held a small shovel, or an axe." Surely an honest seeker would come out openly now, and say *I am looking for a Sword.*

"And I suppose you never saw the bundle opened?"

"That is correct." Ardneh was not picky about the letter of the truth, Gelimer had always thought; rather it was the underlying goal of speech that counted with the benign god. "He stayed in my house for a single night, ate sparingly, and was on his way again at first light, taking his bundle with him." That of course was the point Gelimer had been anxious to establish if he could. "Although the weather was foul at that time and the trails exceedingly dangerous, nothing I could say would induce him to delay his departure."

"You say the weather was foul, good hermit. On the night when this visitor came to you, was there in fact a notably heavy snowstorm, with enough wind to make it almost a blizzard?"

Gelimer tried his best to give the appearance of a man trying to remember, succeeding a little at a time, recovering something he had thought of small importance when it happened. "Why, I suppose that is a fair description of the weather, now that I think about it."

"And was this strange visitor traveling mounted or on foot?"

"He had a riding-beast. Yes. I didn't really notice much about the animal—but yes, that visitor traveled mounted."

"And in which direction did he go on his departure?" All pretense of a merely casual interest on the questioner's part was gradually being discarded.

"He was heading downslope, as I recall, toward the river. Of course he could easily have changed directions once he was out of my sight. He never said anything about where he was going. He did not even give me his name, which I thought odd."

"But not surprising, in his case—his name, or at least the name I have known him to use, is Cosmo Biondo, and he is a great rogue."

"A rogue, you say."

"I do. You may count yourself fortunate, Sir Hermit, that he didn't cut your throat while you were sleeping."

Gelimer, blinking to give his best impression of being mildly shocked, brought out from under his robes an amulet of Ardneh, which hung always around his neck. He held the talisman in his hand and rubbed it. "Then I truly wish that I were able to tell you more about him. I wish that you were indeed trying to bring him to justice."

Chilperic shook his head, dismissing that idea, and sat back in his chair once more. But presently he leaned forward again to pose another question: "As I recall, you said you have been visited by two other travelers this month as well?"

"Yes. They were two pilgrims, who came through here only yesterday. The riverboat they were traveling on, they said, had come to grief on the rocks below. The crew, I understand, were trying to tow the craft upstream again with a rope. But I really doubt that the two I met could have had anything to do with this Biondo fellow."

"Perhaps not. Headed upstream or down?"

"They said that they were going down."

"What were they like?"

Gelimer, seeing no reason not to do so, described yesterday morning's pair of visitors in some detail. But he thoughtfully omitted to mention the conversation he had had with them on the subject of Swords.

When today's visitor had finished his refreshment, and stretched, and looked about the house, he expressed a wish to be on his way while the light and the weather remained good.

Doing his best to pretend a certain reluctance to lose a temporary companion, the hermit at last bade his guest goodbye. "And good luck in your search—I would like sometime to hear the rest of this Biondo's story."

Chilperic, already mounted, looked down at Gelimer and shook his head. "It might not be safe for you to know that story, good hermit—as for me, I already know the dangerous parts of the tale, and so am free to indulge my further curiosity."

And in a moment, with a final wave, this latest visitor too was gone, having said not a word during his visit on the subject of his own goals and business. He rode downslope, in the direction of the suspension bridge that would take him across the Tungri. Would he be reporting to the Senones, then? Or perhaps seeking to question them? But it would be as easy for this traveler as for the other one to change directions once he was out of sight, and Gelimer was not minded to follow him to be sure which way he went.

FIVE

O N the morning after their arrival at the fishing
village, Zoltan and Yambu were treated to a fine
breakfast, an expression of the villagers' gratitude for
Zoltan's part in last night's modest victory. Having done
justice to this homely feast of fish, beans, and the eggs
of waterfowl, the travelers thanked their hosts, bade
them farewell, and pressed forward on foot toward the
hilltop stronghold or manor where dwelt the Malolo
overlords.

Patches of forest engulfed the path, between areas of
cultivated land. As they walked, Zoltan told his companion the story of his encounter with Black Pearl during
the night. She listened in silence and made no comment.
He also warned Lady Yambu that when they reached the
manor he was determined to raise the mermaid question
with the authorities there, in one way or another, with
whatever degree of diplomacy he could manage. Now
that he knew the name of Black Pearl, and was certain
that she was still alive, and here, somewhere close—
well, whatever happened, he was not going to let her get
away from him again.

"Well, of course you must make every effort to find
out more, since now you have actually seen her." Yambu
sighed. She believed what the lad had told her about last

night—and she had really believed him about the mermaid all along—but still there were things about the business she did not like.

Zoltan persisted. "Not only to find out more. If this mermaid curse was put upon her by some magician, then there must exist some magic that can take it off. I mean to restore her to true womanhood."

Yambu sighed again, this time silently, at the young man's obvious determination. "When the time comes, then, to speak to the Malolo leaders on the subject, will you let me try my hand at the diplomacy? I do have somewhat more experience in the field than you."

"Would you, my lady?" Zoltan cried with sincere relief. "I would be immensely grateful."

Having reached that agreement, the two trudged on in silence for a time, proceeding through the woods along a well-trodden path at the moment empty of all other traffic. Presently Zoltan spoke again. "I wonder what the leaders of this Malolo clan are like."

"It is impossible to tell until we meet them. Something like other minor lordlings elsewhere, I suppose," Yambu added with faint distaste. The lady took a dozen strides in thoughtful silence before she added: "The village leader back there gave me the impression that he thought something strange had been going on in the clan's stronghold for some time, at least a month."

"Something strange?"

"He really said nothing specific on the subject. But that was the impression I received."

Zoltan pondered this news in concerned silence.

"I wonder where everyone is?" the lady remarked suddenly in a different voice.

Indeed, the crude road which the two travelers were following had remained completely empty of other traffic, and this fact now began to take on an ominous aspect in Zoltan's eyes. At each turn, as the rutted track wound back and forth through fields and forest, he kept expecting to encounter a farmer's cart, a peddler, a goatherd, someone. But there was never anyone else in sight.

"Have all the farmers fled their lands? It should be time for planting."

Yambu shook her head. "Not a good sign."

In due time, and without ever meeting anyone, the two travelers came upon the house, which stood less than an hour's walk from the lakeside village where they had spent the night. The hill, upon which the Malolo clan had chosen to build their manor, had long ago been denuded of trees, leaving only a myriad of ancient stumps. Within a low wall, the stone and timber of the house were dark, and the grounds around the house long uncared-for and eroded. Even in the clear light of day, the whole establishment had a forbidding aspect to Zoltan.

Still no other people were in sight. And everything was silent except for the lowing of cattle, which seemed to be coming from outbuildings in the rear. The animals sounded as if they were in need of being milked.

The front entrance of the manor was protected by a small drawbridge, let down over a long-dry moat. The outer end of the drawbridge, now resting on the earth, had crushed a new spring growth of weeds beneath it. From this fact Zoltan deduced that the bridge must commonly be kept raised at least as much as it was lowered. Evidently the long-standing feud sometimes included direct assaults upon the strongholds of the chief participants.

However that might be, no one had bothered to raise the bridge today. Trudging on across its weathered timbers, the two travelers found themselves immediately before the manor's great front door. Still they had not been challenged, or even observed as far as they could tell. They had seen no one since leaving the vicinity of the village. This absence of human activity caused them to once more exchange puzzled glances.

Then Zoltan shrugged, raised his sword hilt, and rapped firmly, loudly, three times on the door.

For a time, a period of time that became noticeably extended, there was no answer.

He was just about to knock again, and louder still, when at last a small peephole, heavily protected by iron grillwork, opened near the middle of the door. "Who is it?" a crabbed and cracking tenor demanded from within.

"Two pilgrims," the lady on the doorstep answered, putting authority and volume into her voice. "The Lady Yambu and her attendant. We bring certain information that the chief of the Malolo clan should be glad to hear."

There followed a protracted and suspicious silence. Zoltan supposed that the speaker inside—he could not be sure from the voice whether it was a man or a woman—was probably using the peephole to inspect the two on the doorstep.

"You can give me the information," the voice said next, adopting now a different but still peculiar tone, somewhere between wheedling and mindless threat.

Yambu glared at the wooden barrier. "I do not conduct conversations through a door." This time no one would have doubted that a queen was speaking.

Response from inside was immediate, in the form of a tentative rattling, as of a heavy doorbar in its sockets. Then came a brief silence as of hesitation, or perhaps a consultation carried on too quietly to be audible outside. Then the bar rattled again, this time banging decisively as it was thrown aside. Bolts clattered, and a moment later the left half of the double door was creaking open.

Standing before the travelers was one man, unarmed and not very large, his gray beard and hair in wild disarray, his watery blue eyes blinking in the morning sun. The man's clothes—leather trousers, leather vest over a once-white shirt—were so stained and generally shabby that Zoltan was ready at first to take the fellow for a servant. Behind the entranceway in which he stood stretched the dim length of a great hall, where the littered condition of floor and tables, along with a few overturned chairs, suggested at first glance that a notable revel of some kind might have been held here last night.

The fellow who had opened the door looked at the Lady Yambu again, face-to-face this time, and bowed to her at once. "Welcome," he said, in a somewhat more courteous tone than before. He stood aside. "Come in, my lady, come in." But having said that much he stopped, seeming not to know how to proceed.

"Thank you, Sir Wizard," said the lady dryly, entering the house. And Zoltan, turning his head suddenly to look at the man once more, could see that the rings on his stained fingers were marked with insignia of power, and were of a richness that certainly no menial servant wore; and that a chain of thin gold encircled the man's wrinkled neck and went down inside his dirty shirt.

Yambu grabbed her companion by the sleeve and pulled him forward. "This is Zoltan of Tasavalta, who travels with me. Now may we know your name? Your public name at least?" It was a common practice for wizards of any rank to keep their true names unknown to any besides themselves.

Their reluctant host nodded abstractedly in Zoltan's direction, acknowledging the introduction. Then he turned back to his more important guest. "Call me Gesner, Lady Yambu. May I ask, what is this information that you have?"

The lady told him briefly of the incidents in the village last night. Meanwhile, not waiting for any further invitation, she moved on into the great hall, the graybeard moving at her side. Zoltan followed. Seen at closer range, the disorder was more evident than ever. And it was older—as if some feasting might have been suddenly interrupted many days ago, and only a minimum of serious housekeeping performed since. Leftover food in dishes had long since dried, and there was a smell in the air of stale drink and garbage. The ashes in the enormous hearth looked utterly cold and dead.

"And is that all, my lady?" The decrepit-looking magician sounded disappointed. "I mean—skirmishes like that are common. Why should you think my master would consider it vital news?"

Ignoring Gesner's question, Yambu looked about her and asked him in turn: "Where is your master? You are certainly not the lord of the manor here?"

A different voice replied, speaking from behind her: "No, he's not. I—I am here."

Turning to a broad stairway that came down at one end of the hall, Zoltan to his surprise saw a somewhat overweight adolescent boy, two or three years younger than himself, dressed in rich clothing but looking nervous and incompetent and frightened.

At this point two girls, also well dressed, and both somewhat younger than the boy, appeared on the stairs above him. These girls, moving like people who were reluctant to advance but still more frightened of being left behind, edged slowly downward on the stairs, keeping close behind the youth who had spoken.

And the fat boy continued his own uncertain descent of the stairs. He paused, shortly before reaching the bottom, to repeat his claim, as if he thought it quite natural that his audience should doubt him. "I am

Bonar, the chief of Clan Malolo." At his side he wore a small sword, hung from a belt that did not quite appear to fit.

Yambu, the experienced diplomat, surveyed the situation, and appeared to be ready to take the young man at his word, at least for now. Addressing him politely, she related again, with more detail, what had happened in the village last night, with emphasis on how the alarm raised by Zoltan had prevented harm. This time she included the visit of the mermaids and their warning.

The lady's manner, more than the content of what she said, had a soothing and reassuring effect upon the frightened inmates of the manor. Zoltan got the impression that they were beginning to be willing, perhaps irrationally, to trust her now; that these representatives of the Malolo clan were looking for someone they could trust.

Before Lady Yambu had finished relating her story, the young people had all completed their descent of the stairs and were surrounding her and Zoltan in the great hall. The two girls, who were Bonar's sisters as Zoltan had suspected from the first, were named Rose and Violet. Now, while Gesner stood back frowning silently, the three family members bombarded the two visitors with questions.

What had Yambu and Zoltan seen on the other side of the river? What evidence was there of military activity in that direction? On these points the travelers could be reassuring, at least in a negative sense. They had not traveled on the far bank, and had not seen a living soul over there for several days. Nor had either of them observed anything at all military in that direction, unless last night's disturbance at the fishing village was to be counted. Zoltan and Yambu now related that story again, and hearing it seemed to reassure their hosts slightly.

There was a brief silence.

"What is wrong here?" Yambu asked the young people finally. "It is plain that this house has been engulfed by some crisis. Where are all the older members of this family?"

The inhabitants of the manor looked at one another. Then Bonar, nervously clenching his white hands together, suddenly blurted out what might have been the beginning of an answer: "We haven't been out of this house for days. For a good many days. Not since that man came here asking questions."

"What man was that?" Yambu inquired patiently.

"A traveler. Someone of good birth, I'm sure. He called himself Chilperic, and at first we had hopes that he was going to help us. I think he was—I don't know, a soldier of some kind. He claimed to be some kind of distant relative of ours." The speaker looked around at his companions as if for confirmation. They nodded vaguely.

"And what questions did he ask?"

Bonar and his sisters looked at each other in a silent struggle.

"But where are your own soldiers?" Zoltan demanded abruptly. Since these people were so worried about something, and since they were supposed to be engaged in a permanent feud with some other clan, it puzzled him all the more that he had not seen a sentry or armed attendant of any kind since his arrival. "Surely you have armed retainers of some kind about?"

Gesner spoke up quickly. "Of course we do. They are all on watch, at the moment."

"Most of them are out on patrol just now," said Rose, the older sister, speaking simultaneously with the wizard. Rose had fine dark hair, a face that was pleasant if somewhat long, and a figure that Zoltan under less tense conditions might have found distracting. She had come up behind her brother Bonar, and with a gesture that might have been meant as a warning laid her hand upon his arm.

Zoltan and Yambu exchanged glances.

Evidently the former queen and skilled diplomatist thought it was best to let the subject of soldiers drop for the time being. She looked at Bonar and said: "Young man, the people in the fishing village mentioned a different name than yours when they spoke to us of the chief of the Malolo."

Bonar turned paler than ever. Only the shabby magician responded verbally to the implied question. "Yes," said Gesner wearily. "Yes, no doubt they did."

An awkward silence ensued, as if the inhabitants of the house were on the verge of offering some explanation, but none of them quite dared to try.

Zoltan decided at last that diplomacy had had its chance, and he might as well attempt a blunt interrogation. "Chief Bonar—is that what we should call you?"

"It will do."

"Then, Chief, you obviously have some serious problem here. Is there some way that we can be of help?"

"We do need help," Bonar admitted at last, after having looked again at both his sisters and found none. His pale and pudgy hands were held together in front of him, and he gazed down at them as if wondering how he might be able to get the intertwined fingers apart again. "We've had . . . Well, a terrible thing has happened."

"I am not surprised to hear it. Now I invite you to tell us what it was," said Yambu, in a soft and yet commanding voice.

After much continued hesitation, the four members of the household, including Gesner, decided to hold a meeting among themselves. Having first remembered to make sure that the front door was securely closed again and locked, they withdrew to another room, with some apologies, leaving Yambu and Zoltan alone. Soon, from the other room, their muffled voices could be heard, rising now and then in argument, as they debated some matter earnestly. Zoltan and Yambu paced about, looking at each other and shrugging their shoulders.

At length the four, with the air of having come to an agreement, rejoined their visitors in the great hall. Then Bonar, the new chief of the clan, with Gesner at his back, silently motioned Yambu and Zoltan to follow him into an adjoining corridor. There the chief drew a key from inside his shirt and unlocked a door leading to a descending stair.

Zoltan went down cautiously, a hand on his sword hilt. A few moments later Bonar was escorting him and Yambu into a large vaulted room on a windowless below-ground level of the huge house. The door of this room too was doubly locked before they entered it, and it was guarded on the outside by a couple of elderly people who glared suspiciously at the intruders, and whom Zoltan had no trouble identifying as faithful old family retainers. There were a few of the same type back home at High Manor, where he had been born.

As the group of visitors filed into the vault one of the attendant servants held up a torch, revealing that they were in a windowless chamber almost as large as the great hall above.

There was a faint perception of magic in the air, and for a moment Zoltan thought that the dozen or so fully clothed people who were lying stretched out on the tables that almost filled the room were all sleeping some enchanted slumber—but only for a moment. Then he realized that all of them were dead.

Arrayed before the visitors, with some effort at neat arrangement, were eleven corpses—Zoltan quickly took an exact count. If this was a collection of combat casualties, it fit the usual pattern in that young males were in the majority. All the dead were fully clothed adults, all of them laid out on tables, or, in some cases, biers improvised from smaller furniture, chests, and chairs.

A faintly sweetish aroma hung in the air, along with the impression of simple magic in operation. Zoltan, who was no magician but who had seen more magic in his young life than many people ever saw, suspected strongly that some preservative spell was in action here, and also that the spell was neither very well designed nor very well cast. These bodies were going to have to be buried soon, or otherwise permanently disposed of.

Judging by the expression on Lady Yambu's face, and the sidelong look she cast at Gesner, she evidently shared Zoltan's thoughts. He supposed the wobbly preservative spell was the work of Gesner, who did not exactly give forth an aura of competence.

Violet, Bonar's younger sister, had begun sobbing quietly as soon as she entered the room of death. With dull brown hair and a thin body, Violet was plainer than Rose, and also had a fiercer look.

"What happened?" Lady Yambu asked, turning from the bodies to stare curiously at the young chief of the clan.

"We fought." Bonar gestured helplessly at the carnage before him. "It was about a month ago."

"Fought whom? Only among yourselves?"

"Of course not." The youth's cheeks reddened and suddenly he looked sullenly angry. "Against the damned Senones. The clan of scoundrels across the river. Our ancient enemies."

The lady looked at the crowded tables. "Would it be fair to say that your enemies won that fight?"

"I think not." Now the lad's pride was stung. "We killed as many of them as they of us."

"And where did this fight take place?" asked Zoltan,

walking now between the rows of tables, looking at first one and then another of the bodies. As he inspected the dead more methodically he realized that each of them had been slain by a single thrust, through the torso, from some broad-bladed weapon. No other wounds of any kind were in evidence on any of the bodies.

Violet spoke up suddenly. "It happened here, in our house. And also in the stronghold of those scum across the river."

Yambu turned to her. "Here *and* there? I don't quite—?"

"Have you ever heard of the magical weapon called Farslayer, or the Sword of Vengeance?" Bonar's question came out in a bitter monotone, between clenched teeth.

Zoltan had to make an effort to keep himself from flashing Yambu a sudden, almost triumphant look of understanding. But he kept his eyes on Bonar. "Yes," he said. "I have heard of it."

"Good. Then you will understand. Our two clans, neither leaving its own stronghold, fought the whole battle with that single weapon." Bonar's gesture was an aborted movement of one hand, directed toward the tables and their burdens. "My own father lies here, and two of my uncles. And—" For a moment it seemed that the new chief of the Malolo clan might be about to break down and weep.

Rose, who was now bearing up better than before, took over the job of adding details. She related in a muddled way how, a month ago, the people of this clan and those across the river, each at the time locked into their own fortress, had engaged at long range in an hour or more of terrible slaughter.

Zoltan nodded. "There's no doubt about it being Farslayer, then. Of course. And you just kept casting it back and forth . . ."

"Yes," said Bonar. "Yes. I'll see them all dead yet."

"And where is the Sword now?" the Lady Yambu asked.

"We don't know," said Violet. "We haven't seen it since that night. For a while we thought that our cousin Cosmo had taken it to the enemy. But—many days have passed now, almost a month, and no more of us has been struck down."

There was a silence in the room. Everyone was looking thoughtfully at the bodies.

"Well, if your enemies have the Sword, they are hesitating to use it," Yambu agreed at last. "But where did it come from on that night of slaughter? Did the enemy have it first, or you?"

None of the household's survivors could offer a certain explanation of how the fight had started. But when the Sword struck its first victim in this house, a number of people had been on hand who could recognize the magical weapon for what it was, and explain its dreadfully simple use to the others. Almost immediately everyone had known how to use it to strike back at the enemy.

"You hold it—so," Rose was explaining, her two delicate wrists crossed in front of her, small white fingers clenched on an imaginary hilt. "Then you spin around —in a kind of dance—" And her feet stepped daintily in dainty shoes, performing a demonstration. "Maybe the dance isn't even necessary, but most did it that way. Some of the people chanted before they threw the Sword: *'For thy heart, for thy heart . . .'* and they would name a name—someone on the Senones side, you see.

"My father and brothers knew all their names over there, they knew just who they wanted to kill the most. And then, when you have chanted and spun the Sword, you just—let go."

The dainty dance came to an unsteady halt. The small white fingers opened, at the end of the extended wrists.

"And then—the Sword would leap from the thrower's hands, and vanish. Each time I saw it go, it made a splash of color in the air, as pretty as a rainbow. And an ugly little howling sound, like a hurt cat.

"And then, sometimes sooner, sometimes later, it would always come back—the same way. Over there, they knew all of our names, too."

Rose sat down suddenly, rocking gently on a bench, and covered her eyes with her small white hands.

Violet and Bonar each had a few random details of that night's battle to add. So the bloody exchange of death at long range had gone on, and long before morning most of the family on each side were dead.

Zoltan took another walk among the tables, looking and thinking. This corpse must be the survivors' father, and these two—there was a family resemblance—their dead brothers. The great majority of the dead in this vaulted room were men. But not all. Evidently there had been more than one woman living in this manor who had made herself deeply hated across the water.

One, at least, of the trestled bodies was wearing a heavy steel breastplate. Probably this was the previous clan chief—had he been the first to fall that night, had he put this armor on as a decoration? If the object had been protection, the armor had done him no good, for just over his heart a broad-bladed weapon had punched through as if the steel were so much paper.

Zoltan, still walking thoughtfully among the tables, gently touched a dead arm chosen randomly. It was as stiff as wood. Gesner, now moving quietly at his side, informed him that these bodies had been here on these tables since the morning after the slaughter. Ever since then, the surviving family members, all half-demented, had been trying to think of a way to conduct a secret burial or at least a mass cremation, without giving away the extent of the clan's loss.

"We'd need help to bury or burn them all, you see. And then outsiders would be certain to find out how many were dead."

"The Lady Yambu and I are outsiders."

"We must begin to do something. Better to trust complete outsiders like yourselves than—"

A servant chose that moment to enter the vault, bringing a private message for Bonar.

Bonar, after the man had whispered in his ear, turned to his sisters. "The mercenaries are at the back door. Two of them, anyway, Koszalin and his sergeant."

SIX

YAMBU asked: "Mercenaries?"

Violet spoke up. "Fourteen or fifteen men and their commander, whom we've had in our pay since before the slaughter. They're camped in the woods nearby, and I'm sure they know by now that we've been seriously weakened. We've been refusing to talk to them. If those blackguards ever find out exactly how much the clan has been reduced, they'll turn on us and rob us. Then the damned Senones will attack."

"It seems to me," said Zoltan, "that if you and the Senones exchanged blow for blow with Farslayer, as you say, then your enemies can hardly be in any better shape than you are. They'll have trouble carrying out an attack."

Violet glowered. "They were a larger family than us to begin with."

Yambu indicated the bodies. "Did I understand you to say that none of these is the man Cosmo, who you say began the fight?"

The surviving family were uniformly scornful. Bonar said: "No, that coward is not here. When it should have been his turn to use the Sword, he seized it, pulled it out of a dead kinsman's body, and ran out of the house. He mounted a riding-beast and was gone before we realized what was happening."

Talk of Cosmo ended when another one of the old retainers came into the vaulted room to report fearfully that the two mercenaries at the rear door of the house were growing impatient, demanding to be admitted to present their demands.

Rose was fearful. "Demands? That's new. What demands will they have now?"

"I suppose you ought to ask them," said Yambu. Then she volunteered: "If you like, I will speak to them. I have handled a few rebellious soldiers in my time."

The offer was accepted by default; at least none of the family spoke up to reject it out of hand, and none appeared really ready to assume leadership of their own cause. So, with Zoltan at her side, and guided by a servant, the former queen proceeded through the kitchen to deal with the mercenaries. Lady Yambu took her time about getting to the door, while Bonar brought her up to date on the clan's relationship with their hired soldiers.

"You said there were fourteen or fifteen of them. Are you sure that number's accurate?" Yambu asked him.

The siblings conferred briefly among themselves. "Can't be more than a dozen," Bonar reported.

"Too many for us to overawe, I suppose. Then let us buy them off with gold, for the time being at least," Yambu suggested. "I suppose you do have some modest stock of gold available?"

"Gold?" Violet looked almost shocked. "Hardly."

"But there are pearls." This came from Rose in a fearful whisper.

"Do you mean freshwater pearls?" asked Zoltan. "Not worth much, are they?"

"These are." Violet expressed a certain indignation. "Of high quality indeed."

The other family members, after some hesitation, admitted that a few good-quality pearls were available.

Urged on by a savage pounding on the door, they at last produced a small handful of pale rounded gems, which Yambu pronounced more than sufficient to buy off a dozen rascals. Shaking her head, she thrust most of the gems back into Bonar's unsteady hands. "To offer them too much at this stage would be worse than to give them too little. Now, Zoltan, attend me. Stand here, and let them see that you are armed and ready!"

When Gesner unbarred and opened the door at last, the two men outside started to push their way into the house. But then they halted on the threshold. The appearance in the kitchen of an unexpected stranger, armed and resolute, and of an unknown lady of queenly bearing, was enough to delay them momentarily. And that moment was long enough for the Lady Yambu's commanding presence to take over. In a firm voice she demanded to know just who these intruders thought they were and what they thought they wanted.

"Captain Koszalin, ma'am. I'm in charge of the defenses here. This is Shotoku, first sergeant in my company."

"Are you indeed? Those defenses seem singularly ineffective, not to say inoperative. My party was not challenged approaching the house, and I daresay that if we had been a full company bent on an attack, the result would have been the same. Were I your commanding officer, you'd be in trouble."

Zoltan grinned inwardly, in admiration of the way Yambu had managed to suggest the presence of an armed escort besides himself.

Koszalin was not a large man, but gave the impression of fierce energy, now under tight control. He and the massive Sergeant Shotoku, who stood stoically behind him, both wore scraps of armor and dirty green scarves, evidently as a kind of company insignia.

Under pointed questioning by Lady Yambu, Koszalin

claimed to have twenty men at his command. He had come pounding on the door, he said, to collect the gold that was due him in back pay. But after a brief hesitation he accepted four small pearls, and then withdrew with his sergeant.

"He'll need a conference with his men now, I suppose," said Yambu when the door was closed. "Very unreliable troops, in my judgment. Doubtless the two of them will now hold a conference with their men on how best to enjoy their sudden wealth. From our point of view it will be best if they go to the nearest large town to spend it—how far is that?"

"A good day's journey," said Rose, thoughtfully.

Within a few minutes after the two mercenaries had left the house, a servant looking from an upstairs window reported that eight or ten of the ruffians, all heavily armed and moving on foot, could be seen at the bottom of the hill. They appeared to be going upon their way.

For a minute or two the members of the family were loud in their rejoicing. But the celebration was brief. First Bonar and then Violet began to voice their misgivings that the mercenaries would be likely to come back, as soon as they had spent the pearls.

Yambu nodded. "But in the meantime we can expect to enjoy a respite of about three days—that should give us the time we need to decide upon our next move."

When the servant on lookout reported that the irregular soldiers were now completely out of sight, the brother and two sisters more volubly expressed their gratitude to Yambu and Zoltan.

Meanwhile the party was drifting back into the great hall. There, some of the few active servants remaining in the household were called upon to begin a belated cleanup, and provide something in the way of hospitality for the honored guests.

But the survivors of the Clan Malolo and their visitors

had not been seated long at the table before Bonar, unable to relax for any length of time, began to have doubts as to whether they might need the mercenaries after all, and before the three days were up. The damned Senones, he felt sure, were almost certain to mount a fresh attack by then.

Yambu spoke sharply to the young chief. Would he prefer that she and her companion moved on at once?

No, all three family members protested hastily. On that point all three siblings and Gesner were in agreement.

Thinking it would be hard to find a more propitious moment, Zoltan decided the time had come to let his hosts know the real reason he had come calling on them.

He cleared his throat and addressed the chief. "I wish to speak to you on a matter of some importance. To you in particular, Chief Bonar." Zoltan avoided the eyes of Lady Yambu, though he could see that her face was turned toward him.

"Of course, friend Zoltan," said Bonar in mild surprise. "What is the matter of importance?"

"It's about a mermaid."

Bonar blinked. There was a silence in the room. Lady Yambu, when Zoltan glanced her way at last, looked as if she were ready to tell him *I told you so.*

The clan chief cleared his throat. "Well, of course, if you wish to have a mermaid, friend Zoltan, we will do what we can to get one for you." Bonar sounded dubious. "Usually only entertainers and magicians find those creatures of much interest."

"I don't think you understand yet, Chief Bonar. I do want to talk about a mermaid, and the subject will not keep indefinitely. It is a particular mermaid that I wish to talk about. Black Pearl is her name."

The faces of the family members and Gesner grew even blanker than before, with incomprehension and vague anxiety. It was obvious that the name of Black Pearl meant nothing to anyone in the household. But before Zoltan could press his hosts on the topic, a renewed argument had broken out among them on the subject of the mercenaries.

He could see that it was going to be difficult to get them to think seriously on the subject of mermaids.

Turning back to face the sharp look Yambu continued to level at him, Zoltan sighed, and nodded his acquiescence. Any discussion of Black Pearl was going to have to wait.

Dinner began to arrive, piecemeal. And while the group was still at the table, Rose mentioned the subject of mermaids in passing once again. She thought vaguely that Cousin Cosmo, who had been the only current member of the clan much interested in magical research, had once tried to do something to counteract the evil spell that kept the poor fishgirls in their bondage. But all agreed with Rose that Cosmo had got nowhere in his efforts. There were just as many mermaids in the river as ever—or there seemed to be. No one was actually counting them, of course.

Gradually the remnants of the meal were cleared away, and winecups were refilled. As desultory efforts to clean up the room continued around them, talk among the surviving family members turned, as it was wont to do again and again, to that damned cowardly relative of theirs, Cosmo. Bonar and Violet were particularly incensed. That scoundrel Cosmo, instead of retaliating like a man when he'd finally had the chance to do so on the Night of Death, had stolen the Sword and run away with it like a coward.

"He ran away?" asked Yambu. "Where?"

"We don't know."

Toward the end of that terrible night, Bonar, having become clan chief by default, and pressed by the other survivors to do something, had sent a search party of mercenaries after Cosmo. At the time the only conceivable explanation of his cousin's behavior was that Cosmo had defected to the enemy. But the searchers had come back empty-handed, reporting failure to find any trace of Cosmo along the lake or river. And in the long days since then nothing had happened to confirm the supposed defection.

"I wonder if the mercenaries killed him. I wonder if they have the Sword now," said Rose, and shuddered.

"If any of those men had come into possession of the Sword," Lady Yambu sniffed, "they would have begun to kill each other over it by now. Whichever of them survived with such a treasure would take it to a city to sell. We wouldn't have seen two of them begging at your back door today."

"No," said Violet. "The Senones must have it. But they're waiting for something before they strike again."

"Waiting for what?" asked Yambu. There was no answer.

Zoltan thought to himself that there had evidently been no more active feuding of any kind since that terrible night, unless you counted the aborted attack on the fishing village. But despite that fact, the people in this stronghold were maintaining at a high level their fears that a formidable force of their enemies must still exist, and that an attack by that force must be impending at any moment.

Rose had now begun to explain how she, her brother and sister, and Gesner, had been staying in each other's company almost continuously, day and night, ever since the massacre. If at any moment the Sword should claim a new victim from among them, someone would be on hand immediately to exact revenge.

Listening to the hatred and determination in her youthful voice, Zoltan wondered if he ought to try to argue her and her siblings into a different frame of mind. But he decided to concentrate on his own problems, at least for now.

Winecups were refilled again, and presently it began to look as if Bonar at least might be on the way to serious drunkenness. Yambu and Zoltan sipped moderately from their cups—the vintage was passable—and Bonar's two sisters drank even less than their visitors. Meanwhile Gesner, seated at the far end of a table by himself, clutched a forgotten flagon and stared at nothing, while the servitors, still looking frightened by the presence of the visitors and the authority of Yambu, continued working on their belated job of cleanup.

Wondering if the wine could be enlisted as his ally, Zoltan made one more attempt to bring up the subject of mermaids with the chief. But at his first words, Bonar gave him a single, scornful, drunken look that said: *Mermaids again? Forget it. We have more important things than that to worry about.*

Zoltan sighed, and once more abandoned his efforts. But he had already decided that if the survivors of the Malolo clan wanted his continued help, and that of the Lady Yambu, they would eventually have to help him in turn.

Yambu, drawing her young companion aside when the opportunity arose, cautioned him again against impatience. "If you want the active help of these people for your Black Pearl, there is no point in irritating them unnecessarily on the subject. Also it may be better not to let them see how important she is to you."

With that, Zoltan had to agree.

Perversely, just after this private exchange, Bonar raised the subject of mermaids yet again himself. After he had rambled on about it for a while, spilling and drinking his wine meanwhile, all of the members of the household were firmly under the impression that Zoltan wanted to rent a mermaid for some magical stunt or entertainment somewhere.

Zoltan suppressed his angry reaction to this idea. Outwardly he decided to go along with it, hoping such a plan would offer some way to get Black Pearl away. If he could not present himself convincingly to these half-mad people as a magician, maybe they would take him seriously as the proprietor of a traveling show.

Of course, Zoltan meditated, even if he were able to take Black Pearl away from here, she would still be a mermaid. So simply to take her away would be of doubtful help. If he brought her back to Tasavalta, would Old Karel or some other wizard be able to cure her?

Zoltan had no idea.

Now Bonar, who should have fallen asleep or gotten sick some time ago, was instead working himself up to a drunken effort at diplomacy. He made a formal offer of alliance to Lady Yambu.

She responded vaguely and diplomatically. Very diplomatically, Zoltan thought, considering the chief's condition.

Gradually the day had passed, and sunset was now imminent. Zoltan walked out by himself to scout the grounds before darkness fell. When he returned to the house, he found Bonar at last snoring with his head down on the table. Violet, the more diplomatic and practical sister, issued a formal invitation to the two visitors to stay indefinitely. Then Yambu and Zoltan were assigned sleeping rooms upstairs—since last month there were plenty of rooms available—and a dour servant to wait upon them.

As they were on their way upstairs to bed, Zoltan whispered privately to Yambu: "If only there were some trustworthy and halfway competent magician available, closer than Tasavalta!"

The lady only shook her head. Both of them knew

there wasn't a wizard available that either of them would want to trust, not just now. Certainly not Gesner. It appeared that for the time being any direct attempt to help Black Pearl by means of countermagic would have to wait.

Zoltan looked forward to his clandestine meeting, scheduled for this very midnight, with Black Pearl.

SEVEN

AT nightfall on that same day, just after Zoltan had finished his reconnaissance of the Malolo grounds, the man who had called himself Chilperic was making his lonely camp in a small clearing on the wooded north bank of the Tungri. Shortly before sunset Chilperic had crossed the river from south to north, making use of a rope suspension bridge that for some years had spanned the lower end of the gorge. The bridge spanned the river just above the deep pool in which the Tungri at last ceased its deadly plunging, its white self-laceration upon rocks, and widened out again into a calm flow.

Despite the feud—so Chilperic had been informed by a chance-met peasant—the bridge had remained in place for many years. Members of both feuding clans sometimes found it advantageous to have the means of a dry crossing, and so except on rare occasions both sides were willing to let the span of ropes hang there unmolested, though often they posted sentries to warn of an enemy crossing in force. Today there had not been a sentry in sight at either end.

Chilperic had been reasonably cautious in choosing a site in deep woods where his little camp would not readily be seen. With practiced and efficient movements, he erected a small shelter tent of magically thin, strong fabric in an inconspicuous place. He also took care to keep his fire small. The one visitor that he was more or less expecting would need no help in locating his bivouac. Meanwhile Chilperic's mount, also an experienced campaigner, moved about on its hobble calmly, foraging as best it could upon the new spring growth.

The man's face, as he went about the routine chores of making himself comfortable in the woods, was set in a thoughtfully attentive expression. He looked like a man who was waiting to receive some special signal, but uncertain of at just what moment or even in what form the signal might come to him.

And then Chilperic paused in the act of gathering firewood; a frown came over his face and he stared at nothing. The signal he had both feared and anticipated had arrived at last.

The first indication of his visitor's approach was neither a visual appearance nor a sound. Rather an aura of sickness began to grow in the very atmosphere Chilperic breathed, and a special gloom, which had nothing to do with clouds or sunset, seemed to fall over the earth around him. Very quickly he also began to experience a sensation of unnatural cold. His riding-beast, hardened as it was to these matters, ceased to browse and stood still and silent, quivering lightly. The cries of animals in the surrounding forest changed, and presently fell silent. Even the insects quieted.

No more than a few minutes passed from the first manifestation of the demon until the creature made its presence known in a more localized and immediate way. But somehow to the man, shivering involuntarily, the interval seemed considerably longer.

The full manifestation, as he knew well, was apt to

vary substantially from one occasion to the next. On this occasion there was not very much at all in the way of an optical appearance. There was only a cloudiness that might under ordinary circumstances have been taken for a temporary blurring of vision, a little water in the eyes. And simultaneously with the cloudiness there came a strange unearthly smell and a slight sensation that the world was tilting. Had there been any lingering doubts about the nature of the presence thus establishing itself, those doubts would have been dispelled by what came next, a rain of filth falling out of nowhere into the light of the man's small fire, and into the pan of food that he had begun to prepare beside the fire.

Chilperic's expression did not change as he picked up the pan and with a snap of his wrist threw the polluted contents into the woods behind him.

"So you have come, Rabisu," he said quietly. He spoke to the ghastly thing without the least surprise, addressing it with the reluctant firmness of a man who wants to avert both his eyes and his thoughts from something horrible, even though he knows the confrontation will be even more difficult and dangerous if he fails to meet it directly and unflinchingly.

And now at last he heard the demon's voice. It sounded more in the mind of Chilperic than in his ears, and it came in the form of a noise that reminded the man of the chittering of insects, and also of the tearing of live flesh. Still, the words which modulated this noise were clear enough: "I have come to learn what you have to report to the master."

"I want you to tell our master this." As he spoke, Chilperic sat down on a log beside his fire, put his head down, let his eyes close, and rubbed his temples. He spoke in a tired voice. "Tell him all indications are that the Sword he seeks is still somewhere in this area, between the Second and Third Cataracts and near the river Tungri. But whether it will be found north or south of the river I know not."

The insect-chittering took on an ominous overtone. "There is nothing new in this report."

The man who sat by the fire frowned at the empty pan he was still holding in his right hand. Then he put it in the fire, concave side down, to cleanse it. He retained his calm. He said: "I am aware of that. The situation still holds. And tell him that the fight between the two contending clans, using Farslayer, did indeed take place just as some of his powers reported to him. Since my own last report I have visited the stronghold of the Malolo clan and made sure of that."

"A small accomplishment. And you have not visited the clan of the Senones?"

"I am on my way there now. I intend to talk with the leaders of that clan tomorrow."

"But the Sword is still missing," said the demon, as if that were the most reasonable remark in the world to make, making a point that the man might never have thought of for himself.

"I am aware that the Sword is missing." The man with an effort retained his patience. Suddenly he looked up from the fire, into the heart of the nearby aerial disturbance, as if to demonstrate that he was not afraid to do so. "That is why I am here."

"The Dark Master requires that you shall find the missing Sword for him." Again, the voice of the visitor seemed to imply that the human needed instruction on this point.

"I am aware of that, too." Fear and anger contending in him, the man still managed to control himself. "The fact that the Sword of Vengeance is missing is not my fault."

"Yet the Dark Master will require it from you." There was no doubt about it now. The power hovering over the fire, polluting the darkness among the trees, was seeking to goad Chilperic, to provoke him to some uncontrolled response. After a time its unreal-sounding voice began to repeat mechanically: "Yet the Dark Master—"

"Enough!" Chilperic stood up suddenly.

"You claim the right to give me a command?" The questioner sounded pleased at the idea.

"I do claim that right." The man drew in a deep breath, then went on in a firm voice. "If one of us two must be subordinate to the other, then know that the lowly one will not be me. I carry with me a certain thing that I would have preferred not to show to you. But I will show it now, that you may know I am not subject to your terrors."

And in his right hand the man suddenly held up a small object, a thing he had just drawn out from under his belt. It looked like a thin, folded wallet of peculiar leather, grayish and wrinkled.

He said: "Observe it closely. I have been entrusted with this by the Dark Master himself. I think you have seen it before. Whether you have seen it or not, you must know that it contains your life. If I were to hurl this little package into my fire now, or even hold it close above the flames—"

"I was but jesting, Master, when I challenged you." And the voice of the demon was suddenly clear and silvery, a joy to hear. "Surely you know that. Can you not tell when one of my poor kind is jesting?"

"Aye, I think I can tell that. Rabisu, I did not want you to know that I held your life, for I suspected the knowledge might provoke you to more dangerous and subtle tricks than these you have played for mere annoyance." Chilperic kicked his pan out of the fire.

"I, Master? To attempt to play dangerous and subtle tricks with one of your experience and wisdom? Not I, Master, never I. If—"

"Enough. Understand, evil babbler, that I keep this small pouch that holds your life close by me at all times. If you contemplate any serious action against me, I will know it, whether I am awake or asleep. That is part of the power of control our master has bestowed upon me. I will know in time to get out my knife and begin to carve—"

"Enough, Great Master! More than enough! From this moment forward I am your humble servant."

"I rejoice to hear it." The man sounded far from convinced. "But leave me now. Do not come to me again until I summon you, or the Dark Master sends you with a message."

"I hear and obey." But before the demon vanished, it caused a plate of delicious-looking and aromatic food to appear sitting on a flat rock beside the fire, just where the other food had been.

The man picked up the offering and sniffed at it briefly. The dish was, or appeared to be, of fine porcelain. The food upon it smelled delicious. But in the next moment he threw plate and all behind him into the woods.

Then patiently, squatting beside the fire, he once again began to prepare his evening meal.

The next morning Chilperic was up at dawn, busy with breaking camp. Once that routine chore was accomplished, he mounted his riding-beast and moved on to the stronghold of the Sonones clan. This he had no difficulty in finding; it was a large rambling house which stood conspicuously upon a hill only a few kilometers away from where he had spent the night.

At the edge of the clearing surrounding this rural stronghold the traveler stopped briefly to survey the layout before him. Guards were in evidence, and in a few moments Chilperic had decided that these were not mercenaries, like the ones he'd encountered at the Malolo manor across the river. These looked more like conscripted locals: too poor and ineffective to be mercenaries.

They were also too nervous in their behavior, too close to the edge of fear, when there was no obvious danger in sight. Two of them, gripping their weapons spasmodically, challenged Chilperic as he rode slowly forward. Obviously the men were impressed by his clothing, his weapons, and his mount, all of which were of the highest quality. But still, to get them to do what he required, he was required to display some patience, firmness, and a certain degree of courage.

Eventually Chilperic was able to talk himself past the outer defenders of the fortified manor, by claiming to be a friend of two of the family members. Both of these people were, as Chilperic was secretly aware, very recently deceased. He of course pretended to great surprise and horror when the guards informed him that his friends were dead.

He managed also to drop a hint or two establishing himself as a bitter enemy of the Malolo.

Soon the officer of the local guards, finding himself outtalked and outthought, and not knowing what else to do, conducted this impressive visitor up to the main house. Once admitted there, Chilperic was soon able to confer with the new Tyrant of the Senones, a very young man named Hissarlik, who had taken over as head of the clan following the great slaughter.

Naturally Chilperic pretended to be greatly surprised and dismayed when he heard from Hissarlik of the carnage inflicted upon his friends and others of this household, scarcely a month ago, by the terrible Sword of Vengeance.

The two men sat talking in the main hall, on the ground floor of the manor. Two or three other surviving members of the Senones family were gathering around now to listen to the visitor, and look him over, and evaluate what he had to say.

One of the survivors present was a vengeful-sounding youth named Anselm, Hissarlik's cousin. Anselm's face tended to twitch, and he limped badly. Chilperic gathered the youth had been crippled in some atrocity performed by a Malolo gang several years ago.

Anselm's sister or cousin—Chilperic was not sure at first—a young lady named Alicia, made an appearance also.

"A dozen dead on that night," Alicia proclaimed. "And our aunt Megara still has not recovered her wits, a month later." Her eyes glittered venomously. "We owe a huge debt to those Malolo slime, and we mean to pay it."

"Your aunt Megara?" Chilperic murmured sympathetically.

"Mine, too," said Hissarlik. "She saw her father—he was the clan chief—struck down before her eyes."

"Oh, I see. Terrible, terrible." And Chilperic, looking appropriately grim, gave his head a shake.

Hissarlik, the nominal leader of this immature and yet dangerous-looking crew, seemed to have a few years to go before turning twenty, but still he gave a first impression of inward maturity. Only after Chilperic had talked with him for a while did he begin to suspect why this young man had been so far down the structure of leadership and responsibility as to be still surviving after that great exchange of Sword blows. This young fellow talked so boldly yet vaguely about the feats of arms for which he was responsible—bragging about a raid he'd ordered two nights ago against a Malolo fishing village —that Chilperic suspected that the problem, or one of the problems, might well be cowardice.

Refreshments were brought in after a while, and the talk went on. Chilperic, when he thought the proper moment had arrived, and without dropping his pretense of being an old friend of some deceased members of the family, revealed himself as an agent of the macrowizard Wood. He expected that these people, or at least their best surviving magician, would have heard of Wood, and he was not wrong.

That claim, as he had expected, somewhat perturbed and perhaps frightened his new acquaintances. Chilperic was ready to offer some kind of demonstration to back up his words. He reached inside his coat to touch the leather wallet at his belt; he was just magician enough himself to be able to detect the powerful demonic life that throbbed so vulnerably within.

As soon as he saw that Hissarlik was groping for some way of expressing polite doubt about his relationship with the famous Wood, Chilperic once more touched glossy but wrinkled leather. Muttering a few words he'd had from the Ancient One himself, he called up the demon.

This time the manifestation was much quicker, and distinctly visual. While the owners of the house shrank back, the demon appeared in their great hall in afternoon sunlight, blocking out some of the bright beams that came slanting in through the high windows. Rabisu, taking the image of a gigantic though transparent warrior—a demon could look like almost anything it chose—acquitted himself impressively, offering a demonstration of obedient power that would have gladdened the heart of any magician-master. He bent a steel bar into a loop, and caught a rat somewhere inside the wainscotting, and turned the little creature inside out, at the same time sucking it dry of life and blood, so deftly that there was hardly any mess.

It was about an hour after this demonstration when Chilperic, feeling that he had now established himself with the Senones leadership, decided to strike while the iron was hot, and began asking important questions.

Anselm, in response to a direct query, told him that the last person to be struck down by Farslayer on that night a month ago must have been some Malolo youth. Cosmo's name did not come up here directly.

Hissarlik, Alicia, and Anselm each laid claim to having killed one of the Malolo on that night, but they could not agree exactly on each other's claims. Chilperic soon lost interest in the details, and managed to switch the conversation.

An hour after that, Chilperic and his hosts were halfway through a banquet celebrating their new alliance.

Chilperic had seen to it that their talk never strayed far from the Sword for very long. Chewing thoughtfully on a tough piece of fowl, he remarked: "And it never came back into this house again."

"No." Anselm hissed a sigh of exasperation. "It appears that our enemies still have it."

His sister murmured tensely: "They're trying to break our nerves. Well, we won't break."

Their cousin Hissarlik, seated at the head of the table, shook his head slowly. "I think they may not have it after all. Their last man to be struck down may have been away from the others when it happened. It's possible that they just have never found him, or the weapon, either."

"Where else would he have been?" Alicia challenged him at once. "We searched the islands. We searched all over our side of the river, and they would have searched on theirs."

The chief could only shake his head. And Chilperic had no intention of enlightening his hosts at the moment.

The story Chilperic had heard in the Malolo stronghold was of course not about their last man to be struck down, but rather about the misfit Cosmo. Cosmo Malolo, the mysterious one in that family, misfit and leading magician as well. Cosmo, who on that night of terror had simply grabbed up the Sword and ridden off with it, effectively putting an end to the cycle of revenge. It appeared that no one, except the hermit whom Chilperic had stopped to question, had seen Cosmo since that night.

Chilperic wondered now whether he should have questioned the hermit further.

In any event, it would seem that Cosmo had not been a simple defector, bound for enemy headquarters. Or, if so, he had never reached it. It would not have been reasonable for Cosmo to stop at the hermit's at all if he intended to go no farther than the Senones manor. But then everyone agreed the weather on the night of the massacre had been terrible, the mountain trails deadly dangerous, and that might have been a factor in his whereabouts.

Chilperic was increasingly sure that the Sword had not been carried here by Cosmo, and that none of these frightened but still bitterly determined Senones fanatics had made any systematic attempt to locate Farslayer since that horrible night of slaughter. The shock had perhaps disabled them more severely than was at first apparent.

The more Chilperic talked to these people, the more their situation appeared to resemble that obtaining among the Malolo on the other side of the river. But of course Chilperic was not going to offer that comment aloud.

"But where is the Sword now?" young Hissarlik asked him, plaintively and suddenly. It sounded almost as if the question were now occurring to him for the first time, or perhaps it was that he now felt for the first time that there was some point in asking it.

"That question," responded Chilperic with slow emphasis, "is also of great interest to my master, Wood."

"I see," said Hissarlik after a pause, not really sounding as if he saw. "But I was just thinking, suppose . . . suppose that one of those poor peasants or fishermen over on the other side of the river should happen to come across this lost Sword. What would someone like that be likely to do with such a weapon?"

Anselm tried for once to be reassuring. "The peasants? People like that wouldn't know what to do with such a thing, cousin. Take my word, they'd be too frightened to do anything."

"But just suppose . . ."

Chilperic, taking every opportunity to establish himself as a useful friend, concealed his contempt for this lack of fortitude and also did his best to be comforting. "Why, sire, there are every bit as many old enmities in villages as in castles. Farslayer would be used again, and soon, depend upon it. And then any magician worth his salt—assuming of course that he was alert and looking for the Sword—should be able to tell that it had been used again. Once that happened we'd be well on our way to getting our hands on it."

The Tyrant cast a look, eloquent of hopelessness, toward his two surviving relatives, neither of whom had any magical ability at all, if Chilperic was any judge. Chilperic had already been told in further detail how the most competent magician in the clan, Hissarlik's Aunt Megara, had been paralyzed, thrown into a trance on the night of terror, and her first replacement had been among those slain by the Sword. That junior sorcerer, according to Hissarlik's description of events, had just finished casting a spell intended to stop the Sword moments before it struck him down. There had been no indication that the magician's efforts had slowed his own doom in the slightest.

"But your most competent magician—this sorceress, your aunt—was thrown into a trance, you say? Not killed?"

"Yes. Our aunt Megara," said Hissarlik with dignity. "She's been confined to her room ever since. She still exists almost as in a trance, scarcely able to talk or move about."

"Might I see her?" asked Chilperic, in his very most helpful and friendly voice. "I am of course no healer. But I have been present once or twice at similar cases, and . . ."

By now Chilperic had been accepted as an old friend of the family. Its three surviving members now conducted him upstairs. On the second floor they entered a room half-choked with incense. No doubt these fumes were somehow intended to be magically helpful, but if the air was always like this Chilperic was not surprised that the occupant of the room had remained practically comatose.

A woman lay in the single bed, between white sheets, being watched over by a faithful maid. Chilperic was surprised at first glance by the patient's obvious youth. Her face was drawn and pale, but certainly not lined. It was not uncommon, of course, for a sorceress of skill to appear much younger than she really was. But such cheating of the calendar tended to fail in such a collapse as this.

The woman in the bed ignored her visitor, though at intervals while he was there she managed to rouse herself enough to murmur a few words, usually something that sounded as if it might express some magical intention.

These words never had any effect, as far as Chilperic could see.

None of the family or servants, according to Hissarlik, had been able to do much for her.

Chilperic, looking at her, was sure that he personally could not do much for her, either. But he knew someone who almost certainly could. He nodded to himself, and turned away.

"Can you be of any help?" Alicia, with her burning eyes, demanded of him at once.

"Not immediately, no, I'm sorry. But given a day or two it may very well be possible to help."

"Do you mean it?"

"Yes indeed. Can you tell me more exactly what happened? Was your aunt in the manor house with you when she was stricken? You say it happened on the night of the great slaughter, and she saw her father killed beside her?"

"No, it did not happen in the house. Rather she was found by some of our militiamen, out on Magicians' Island. There's a cave, a sort of a grotto out there, where magicians from both clans sometimes go to practice. They have warning spells or something to keep them from encountering each other. Aunt Meg was found lying unconscious with our father's body beside her, the Sword through his heart. Farslayer had struck him down from behind. He was the first victim of the treacherous Malolo on that night.

"The militia brought Megara home, along with her father's body. For a while we were all afraid that she was going to die, too. Oh gods, I was afraid we were going to have to bury her at night, under the stones out in the courtyard, with all the rest who died that night." Alicia covered her face with her hands.

"*Can* you help us?" This time the question came from Hissarlik.

Chilperic faced him thoughtfully. "I think I can. I certainly intend to try."

Invited to stay the night, with a strong implication that he would be welcome to remain indefinitely, Chilperic lost no time in moving his few personal effects into a snug bedroom on the manor's upper level. There a sobering number of well-furnished rooms were vacant now. As soon as he was installed, he began to plan how to convince this puny Tyrant that he and his demon could overwhelm the Tyrant's enemies—provided, of course, that the Tyrant helped Chilperic to recover the missing Sword.

In the privacy of his room, where the demon was able to visit him without disturbing other members of the household, Chilperic was able to make certain other arrangements as well.

Next morning, as he joined his hosts for breakfast, Chilperic felt confident enough to hint strongly that some real help ought soon to be available.

Hissarlik and those with him were pleased and startled at the same time. "Then you have communicated with your master during the night?"

"Of course."

"But how?"

"To a magician of the stature of my master, the great Wood, there are always means of communication." Chilperic did not say that the means employed in this case had involved several nocturnal visits to the manor by the demon, carrying messages back and forth.

"This help you mention—how long do you think it will be before it becomes truly effective?"

Chilperic smiled encouragingly. "Perhaps I will be able to do something for you, and for your poor aunt, tomorrow. Perhaps it will take a day or two longer."

"As soon as that?" The Tyrant seemed to be struggling with mixed feelings. Pleased, of course, as well he might be, but also a touch alarmed. "How near is your master himself, then?"

"Alas, the mighty Wood is still almost a continent away. But he has rapid means of transport available, when he wants to use them."

The assurance did little to allay his host's uneasiness. Still, to Chilperic, everything seemed fairly well under control.

EIGHT

HALF an hour before midnight on his first night in Malolo manor, Zoltan, having listened patiently to the last ineffective warnings Lady Yambu felt bound to deliver, slipped out of a back door of the stronghold. He went quietly over the outer wall of the compound, which was no higher than his head, then moved as silently as possible through the moonlight toward the nearby forest, intent upon keeping his rendezvous with Black Pearl. Yambu's disapproval of this midnight sortie made him uncomfortable, but a much greater degree of discomfort would have been required to keep him from going.

If the disgruntled mercenaries, Senones agents, or anyone else, were spying on the Malolo manor tonight, Zoltan observed no sign of their presence as he crossed the moonlit clearing. Once in among the trees he paused to let his eyes adjust to the deeper darkness. Then he moved along, steadily following a gradually descending slope. On his jaunt around the grounds late in the afternoon he had made certain where the creek ran near the manor house; and once he reached the creek tonight it ought to be easy to follow it downstream to the spot along the riverbank where Black Pearl had said she would meet him. Fortunately Zoltan possessed a natural talent for finding his way to any desired geographical goal.

The creek was just where he thought it ought to be, and when he had followed the path beside it for less than a kilometer, he emerged on the bank of the river. No mist had risen from the Tungri tonight, or else it had all dispersed again by this late hour, and the broad surface of the stream, a hundred meters wide, lay clear before him in the moonlight.

There was no house or dock in sight, nor had anyone been considerate enough to leave a boat where he might borrow it to go paddling out in search of his love. Zoltan found a smooth fallen log conveniently close to the water's edge, and sat on it, doing his best to quiet his impatience, preparing himself to wait.

While he was waiting, Zoltan thought over the general situation. It could have been better, but certainly it also could have been worse. The great thing was that he had now found Black Pearl, and he now knew her name. There had been moments during the past three years when such an achievement had seemed impossible.

He was almost lost in thought, enjoying in his imagination the glowing possibilities of the future, when the dark water rippled directly in his line of vision, and she was in front of him again.

Zoltan slid from his rock and splashed thigh-deep into the cold, dark stream. "Black Pearl—I was afraid that you weren't coming."

Two meters farther from the shore than he, the mermaid tossed a spray of moonlit silver from her hair. Swimming without apparent effort she held her head and shoulders out of the moonlit water. It looked as if a girl with two legs was simply standing in a greater depth of water.

"Zoltan." There was great tension in the mermaid's voice. "I am pleased that you have not forgotten me."

The young man blinked at that; it seemed a quite unnatural suggestion for the object of his love to make. "Forget you? How could I ever do that?" Zoltan waded forward until the water was waist deep, and he could feel the full strength of the cold current. Reaching out with his right hand, he touched her wet hair, as before. The skin of Pearl's shoulder, when his finger only brushed against it, felt very cold. Suddenly he burst out: "And are you doomed to remain always—like this? I can't believe that, or accept it. There must be some way—"

His fingers encountered the thin chain of the amulet she wore around her neck. "Where did you get this? You didn't have this when I knew you before."

"It's nothing, many of the girls wear them. I found it on the bottom of the river, that's all." Her dark eyes held his, and she seemed to be trying to find words. "Oh, Zoltan, are you so jealous? What man would love a mermaid, and give her pretty things to wear?"

"I can love a mermaid, I've discovered. I can love you. I wish that I had pretty things to give you. I wish . . ."

The mermaid was silent for a few moments. Then she took his hand in her cold fingers, asking: "And if there should be no way for me to change, to ever be a normal woman? If I must remain like this until I die?"

"I love you," he repeated, as if that meant some means of solving any problem must exist. And if there was the slightest pause before Zoltan gave his answer, the pause might very well have been only the kind in which a speaker tries to find the most forceful words in which it was possible to express an idea.

"But you would be happier if you had two legs," he added a few seconds later, feeling that he sounded foolish. "And how can I ever love you as a man should love a woman, unless . . ."

"There might be a way for me to have two legs again,"

she said. "I say there *might* be. If we can find it. Often I dream I am a little girl again, with legs."

"Then when you were a little girl you were not a mermaid?"

"Oh no." Black Pearl shook her head decisively. "That happened to me later. It is a result of evil magic."

"So I have heard. Then I say there must be good magic to counteract it. Tell me what happened. Tell me how this curse ever came to fall upon your people."

Briefly the mermaid did as Zoltan asked. The feud, and the curse it brought, had fallen upon Black Pearl's people long before she was born. She could only tell Zoltan something of the early years of the feud, as she, when a small girl with two legs, had heard the story from the elders of her people. And tonight she also gave her lover an idea of what life was like for someone upon whom the curse had fallen.

All girls born in the two or three afflicted villages lived seemingly normal lives up until puberty. Then, at about the time of commencement of the menses, perhaps one out of ten of the young women underwent what could only be described as a magical seizure. There was no telling ahead of time which girls would be afflicted.

"Sometimes the change will strike by day, sometimes by night. Always it is very sudden. No one knows who will be taken and who will be spared. Except that if a girl has already been a woman for three cycles of the moon, or if she becomes pregnant, she is certain to be spared."

"Why don't the people of these villages pack up and go somewhere else when they have daughters? Just to get away from this?"

"The villages are their homes. Anyway, people say that in my grandmother's time some people tried that. The only effect was that when the change struck their daughters they were far from home, in some cases far from any river, among people who did not understand, and who wanted to burn the helpless girls as witches."

"I see."

Black Pearl looked sharply at Zoltan. "You must come in a boat next time. The water will freeze you, my poor Zoltan, your teeth are starting to chatter already."

"I'll be all right. But what about you? The water is so cold—"

Black Pearl laughed; it was a cheerful and wholly human sound. "My poor man, I live in this water all winter; it would have to turn to ice before its coldness bothered me. Next time, tomorrow night, let us meet out there." And Black Pearl, pointing out over the dark water, indicated to her lover what she called the Isle of Mermaids, and said that it was easily reachable by boat. "There are two islands. The small one is the Isle of Magicians, and we had better avoid that."

"Are there magicians on it?"

Black Pearl hesitated. "Sometimes there are. And there are other things, which can be unpleasant. The Isle of Mermaids is much nicer. Any of the maids you find there ought to be willing to pass a message on to me, if for some reason I'm not there."

"What would happen if I did go to Magicians' Island?"

Again she seemed uncertain. "Probably nothing bad. But sometimes, when people go there, there is unpleasantness."

He decided to let that subject drop for the time being. "Wouldn't it be easier for us to meet by day?"

"Yes." The mermaid's evident uneasiness remained. "But if the lords of the Malolo manor find out that you are meeting me, they will want to charge you a price for my company. You are not a wealthy man, are you?"

"No, I am not. But in any case I would not be inclined

to pay them a price for that. You're not their slave, are you?" The mere thought made him angry.

"I'm no one's slave. But it will be better if you can avoid dealing with those people altogether."

"Can't do that very well," he announced cheerfully. "I'm living in their house now."

Black Pearl's confusion only increased. "If you refuse to pay them, Zoltan, then you will have to fight with them. They do consider mermaids slaves if someone else wants one of them. I have already been sold once, as you know."

"My poor girl, there aren't enough Malolo manor-lords left to fight very successfully with anyone. The Sword called Farslayer has taken care of that."

Black Pearl considered this in silence, running fingers through her long dark hair, tossing her head. She said: "Even mermaids have heard about the fight." After a pause she asked: "Which ones are dead?"

"Quite a number. I didn't get any list of their names. Why?"

"Nothing. Is there—is there a man named Cosmo among them?"

"No. Not among those still living at the manor or among their dead. He's missing. Why?"

"Why? I don't know. I don't suppose it matters."

Zoltan hesitated for a moment, trying to understand. Then he asked: "I don't suppose you can tell me anything about the Sword that killed them all? I would like very much to get my hands on it."

Black Pearl splashed water with her hands, nervously. It was a gesture that an ordinary girl might have made in swimming. "Whom do you want to kill?"

"I? No one, at the moment. No, it's a matter of seeing that certain people don't come into possession of Farslayer."

"Well, I know something, perhaps. But I am not sure that I should tell you."

"Why not? Yes, absolutely you should tell me. Where's Farslayer now? Can you tell me that?"

"No, I can't. Not right now."

He took a step toward the mermaid, but she slid effortlessly out of his reach in the water. "Black Pearl?"

"Zoltan, at our next meeting I will tell you something, I promise. Maybe that meeting will have to take place at night again."

There was a gentle disturbance in the surface of the water nearby. Another mermaid surfaced; this one had lighter hair, but in the darkness Zoltan could not otherwise distinguish her.

"It's only Soft Ripple," said Black Pearl. "You remember, she's my best friend, who came to the bachelors' hut with me."

"I remember," said Zoltan and nodded politely in the direction of the newcomer. Then he resumed his conversation with Black Pearl. "I'll seek you out again by night if need be. But if I come out here looking for you by day, I hope you don't intend to hide."

"I will not hide, by day or night. Zoltan, you have really come all this way downriver seeking me." Black Pearl's voice was gently marveling.

"Of course I have. What did you expect?"

But Black Pearl would not tell him what she had expected. Again, with Soft Ripple looking on, the lovers embraced, and this time exchanged passionate kisses. Zoltan thought he had been ready for the coldness of her mouth, but still his own nerves felt it as a shock. And another shock—though it was hardly a surprise—came when his hand, sliding down Pearl's bare back in the moment before they separated, encountered the border where smooth skin abruptly changed to scales. It felt as if her lower body were completely encased in some flexible kind of armor.

Hastily they arranged another meeting. Then, his body feeling shriveled and numb with cold from the waist down, Zoltan slowly and unhappily waded back to shore. Then he turned his steps uphill in the direction of the Malolo manor house.

Ascending the rough path that followed beside the little stream, he crossed a small clearing in bright moonlight. Looking back from the uphill end of the open space, Zoltan realized abruptly that he was being watched and shadowed. At least it looked that way. First there was one, and then, he thought, there were two dark and nimble figures just visible at the edge of moonlight at the lower end.

Zoltan wasted no time. He turned, ducked into the shadow of the trees again, and ran. The people who might be trying to follow him were not going to get any closer if he could help it. The path was very dark in stretches, but it was basically familiar to him after his trip down, and if the two figures were trying to catch up they were having no success. Now and then, looking downhill behind him, he caught a glimpse of one or another of them in moonlight, and was satisfied that they were gaining little if any distance on him.

Zoltan did not slacken his pace. Running softly, dodging among trees like a shadow, he soon drew near the cleared area around the manor. Here, to his surprise, he came close to running into several more mysterious figures. These were keeping watch on the house from the shadowed edge of the forest.

Zoltan got past these additional complications without incident. As he entered the clearing, a man's voice, its owner invisible in the darkness, called softly from somewhere off to his right. Zoltan thought that he could recognize the voice of the mercenary officer Koszalin. If this identification was correct, the mercenaries had come back from spending their pearl money sooner than expected. Or else something had happened to keep them from ever going as far as the nearest town.

Whoever the watchers at the edge of the clearing were, they must have been aware of Zoltan's passage. But they made no attempt to stop or overtake him. In a few score running paces he had reached the back door of the manor.

Lady Yambu had evidently been listening for Zoltan's return, for the moment he gave the agreed-upon signal, the door swung open to admit him to the house.

Bonar and his sisters were waiting in the kitchen along with Yambu, and the clan chief and his sister Rose were openly relieved to see that Zoltan had returned. Violet, on the other hand, immediately expressed her suspicions that he had been treating with the enemy.

Zoltan denied this flatly.

"Then where were you?"

"If I told you I was visiting a mermaid, would you believe it? I'll give you the details, if you like."

There was silence; at least the accusation of treating with the Senones was not immediately renewed. Meanwhile Yambu, not bothering to ask Zoltan what success he'd had with his mermaid, hastened to bring him up to date. For whatever reason, at least some of the mercenaries, Koszalin among them, were here instead of enjoying their binge in town. Possibly their captain had decided that much more treasure could be extracted here, and had been able to enforce patience on his men. Whatever the reason, they had returned a little after midnight, to hammer on both doors of the manor, demanding what they called their fair share of the wealth.

Zoltan, mindful of possible flanking movements, started upstairs to check on the manor's defenses there.

Somewhat to his surprise, dark-haired Rose volunteered to come with him, saying that he might need help finding his way about through the darkened rooms.

"I might well need some help. Are all the windows protected with good gratings?"

"I'm almost sure they are. Let me come with you and we'll make certain."

A few moments later, as Zoltan turned to make his way out of a small bedroom whose windows were indeed securely barred, he found Rose gently but firmly blocking the narrow doorway.

Her hand came to rest on his arm; her voice was hardly louder than a whisper. "I feel safe as long as you're here. But you're wearing pilgrim clothes, and that means you don't intend to stay here very long. Doesn't it?"

"Being a pilgrim generally means not staying in one place, that's right."

"There's nothing for me here either, not really. With all the elders in the family dead, Bonar inherits the manor, the villages, everything." Rose was looking at him through narrowed eyes; in candlelight she was far from unattractive. Suddenly he realized that she must have recently put on some kind of perfume.

Just now, thought Zoltan, was not the time for him to say that he had committed his thoughts and his entire future to someone else.

Now his attractive companion, still obstructing the exit, had him by the sleeve, which she fondled as if testing the gray fabric. "Sometimes I think I'd like to be a pilgrim, too."

"Really?"

"Yes. What else is there? There's nothing else for me around here."

"The life of a pilgrim is not easy, either."

He tried to put her gently aside. Rose grabbed him,

and made her plea more openly than before. "Zoltan. When you leave here, take me with you."

Zoltan was doing his best to frame an answer that would not provoke a crisis, when, to his considerable relief, another candle appeared down the dim hallway. It was Violet, in a hurry, obviously bringing some kind of news.

Violet looked at the two of them sharply, as if she suspected what her older sister was up to. Zoltan was beginning to believe that Violet tended to see everything in terms of jealousy and suspicion. She was an anti-Senones fanatic, always ready to suspect some betrayal in that direction. At the same time, Zoltan thought, she might be somewhat jealously attracted to him, too.

And in the privacy of his own thoughts he tried to imagine how outraged both women would be at the idea that any man they considered at all interesting could be as obsessively smitten as he was—with a creature they considered little more than a fish.

But the message brought upstairs by Violet allowed little time for debate. The disgruntled soldiers had renewed their pounding on the rear door. It sounded this time like a serious attempt to break it down.

The upstairs seemed secure, as far as Zoltan could tell. So he hurried back downstairs. As he arrived in the kitchen he could hear the mercenaries outside, threatening now to burn the whole manor to the ground if their demands for more treasure were not met.

The doors themselves were truly strong, and for the moment seemed secure. Gesner, the claimed magician, was at least keeping his head well, even if not contributing much beyond that. He now assured the visitors that the manor's sloping roof was of slate tiles. Most of the rest of the building was stone, and it would not be easy to burn. Gesner had now equipped himself with some serious-looking magician's paraphernalia, and

announced that he intended to do what he could with
fire-preventing spells. And if a fire was started by anyone
outside the house, he'd attempt to make the flames snap
back at and burn the fingers that had ignited them.

Yambu approved this plan. Then she and Zoltan
concentrated for the moment on organizing a more
mundane line of defense, ordering servants to stand by
in key locations with buckets of water. A well-filled
cistern on the roof offered some prospects of success.

Bonar meanwhile had unlocked an armory on the
lowest level of the house, next to the improvised mortu-
ary, and was passing out weapons to his sisters and the
remaining servants, or at least to those among the
servants he could persuade to take them. Violet armed
herself eagerly, and Rose with some reluctance followed
suit.

Entering the arsenal himself, Zoltan selected a bow
and some arrows from the supply available. Thus
equipped, he ran upstairs again and stationed himself in
a high window that gave him a good view of the rear
yard. The fools out there were getting a fire going in the
rear of one of the outbuildings, and a moment later
Zoltan shot a man who came running with a torch
toward the manor itself. The fellow screamed so loudly
when he was hit that Zoltan doubted he was mortally
hurt.

Another pair of mercenaries came to drag their
wounded comrade away, and Zoltan let them do so
unmolested, thinking they might be ready for a general
retreat. The barn, or shed, or whatever it was, was
burning merrily now. Fortunately it stood just outside
the compound wall, and far enough from all other
buildings that the spread of the fire did not seem to
present an immediate danger.

Meanwhile the fire was giving him plenty of light to
aim by, which put the attackers at a definite disadvan-

tage. But Kosazlin's shouts could be heard, rallying his men, and they were not yet ready for a general retreat. Taking shelter as best they could, they began to send a desultory drizzle of stones and arrows against the house.

When this had been going on for some time, Bonar, in a fever of martial excitement, entered the room where Zoltan was, crouched beside him and looked out. This window afforded the best view of what was going on outside.

"What's burning? Oh, the old barn, that's nothing much. How many of them have we killed?"

"None, that I know of. I hit one but I doubt he's dead. Is the rest of the house still secure?"

"The ground floor is fine, I've just made the rounds down there."

There was a sound in the hallway, just outside the bedroom, as of a servant running, calling. Then a brief scuffle.

Bonar and Zoltan both leaped up, leveling their weapons at the doorway. The door pushed open—

Zoltan found himself confronting a tall and powerful man who gripped a drawn Sword in his right hand. In the firelight that flared in through the open window Zoltan had no trouble recognizing his uncle, Prince Mark of Tasavalta.

NINE

ZOLTAN'S hands sagged holding the half-drawn bow, and the ready arrow fell from his fingers to the floor. For a moment he could only stare at this apparition blankly, and for that moment he was sure that it must be some kind of deception, that he was facing some image of sorcery, an effect of the Sword of Stealth or some other magical disguise—and the apparition, if such it was, was lowering the Sword in its right hand.

"No need to think you're seeing visions, nephew," said the tall man, having observed the two occupants of the room carefully for a moment. He spoke in Prince Mark's familiar voice. "I would have hailed you down on the hillside, but I couldn't get close, and I didn't want to yell your name at the top of my voice. You gave us the devil of a chase uphill from the river. After we followed you to this house, we decided we'd look in to make sure that you needed no help." Now Mark sheathed his Sword.

"We?" Zoltan could only repeat the word numbly.

"Ben and I."

Behind Mark, entering from the hallway, appeared another big man. This one was indeed monstrously massive, though somewhat shorter than the prince and a few years older. Ben of Purkinje's ugly face split in a reassuring smile at the sight of the bewildered Zoltan.

And he, the prince's nephew, shaking his head in wonder and relief, at last remembered the chief of the Clan Malolo. "Bonar, put down your sword. This man is my uncle Mark, the Prince of Tasavalta."

While Bonar was managing some kind of greeting, the Lady Yambu put in her appearance, to greet both Mark and Ben with great surprise and equally great relief.

A couple of the more trustworthy servants were posted as lookouts, while a conference of explanations was conducted. Almost the first question the two newcomers were required to answer was how they had gained entrance to the house. Mark explained, and apologized, for the secret violence of their entry. The Sword he carried at his belt was Stonecutter, and he and Ben had used it to carve their way in through the solid stone wall of the manor, a process Stonecutter's magic accomplished swiftly and almost silently.

By now Rose and Violet, as well as Gesner, had joined the conference around the two newcomers, and were being introduced to them with a mixture of relief and apprehension.

Fortunately it now appeared that the mercenaries' assault, such as it had been, had abated at least for the time being.

Ben, scowling out the window, muttered: "Maybe when the fire in back dies down they'll try again."

"Maybe." The prince nodded. "That means we should use our time meanwhile to good advantage."

And now for a time the conference adjourned to the great hall of the manor, where Mark and Ben were provided with food and drink. They found this welcome, having been through some hard traveling in the past few days.

Their riding-beasts, as Ben explained, had been lost in some minor skirmish with unnamed foes "between here and the desert." Ben waved a huge hand in a generally southeast direction. For the past three days they had been on foot.

"But what brings you here?"

In answer to that question Zoltan's uncle Mark explained that he and Ben had been on their way back to Tasavalta after concluding a deal with the desert tribesman Prince al-Farabi, by which al-Farabi had been allowed to borrow the Sword Stonecutter for a time.

With that transaction concluded, and after starting home with Stonecutter, Mark had received, by winged messenger, word from his father the Emperor. In a written message the Emperor informed his son Mark that important matters, requiring almost his full attention, were developing somewhere in the extreme south of the continent.

The Emperor had warned Mark to prepare for urgent action, and to await another message which, Mark hoped, would spell out in some detail just what he was expected to do.

"That still doesn't explain how you and Ben come to be here. Did you mean to follow the river east, or—?"

Mark shook his head. "There was another part to the message. It suggested rather strongly that we might want to locate you. You, Zoltan, and you, Lady Yambu."

The two pilgrims exchanged uncertain glances. "Did the message say why?" Yambu asked.

"It did not. But it did say that a Sword was at stake here, and that Swords should not be allowed to fall into the wrong hands. So, we started for the valley of the Tungri as fast as we conveniently could. And here you are, and here we are."

Zoltan whistled his amazement softly. "My great-uncle is quite a magician."

Prince Mark sighed, but made no other comment.

Ben shrugged. "I've seen enough, that when the Emperor suggests something I'm inclined to listen."

Yambu nodded her head. Meanwhile the folk native to the manor were watching and listening in silence, though Bonar once or twice seemed on the verge of breaking in with some sharp comment.

"How did you recognize me in the dark?" Zoltan wanted to know. "I mean earlier tonight, on the hill down toward the river?"

Huge Ben snorted gently. "Who else would be talking to a mermaid?"

"Oh." Zoltan wondered if everyone in Tasavalta knew of his obsession.

Now Violet asked: "Excuse me—Your Grace? Your Majesty?—you say that the Emperor knew that your nephew and his friend were here? But how?"

Mark only shrugged. The gesture seemed to say that he did not understand his father's purposes or his father's powers. But the prince's continued smile indicated that he had learned to trust those powers; and it no longer surprised him that he did not understand.

Ben asked: "But what's going on here, Zoltan? Yambu?"

The two pilgrims told Mark and Ben of Farslayer's presence here, and how the Sword had wrought such havoc among the clanspeople on both sides of the river.

Mark nodded. "We must do what we can to get it."

A little later, when the people of the clan had left them, Mark also fretted aloud to his nephew about his ten-year-old son Adrian, who had been recently enrolled, or was about to enroll, in a new school, unspecified. There, his father hoped, he would be able safely to master the arts of magic for which he had such a natural aptitude, and which might otherwise prove such a burden to him as he grew up.

To Ben, Zoltan, and Yambu, Mark declared: "Old Karel has arranged something in the way of schooling. This time I expect it'll work out successfully."

Zoltan said: "We could use someone here right now with a little natural aptitude along the line of magic—and a little schooling, too."

No such luck.

Bonar and his sisters gawked at this royal personage when he rejoined them, and made efforts not to be overly impressed. They struggled not to be awed by his presence, or by that of the Sword he carried. Yet, at the same time, the Malolo survivors were more at ease now. If their manor was to be occupied at all, far better that it should be done by a reigning prince and his entourage.

It was easy to see that Bonar, despite his rather hollow protests that it did not matter, was somewhat perturbed by the tunnellike hole carved in the stone wall of his house, and by the ease with which these strangers had penetrated his defenses. But the physical damage could be easily enough repaired, and in the morning the huge man Ben helped the Malolo servants push back into place the blocks of stone that had been cut free.

Zoltan had already told Mark of his, Zoltan's, successful search for Black Pearl, and in the same breath had informed the prince that Black Pearl had said she knew something of the Sword's hiding place.

Bonar and his sisters repeated to Mark and Ben what they had already told Zoltan and Yambu, about the man Chilperic, who had come through here saying that he acted as the agent of the great magician Wood.

That got the prince's full attention. "What did you tell him?"

"There is little enough we can tell anyone. He went on his way dissatisfied."

Yambu and Zoltan also told Mark of the hermit.

Mark, who had of course heard of Black Pearl at great length while Zoltan was still in Tasavalta, listened sympathetically now to his nephew's continued pleas to help her, but could not promise to be of any real assistance. "You're sure it's the same wench, hey?"

"Of course!"

"Pardon, Zoltan. Of course you are. It's just that I have many other things to think of. Like Farslayer."

Still, Mark promised that if another winged messenger should come to him here from Tasavalta, he would use it to send a return message, asking Karel about magical help for mermaids.

Zoltan momentarily regretted bothering his uncle with a personal problem. But only momentarily.

An hour or two before dawn, when the fire in back had burned itself out without any renewal of the mercenaries' attack, and when most of his comrades were asleep, Mark found his way alone up to a flat portion of the manor's roof.

Here he found a comfortable seat, which for a time he occupied in silence and solitude, regarding the night sky and its mysteries. But when a quarter of an hour had passed, there came an almost inaudible whisper of wings. The expected messenger, an owlish, half-intelligent creature, whose wingspan was greater than the span of the prince's arms, came gliding down out of the stars to land beside him on a small parapet.

The prince of Tasavalta was not surprised and did not stir. "Hail, messenger," he murmured in greeting.

"Greetings to the prince of Tasavalta." The words were clearly only a memorized formula, and the thin, small voice in which they were spoken was far from human. Still, the words were clear enough.

"Do you bring me word from my father? From the Emperor?"

"Message for Prince Mark: No news from home. All goes well at home. I stand ready to bear a message back."

No news in this case was good news. The prince had been away from Tasavalta for several months now, and he tended to worry about matters at home.

True, Mark had left the affairs of Tasavalta—as well as the care of his second son, Stephen, now eight years old—in the very capable hands of his wife, Princess Kristin. But still he inevitably worried.

"Any news from the Princess Kristin? Or greetings from either of my sons?"

"No news from home. All goes well at home. I stand ready to bear a message back."

Mark sighed, and began to say the words he wanted the creature to memorize.

TEN

ON the morning after that on which the prince conversed with a winged messenger, the hermit Gelimer was sitting on a block of wood in his dooryard, gazing in the direction of his woodpile, which had been much depleted by winter. But at the moment the hermit was hardly conscious of the wood, or anything else in the yard around him. Gelimer was enjoying the promise of an early spring sun, and thinking back over his life. He found much material there for thought, especially in the days of his youth, before he had become a hermit.

He had become an anchorite long years ago, chiefly out of a sense of the need to withdraw from evil. But from time to time it was borne in upon him that evil, along with much else from his old life, was not to be so easily avoided.

Gelimer possessed, as did many folk who were not magicians, the ability to sense the presence of magical powers. And he could sense that there was a demon in the valley now.

He thought he knew why the foul thing had come. It was the Sword, of course, like any other great material treasure a lodestone drawing all the wickedness of the world about itself. When the hermit thought of demons, and of the men and women who consorted with such creatures and tried to use them, he was tempted to reclaim the Sword from where he had hidden it, and employ it to rid the world of at least some of those evildoers. But so far he had managed to put the intrinsically repulsive thought of violence away from him.

Another aspect of the Sword's presence was inescapable. As long as he, Gelimer, knew where it was, had it virtually in his possession, he could no longer distance himself from the local political and military situation. Ordinarily he ignored the inhabitants of the valley, those of high station as well as low, and neither knew nor cared about the latest developments in the bitter feud between the clans. But now that was no longer an option; Farslayer had brought him an unwanted burden of power and responsibility.

When Gelimer had hidden the Sword, he had thought vaguely that with good luck the terrible weapon might remain where he had put it for years, for generations even, until no one any longer sought it in the valley. But already that had come to seem a foolish hope.

Very well. If he was now inescapably involved, then he must try to be involved as intelligently as possible.

By now Gelimer had logically reconstructed, at least to his own satisfaction, what must have happened in his house on the night of the storm. His visitor, Cosmo Biondo—if that had really been the man's name—must have awakened, perhaps delirious with his head injury, in the middle of the night, while Gelimer himself still slept. Then the visitor, whoever he was and whether delirious or sane, had taken the terrible Sword in hand and carried it outside. What had happened immediately after that was still uncertain, except that the Sword must have passed from the hands of the man Cosmo into the possession of someone else. Possibly, even probably, Cosmo had decided to invoke Farslayer's awful magic against someone at a distance, and had gone outside where he had room to swing the Sword, and privacy to chant whatever words he thought were necessary.

However he had rid himself of Farslayer, Cosmo had had time, before the Sword came back to him, to reenter Gelimer's house. Time to latch the door after himself, and to go to stand beside the bed—as if, having used that Sword, he might be ready to go back to sleep.

As indeed, in a sense, he had done.

Whether the violent death of Cosmo had been merited or not, Gelimer reflected that it had probably done no one any good, and settled nothing. Evil moved on through the world as before, and was now gathering in the vicinity of that hidden grave.

Even if Gelimer had been minded to take up the Sword himself and strike at that evil, he would not know where best to aim the blow. At the demon? Such creatures were notoriously difficult to kill. Gelimer had no idea whether even a Sword would be effective in such an effort, or to what physical location the Sword might go if he tried to slay a demon with it, or into whose hands the Sword of Vengeance would fall next. He knew that demons' lives, their only vulnerability, were apt to be hidden in strange places.

No, he would not try to kill the demon now roaming invisibly through the valley—at least not yet. For decades now everything—or almost everything—in the hermit's nature had shrunk from the deliberate taking of any human life. I have put all that behind me, he thought. I am not a god, to judge and punish humans for their crimes. Even the gods did a very poor job of that when they were still around. Not you, of course, Ardneh, he added in his thoughts. You know I don't mean you. And you know which gods I do mean—the ones who created these damnable, almost indestructible Swords, thirty years ago, for the purposes of their Game. The ones who thought that the entirety of human life was no more than a game carried on for their amusement.

Well, the game of human life had swallowed up what had turned out to be the lesser reality of those gods and goddesses. What those divinities had deemed a mere amusement had destroyed them. And perhaps the limit of what human life was going to accomplish in the universe was not yet in sight.

Sitting by his woodpile now, Gelimer closed his eyes, wincing as if he felt an inner pain. He could tell that the demon had just passed, in some dimension, near him. But at the moment he stood in no immediate peril, for the thing was already gone again.

Even a nonviolent man could hardly scruple to kill a demon, by any means possible. In fact it might be thought a crime against humanity to fail to kill one if you had the power.

Despite its violence, the idea was developing a powerful attraction: *To cleanse the earth of such a foul blot— why should I not for once be willing to use the clean steel of a god-forged blade?*

But he must be very careful. He must be sure of what he was doing before he moved.

Who had the ordering of demons, who employed such difficult and deadly dangerous tools? It was certainly not likely to be any of these local fools, even though one or two of them dared to call themselves wizards. No, it would be some vastly greater power, from outside the valley. And what would bring such a power here? Certainly the Sword Farslayer, as a prize to be won, might do so.

Gelimer's thoughts kept coming back to the same conclusions, but those conclusions never brought him any nearer to knowing what to do.

* * *

Meanwhile, Chilperic on that same morning had no clear idea of where his demon was at the moment or what it was doing—filthy creature, he would like to forget that it existed, if that were only possible. Today Chilperic himself was back on the south side of the river, and in fact he was within a few hundred meters of the hermit's house. He was coming back to question the hermit again, but had decided that it would be wise to look around in the vicinity a little first.

Chilperic did not think the hermit had lied to him. But during his second night at the Scnones manor, it had gradually come to him that neither Cosmo Malolo nor the Sword he had carried might ever have left these high crags. There had been a great deal of killing on that night, and there was really no reason to think that Cosmo had survived it.

And now today the sight of a scavenger bird or two, rising in bright sunlight from somewhere among the rocks that formed the lip of a precipice, suggested to Chilperic that some large creature was lying dead in that location.

To get anywhere near the place Chilperic was forced to dismount, then edge his way forward carefully on foot, until he was standing on the very brink. Forty meters or more below him, the Tungri grumbled and fumed eternally, sawing its way down through rock, day after day infinitesimally deepening its gorge.

Wrinkling his nose at the smell of death, chilly and stale in the spring air, Chilperic reached the last necessary foothold, braced himself with one arm on a rock, leaned over and looked down. Not two meters below him he saw the startling white of bone, protruding from amid coarse hair and decaying flesh. Leaning forward again, even more precariously, he was able to assure himself that the victim had not been human, but a riding-beast; there were no saddlebags, but the saddle and other tack were still in place. The discoverer could remember seeing leather worked in similar patterns when he had poked his curious nose into the Malolo stables.

Interesting. And more than that.

His heart beginning to beat faster, Chilperic looked around him carefully. He clambered back and forth along the rough brink of the cliff, probing into every nearby crevice of rock. He even managed at last to get close enough to the dead animal to move what was left of it, using his own sword as a lever. He shifted the carcass enough to see that there was no man's body, and no resplendent Sword, pinned underneath it.

Cosmo's riding-beast, quite probably. Almost certainly, if Chilperic could find Cosmo's initials or some other identification on the leather. But still the Sword of Vengeance was nowhere to be found.

Reluctantly Chilperic returned at last to his own tethered mount. He swung himself up into the saddle and sat there motionless for a moment, gazing thoughtfully down toward the thundering stream below. It might be a hopeless search down there at the bottom of the river, but then again it might not.

He could, of course, employ Rabisu in the search. But how much help the demon would be was problematical. Chilperic had for some time suspected that the foul creature might prefer, after all, that the Sword never be found. Its own life, however carefully hidden, might be as vulnerable as the life of any puny human to that blade.

Probably, Chilperic concluded, it would be best not to try to use the demon at all. It was his understanding that there were other creatures nearby, just as intelligent and much more docile, who would be even more at home along the bottom of the river.

* * *

Chilperic, on leaving the place where he had discovered the dead riding-beast, hastened to recross the river, and long before nightfall he had returned to the headquarters of the Senones clan.

Today the homegrown militia guards stationed around the perimeter of the clearing in which the Senones manor stood were not as grim and tense as they had been yesterday. And today, Chilperic noted as he handed his riding-beast over to a groom, there was more ordinary activity around the place, as if things might be beginning to return to normal.

But even before he had passed through the gate into the inner grounds, this last impression was firmly contradicted by an apparition in the sky.

Suddenly some of the people around him were gawking upward. Following the direction of their collective gaze, Chilperic beheld a marvel. Outlined against a fluffy cloud was a huge griffin, spiraling in descent. A single human figure was mounted astride the creature, which possessed the head and wings of an oversized eagle, and the four-legged body of a lion. Such creatures were extremely rare, and their flight depended more on magic than on the physical power of their wings.

The griffin's descent was quick, and not many people actually witnessed its arrival. Which was probably just as well, for most of those who did were petrified. The winged beast came down gently and peacefully enough, to land on the flat lawn immediately in front of the manor. Though not one person in a thousand among the general population ever saw one of these uncommon beasts, Chilperic was no stranger to the sight—nor was he, actually, very much surprised by the arrival of a griffin at the Senones manor just now. He had a good idea who the creature's passenger might be.

The gates in the inner wall of the manor had already

been opened to admit Chilperic, and he strode in, practically unnoticed. The new Tyrant, who seemed to have been waiting on the lawn, quite possibly to welcome him, had now instead turned his back on Chilperic and the gate—for which he could scarcely be blamed— and was gaping like a yokel at the unexpected aerial arrival.

The human figure who had just arrived was at this instant in the act of dismounting from the griffin's back. This was a diminutive female with her long blond hair bound up closely, dressed in a close-fitting jacket and trousers, what looked like eminently practical garb for hurtling through the air astride a monster's back. The woman was very young—to all appearances, at least— and very pretty. She could only be the healer that Wood had promised to send.

Meanwhile the griffin was crouching on the lawn in the pose of a docile cat. Still, it managed to impress and even cow most of the local people who were quickly gathering —at a respectful distance—to behold it. Chilperic thought that the monster's presence might well worry the more thoughtful among the local people, offering as it did more evidence that whether they liked it or not they were now closely involved in the affairs of the great world.

The young woman with the neatly controlled blond hair and the small backpack immediately decided— whether through deduction or divination—which of the people present was the clan leader. For the moment she ignored everyone else, including Chilperic, and came walking straight to Hissarlik. Her movements possessed a grace that Chilperic had seldom seen matched. Genuflecting briefly before the Tyrant in a gesture of great respect, the new arrival introduced herself, in a soft voice, as Tigris, physician and surgeon.

The Tyrant, staring distractedly at this beauteous

arrival—as many a more experienced man in his place would have done—murmured and mumbled something in return. Then he recovered himself sufficiently to take the young lady formally by the hand and bid her welcome.

"Thank you, my lord." The healer's eyelashes fluttered demurely, and her gaze became downcast. "Will you now have a servant show me to my quarters—my room will be next to my patient's, I pray—and provide me with a maidservant to attend me? Soon I will be ready to examine the patient."

"I, uh. Yes, of course." The Tyrant, recovering further, clapped his hands and gave the necessary orders.

Meanwhile the griffin, as if it had received some hidden signal, spread its wings again—at a closer look those limbs appeared to be more reptilian than avian— and soared suddenly into the air. The gawking crowd fell back even further, but Tigris ignored the departure of the beast completely. She had now raised her eyes and was gazing, in a way that might be thought inappropriate for a physician, at the man she had greeted as her lord.

Only when she turned away to follow the servant who was to lead her to her quarters did her gaze brush Chilperic's. It was a cool, appraising glance. He supposed it likely that the lady had come with some special orders from Wood having to do with himself. He would have to take the opportunity to meet with her alone as soon as it was practical.

Hissarlik's grim young cousin, Anselm, limped from somewhere to intercept the healer just as she was about to enter the house. At first Chilperic thought that Anselm intended to stop her from going in, but after a few moments' conversation they entered the manor together.

As for the Tyrant himself, his gleaming eyes followed his new guest until she was out of sight. Only then did he turn, with a sigh, and speak to Chilperic. "Though I have scarcely met the woman as yet, I am deeply impressed. Your master, the Ancient One, certainly fulfills his promises quickly."

"Oh, indeed he does," Chilperic assured the Tyrant. "I would not be likely to attach myself to any master who did not."

"Nor would I be."

"I see."

Now the two men, by unspoken agreement, began to stroll. They passed around the side of the sprawling house, and entered what must once have been a flower garden, though it was sadly neglected now.

As they walked, Hissarlik started to discuss his plans for the future. His only real goal, it appeared, was to determine just how, working together, he and his new friend Chilperic were going to wipe out once and for all those infamous Malolo brigands across the river.

The older man smiled at him, gently and agreeably. "Undoubtedly a very worthy objective, sire. But before I can undertake to give you assistance in such a project, there are one or two other matters that I must see to for my master."

"Oh. I see," Hissarlik said vaguely. He did not seem to be paying complete attention. His head turned away and his eyes kept straying toward the house, where certain windows on the second floor seemed likely to be those of the entranced family sorceress, next to those of the beautiful blond physician. "And what would those matters be?"

Patiently Chilperic reiterated the story of how sincerely his own dread master, Wood, wished and pined to possess the Sword of Vengeance. Once that goal had been attained, then certainly the mighty Wood would be ready to reward his friend Hissarlik even more generously than by sending a healer—provided of course that in the meantime Hissarlik had been of help in recovering the Sword.

Chilperic lowered his voice slightly when he imparted the next bit of information, which was that Wood might even have in mind something like the offer of a real partnership.

The Tyrant, now sitting at ease in a worn-out garden chair, under a leafless tree at one end of his neglected garden, scratched his head. "Well, that's all very fine, of course. If I had possession of the Sword, or anything else your master wants, I'd gladly give it to him. I hope he knows that. But the truth is I don't have Farslayer, nor do I know where it is. You don't believe I have it, do you?"

"Of course not, sire. You don't have possession of the Sword now. If you did you would already be attacking the Malolo."

"That's right."

Chilperic paused momentarily. "But I do have an idea as to where it might be found. And how, with some help you can provide, we might be able to recover it."

"Is that so?" Hissarlik still sounded cautious rather than eager. "What sort of help do you need?"

Chilperic explained briefly about his discovery, this very day, of the dead riding-beast, and his idea that the Sword might be lying at the bottom of the Tungri somewhere in that vicinity. "The water runs quite swiftly there, and I suppose that it is deep. But a creature capable of living and moving easily underwater ought not to have too much trouble in examining the bottom."

"Hmm."

"Yes." Chilperic pressed on: "Unless I'm mistaken, you Senones folk are able to call upon the local mermaids for service when you wish, though technically the creatures are supposed to be under the lordship of those fools across the river. Their grip on all their vassals, including even the fishgirls, is evidently weakening."

"Yes, we can call upon mermaids if we wish." But Hissarlik did not seem to be immediately pleased by the idea of doing so. "If you mean by magic, it was Aunt Meg who generally handled that sort of thing, of course, when she was well." Then he brightened. "What about your demon? Couldn't it conduct a search even more swiftly and surely?"

Now it was Chilperic's turn to be less than enchanted by a suggestion. "The demon has many other tasks to accomplish."

"I suppose it must have," the Tyrant agreed somewhat doubtfully.

"Tell me, my friend. Is there something you don't like about the idea of using mermaids?"

"Well, the truth is that those creatures do tend to be somewhat unreliable. They're totally lazy, of course. They can be forced magically to do some things, such as coming when they are called—though it's not always certain that they even do that. And there's no way to force them to obey perfectly when sent out on a mission. Actually they're a pretty rebellious lot, and all in all more trouble than they're worth, though we do manage to sell one once in a while."

Chilperic frowned in thought. "How long have there been mermaids in the river here? I was told their condition was the result of a spell inflicted on some villages by a Senones magician many years ago, in the course of the feud."

"Yes, that's correct." The Tyrant went on to explain that the ancestral magician, whom he claimed as his own great-grandfather, had been still in the process of perfecting the spell when he died. Great-grandfather's ultimate goal had been to develop some similar curse that might be used directly against the vile Malolo leaders, but their magical defenses had remained too strong.

"And no one since his time has devised a way to lift the spell, or to expand and perfect it as he sought to do?"

"Aunt Meg, as I say, was—is—our best magician. She's really the one you ought to talk to, as soon as she's able." Judging from his confident tone, the Tyrant had great faith in the healer Wood had sent him. "But no, friend Chilperic, as far as I know, no one on our side in modern times has been much interested in using the mermaid spell. I have the idea that somehow it's impractical. I suppose the Malolo leaders really haven't cared that much about it, either. It actually doesn't affect enough of their people to do them any harm. Having a few mermaids about is interesting, and sometimes such creatures command big prices as slaves or oddities. Sometimes the Malolo sell one, sometimes we do."

"I see."

"Yes. Now that I come to think of it, I did once hear a rumor that Cosmo, the Malolo who disappeared on the night of the big fight, was tinkering around with the curse, though I don't know why."

"It would have been Cosmo's mount that I found dead today. I think that he was carrying the Sword."

"Yes, that's what you were saying. And I have to admit Cosmo may have been the best magician on either side in modern times. But I doubt that he got anywhere trying to revoke the curse, either. People still see mermaids."

"Indeed. Where, if I may ask, did you hear this rumor about Cosmo's working on the mermaid curse?"

The Tyrant shrugged. "One hears things sometimes among the servants." It was obvious that Hissarlik was really not much interested in the subject.

Chilperic stood for a little time in silent thought. He was increasingly intrigued by the fact that this magician,

Cosmo, was the same man who had so cravenly—or so wisely—terminated the Sword-throwing fight by absconding with the Sword. But Chilperic made no comment on that fact now.

"So, what about the mermaids?" he asked at last. "With your permission, my friend, I would like to have some of them searching the bottom of the river for the Sword as soon as possible."

"Very well. We can go down to the river and call some of them up for you." The Tyrant drummed with his fingers on the arms of the old chair, making no move to get up. "Boats go out to their island more or less regularly. Usually someone in the clan here takes them some food every day or two. We should take food, too. It might work better than such magic as we have available."

"Food?" Chilperic had thought of mermaids as being somehow completely self-supporting.

"Well, as I understand it, having spent their childhood ashore in villages, sleeping under roofs, and eating in most cases from some kind of plates, even when they grow tails they remain reluctant to bite raw fish and chew on snails they've just grubbed up out of the mud. At the same time, since they can't get about on land, cooking and housekeeping in the traditional ways present them with certain difficulties."

"Yes. Now that I think about it, I suppose they would."

"So, in return for some real food, or at least for certain things that pass for real food in the villages, the fishgirls provide us with a few pearls. Or other valuables if they find any. It's a sporadic kind of barter, that happens when both parties have an urge to trade. No really considerable wealth is involved."

"I see. How many mermaids do you suppose will show up when you summon them?"

Hissarlik shrugged his shoulders. "I suppose we'll get a dozen if we're lucky. As I said, there's a minor control spell that will summon them, or at last those who are within range, to attend us at the water's edge. It's related to the spell we use to call up mermaids when we want to sell or rent them out to visiting magicians, or to traveling shows. We rent them, usually. The creatures seldom live beyond the age of thirty, so there's no great bargain for a purchaser in buying one. When we have them at the shore we can give them orders, and bribe them with food. But as I warned you earlier, the magic for obedience is unreliable, and the orders we give them are seldom or never carried out just as we would wish. So, you see, the curse has never been of much value in a military way."

Chilperic brushed aside the problems associated with the regular mermaid trade. "You keep harping on the idea that they'll be unreliable as searchers."

"I'm afraid they will." Hissarlik hesitated. "And then—suppose they do find this Sword."

"Yes?"

"Well then, suppose one of them found it and instead of turning it in decided to try to use it."

"Is that what's bothering you? Consider that if Farslayer does lie at the bottom of the river, one of the fishgirls is likely to discover it there anyway."

"Oh." It was obvious from the Tyrant's sudden change of expression that he hadn't thought of that.

Chilperic pressed his new advantage. "So, it should help if I offer a reward to the fishgirl who brings it to us. And if at the same time I threaten punishment of any who try to conceal the Sword or dispose of it in any other way."

Hissarlik looked reluctantly ready to agree.

"They are at least moderately intelligent, are they not?"

"Hey?"

"The mermaids, man, the mermaids." There were limits to Chilperic's patience.

"Oh yes. As intelligent as any other peasant. Very well, then, let's go." And Hissarlik got to his feet.

Within an hour a small party, consisting of Hissarlik, Chilperic, and an escort of militia, had formed and had moved on to the riverbank, where several boats were being made available for the short jaunt to Mermaids' Island.

"Hissarlik, my friend?"

"Yes?"

"Is there any real advantage in our going out to the island? Can we not lure the creatures, and speak to them, just as successfully from here on shore?"

"Well, it might take a trifle longer that way—but yes, I suppose we can."

"Then let us do so." A handful of soldiers from the Senones Home Guard were standing by, ready to offer armed protection during the boat trip to the island, just in case some of the Malolo forces should be encountered on the island or on the water. But Chilperic, sniffing the air and eyeing suspiciously the fishing boats already on the river, had decided that he would rather not trust in the protective abilities of the Home Guard. He could of course call up the demon for protection, but his reluctance to depend entirely upon that power continued.

"I suppose we can do it just as well from shore. And perhaps we ought to wait for Megara anyway," said Hissarlik vaguely, turning away from the boat he had been about to enter.

Anselm had joined them, and was now serving as stand-in magician. He began to cast a spell. Within a quarter of an hour three or four of the underwater creatures had appeared in the water near shore, where they paddled about looking surprised, as if wondering why they had come here. Within an hour there were about a dozen, and these were all the mermaids that were likely to attend, according to Hissarlik.

A couple of the creatures sat on the muddy shoreline, while the others swam about. By now they all looked sullenly unwilling to be here.

Chilperic had to admit they were all lithe and attractive young women from the waist up. When he was assured that no more were likely to arrive, he stood up on the bank and spoke to them, describing the missing Sword, and promising to heal all of them of their affliction if one of them could bring him such a weapon. Their reaction was subdued; he could not tell to what extent his promise was believed.

So he took care, before dismissing them, and while the food from the hampers was being thrown to them, to threaten them with his demon if none of them did bring him the Sword he sought. He let them see the demon to convince them that it was no empty threat—and this time he got the reaction that he sought.

ELEVEN

THE mermaid named Black Pearl had attended the gathering on the northern shore, more out of curiosity than from any compulsion by the feeble magic of Anselm Senones. She had listened to the arrogant strange man who spoke from the bank after Anselm, but she had not been much impressed by either his promises or his threats. At least not until the demon appeared to give a brief demonstration of its powers. Naturally the people on the north bank wanted the Sword, but they, or their late parents, were the same people who had sold Black Pearl into slavery, and she was not inclined to help them get anything they wanted now. Besides, if she had known where the Sword was, she would have taken it to Zoltan.

When the demon-master had finished his threats and the feeble magic of Anselm had relaxed its grip, Black Pearl had slipped away from the other mermaids, into the swift-flowing depths of the Tungri. And now she was on the south shore. Swimming and scrambling, she was struggling with great difficulty to make headway against a roaring and shallow rush of water. With hands and fins and tail she labored to ascend the rocky bed of a small stream.

This particular stream, much faster than the creek

Zoltan had followed on his way to meet her, came gushing down the mountain through a narrow little canyon in the south side of the river gorge. The mouth of this brook, where it poured into the Tungri, was less than a kilometer from the hermit's house high on the irregular slope above. That house was still invisible from the place where the young mermaid squirmed and struggled.

On this spring day the little stream had been augmented by melting snow in the high country, yet still there were stretches in which its depth was insufficient to keep afloat a swimming creature of the mermaid's size. Black Pearl, in the form to which she had been condemned by enchantment, was only a little smaller than she would have been as a young woman with two legs.

Even this close to the stream's mouth she had already encountered an especially difficult spot. Here, where the water spread out into a mere corrugated sheet stretched over a rocky bed, it was impossible for any creature of her size to swim. Pausing in her efforts, lying on her side in the rushing shallows, she reached for the amulet that hung from a thin chain about her neck, and muttered a few soft words.

Almost unwillingly Black Pearl had memorized the words of the spell, after hearing Cosmo recite it countless times in the secret grotto. Perhaps he would be surprised, she thought now, to see that his magic worked for her alone almost as well as it had ever worked for him. Perhaps he would be surprised to know that it worked away from the grotto as well.

Immediately the spell had its effect. In a puff of watery mist her mermaid tail was gone, replaced by pale but very human-looking hips and legs. Shakily Black Pearl stood up, nakedly vulnerable now to the cold water and completely human. A young woman's body, perfectly normal in appearance, poised now upon two bare and very human feet.

Stepping carefully and with difficulty, yet trying to make the best speed she could, she walked forward over the rough rocks, muttering prayers to all the gods that she had ever heard of.

Barely had Black Pearl reached the next deep pool upstream before the strength of the spell she had just recited collapsed under the burden of the greater magic it labored to counteract. The forces that had for the space of a few breaths maintained her body in a normal human form abruptly dissipated. In an instant, metamorphosis reversed itself. Feet and legs were returned in the twinkling of an eye into the fishtail that she had worn for the past five years, since the age of twelve. She fell with a great splash.

But still she was able to make progress. Here, and upstream for some distance she had yet to discover, there ran a channel deep enough to support her finned body as she swam. Once more she could fight the current with her fins and tail—until she reached the next stretch where the channel disappeared.

Several times during the next few minutes of the mermaid's upstream struggle she was forced to use the secret counterspell and amulet. The trouble was that the effect of the counterspell faded rapidly with frequent repetition. The time Black Pearl was able to spend in fully human form was limited to a few minutes at most with each use of the amulet, and the power had to be carefully husbanded. Only rarely and infrequently could she escape the deforming impact of accursed Senones magic, and regain for a heartbreakingly small time the shape that would have been hers in normal life. And each interval of relief cost her more and more in psychic effort to achieve. It would be necessary to let the power in the amulet lie fallow for days, weeks, or even months before the maximum, comparatively long periods of full

humanity could be attained once more. She had husbanded the power for many days before attempting this
ascent, where she expected that it would be needed in its
fullest form.

She was determined to tell her secrets to someone, and
it certainly would not be those slave dealers on the north
side of the river. Nor would it, could it, be Zoltan. Never
that.

Months ago, Cosmo, lying with Black Pearl in the
secret grotto upon a bed of moss and furs, with his own
gift of her true woman's legs clasped round him, had
murmured into her ear again and again that the secrecy
was part of the spell. That if she revealed the magical
power of changing to another living soul, that power
might be taken from her, beyond even his wizard's
power to restore it.

At that time Black Pearl had assured her lover fiercely
that she would never tell. And until now she had kept the
secret safe, though several times she had come close to
telling Soft Ripple everything.

But today she intended to tell someone. Her confidant
would not be her only real friend, Soft Ripple. Because
Soft Ripple could be of no help to her, and Black Pearl
desperately needed help. The secret had developed a
monstrous complication.

In the intervals when Black Pearl could use her tail
and swim, her progress upstream was swift. But now
already she was entering yet another stretch of the
stream where the water grew too shallow for swimming.
A few moments later Black Pearl was on her magically
restored feet again and walking. This time, while the
change to normalcy still held, she took a moment to look
down at herself, studying fearfully the near-flatness of
her woman's belly, pale and goose-bumped now with
cold.

So far the enlargement was minimal, almost undetectable. But she was more firmly convinced than ever before that she was pregnant.

Cosmo the magician, who had made this desperate upstream journey possible for Black Pearl, was—or had been—also Cosmo the man, who had made the journey necessary. The Malolo magician had been her lover for several months before the night of many killings, the night he had disappeared. Black Pearl was going to have to assume now that he was dead.

Far less than any ordinary woman did Black Pearl have any means of knowing with any certainty what went on inside her own belly, down there on the borderline of magic, the region of her body where five years ago the ancestral curse had imposed itself. Down there, where a true woman would have a womb, what did a fishgirl have? For that matter, what organs did a real fish possess? Daughter of fisherfolk as she was, she could recall no clear image. Her mind refused to think about it.

One fact was obvious. Mermaid bodies were not equipped, any more than the bodies of real fish were, for anything like human pregnancy or human birth. What was going to happen to her as her pregnancy advanced, if she did not get some effective help from somewhere, Black Pearl did not know, could only guess. But each imagined possibility that suggested itself to her was more horrible than the last. She could only be certain that the outcome was going to be monstrous, unnatural, and fatal to herself and to the unborn as well.

And one more thing was very clear to her. Never before in the history of any village, Black Pearl was quite sure, had any mermaid ever become pregnant.

For more than a month now she had been experiencing dull aching pains in her abdomen, pains that could be relieved only by her assuming the fully human form, and which returned the instant she again became half fish. She had been on the verge of telling Cosmo about her difficulty, though she feared his reaction. And then, about a month ago, on the night when manor folk had slaughtered one another across the river, he had disappeared. Terrible as it was, the only assumption she dared make was that her magician-lover was dead.

Within hours of the great slaughter, the news had spread rapidly, first in its essentials and then in its details, among the peasants and fisherfolk along both shores. From some of these legged people the story had diffused quickly to the mermaids. Black Pearl was soon aware that there was no one left in the Malolo clan who might provide effective medical help. Black Pearl didn't think there were any very capable people left in the Senones clan either, and anyway she wouldn't expect anything better from them than being sold into slavery.

So far Black Pearl had not hinted to anyone, not even Soft Ripple—and most certainly not Zoltan—of her fear that she was pregnant. Such a claim would have made no sense to either of them anyway. Neither of them had any idea that even a temporary reversal of a mermaid's condition was now possible.

Oh, if only it could be possible that Cosmo was not dead! Word passed along from the Malolo household servants had said that his body was not among those arrayed in the underground vault, where all the other dead were said to be gathered, still magically preserved. For several hours, for a few days even, that reported absence had given Black Pearl hope, and the hope had been confirmed by Zoltan. But now she realized that Cosmo's absence really proved nothing. If her lover was not dead, where was he? If he had fled the valley permanently, he might as well be dead as far as she was concerned.

With each day that passed without word from her magician lover, Black Pearl became more and more fearfully certain that she was never going to see him again. There were still occasional moments when she nursed hopes that he was alive, but those hopes were growing more and more desperate.

In the midst of her growing despair, her thoughts had fastened on the hermit Gelimer. Black Pearl's only real hope at this point was that the hermit might be able and willing to do something to help her with her pregnancy. She wanted desperately to save the unborn child, which was Cosmo's child too, if that were at all possible. And if she could be granted some assurance that the child was not monstrous. But failing that, she still wanted at least to have a chance of saving her own life. She knew now that at least a temporary cure of her condition was attainable; and now also Zoltan had come to seek her out and had said he loved her. She had begun to forget Zoltan more than a year ago, and he had passed out of her thoughts completely for a time. Now Zoltan offered hope. But if he ever learned that she was pregnant . . .

Black Pearl had never seen the hermit Gelimer, but now she had nowhere else to turn. For all of her young life she had heard that he was a good man, one who often went out of his way to help people. The stories told in the villages said that Gelimer had more than once saved folk who were dying of cold and exposure in the mountains. In Black Pearl's mind this was good evidence that the hermit must possess some medical skills.

Now, compelled yet again to use her amulet and the weary, fading counterspell, she changed her form once more. At a place where only human hands and feet could climb, she briefly bypassed the water altogether, walking on dry land. Again the sun was warm but the breeze numbingly chill against the wet and suddenly vulnerable nakedness of her human skin.

Without warning, moments earlier than she had anticipated it, the spontaneous reversion overtook her.
Abruptly deprived of feet and legs, Black Pearl fell,
rolling fortunately toward the stream and landing in a
small pool that was deep enough to cushion the impact
of her body before it struck sharp rocks. Now suddenly
the water felt comfortably warm again, on fish skin and
woman skin alike.

The hazards of her journey were increasing. There was
no way to exercise the least degree of control over the
spontaneous relapse, no way to guess from one breath to
the next exactly when it was going to strike her.

Once more the water was deep enough. She swam
upstream, only to find almost immediately that her way
was blocked again by a stretch of shallow water. It
seemed hardly possible that any fish bigger than a
minnow could swim upstream through this obstacle. She
was going to have to wait here, all but helpless, letting
the change-power of the amulet rest again until it had
recharged itself sufficiently to let her bring her human
legs back into existence. Then she would be able to rise
and walk on them once more.

And, if she was pregnant, as she was sure she was, and
if by some miracle she could carry the child to full term,
and by some greater miracle give birth—then what kind
of monster would she produce, gripped by this evil
magic as she was? Perhaps the question was meaning-
less. But Black Pearl had had dreams of late, dreams
coming to her below the surface of the river as she slept,
nightmares in which she felt and saw herself giving birth
to clouds of fish eggs, or to a swarm of lively tadpoles.

Even while she waited to continue her climb toward
Gelimer's house, her mind sought feverishly for some-
one besides the hermit to whom she might turn for help.
But she could think of no one. She could imagine

Zoltan's reaction to the news of her pregnancy, and it would not be good. The remnants of her own leg-walking family in her home village had practically disowned her on the day, five years ago, when the evil change came upon her. It was a not uncommon reaction among mermaids' families. And even if her relatives had been willing to help her now, what could they do? They were as lacking in magical powers as they were in mundane wealth.

If only Cosmo were not dead . . . once more Black Pearl reminded herself sternly that such wishes were hopeless, useless.

But suppose that the holy hermit, when she reached him—she could not admit to herself that she might fail today to reach his house—suppose he were to refuse her help? She might be able to pay him with a pearl from a riverbottom clam, or perhaps a gemstone or even a lump of gold obtained at the same source—supposing she could work a minor miracle and find one. Such treasures failing, there was still her body that she might offer him, half-human as it was, and the few doubtful minutes for which she might be fully human. Black Pearl did not know what attitude the hermit, who had evidently chosen to live without women, might take toward an offering like that.

There was only one way to find out. Black Pearl swam and climbed, and fell and climbed again. Her capacity to change was once more almost totally exhausted. Eventually she reached a point from which she could see, still dishearteningly high and distant, what she took to be the hermit's dwelling. It was, at least, a fallen great tree with a stump that looked as if it had a shuttered window in one side, and so she had heard Gelimer's house described.

But the distance still remaining to the house was crushing. On starting upstream from the Tungri the mermaid had had no idea that the hermit's dwelling was so far up the mountainside, or she might never have attempted to reach it. But no, she'd probably have made the effort anyway. Because she had no other choice.

Now once more on the verge of despair, Black Pearl heard a whining and howling, an almost doglike yapping. Looking up in alarm, she beheld a watchbeast shuffling bearlike along a small ridge that paralleled the stream.

She recognized the breed of animal at once. Two or three times before in her short life Black Pearl had seen watchbeasts. Years ago, when she'd had legs and could walk uphill anytime she felt like it, the folk at Malolo manor had had a pair of such beasts to guard their house.

Now the beast had sighted her, or heard or scented her, which came to the same thing. Running for a little distance beside the stream, the animal howled at the unprecedented sight and at the noise of a mermaid's renewed struggling here. Then the watchbeast turned away and ran off, disappearing almost at once among the rocks and scattered vegetation of the uphill slope.

Black Pearl, still unable for the time being to use her amulet effectively, could do nothing but wait for what might happen next. Her hopes rose slightly when the watchbeast reappeared in the distance, still climbing away from her. Obviously the animal was going to the high tree-stump house, and the mermaid could hope that it was going to bring its master to her aid.

When Gelimer heard Geelong's clamor just outside his door he was considerably surprised. That particular sound had always meant a traveler was in distress, an unlikely situation in such fine weather as this.

Relatively unlikely, but of course not impossible. Hastening to follow the anxious beast, the hermit left his house and garden and soon reached the side of the pool in which Black Pearl was now resting.

The sight of a mermaid was so remote from anything the hermit had expected that for several moments he stood on the bank gazing at her stupidly, as if paralyzed. Adding something to Gelimer's difficulty was the fact that he had never spoken with a mermaid before. But her face looked not only intelligent but frightened, and he could only assume that she was much like other people. At last he spoke.

"Young woman—are you in need of help?"

She gazed up at him boldly though fearfully. "I am," she said, with the water sloshing spasmodically around her silver tail. "My need is very great. And I have come to you, come up all the way from the river, to try to get the help I need."

"You've come to me?" Gelimer, still somewhat bewildered by this unheard-of presence so far up the side of the mountain, ran a hand over his bald head. He felt himself to be at a total loss. "I will do what I can. But what can I do?"

The mermaid sat up straighter in the water, with her tail now in front, propping her torso erect on both hands extended behind her. "Sir, if you will only wait a few moments, it will be easier for you to understand my difficulty. I will demonstrate as well as explain. Wait while I rest, and then watch carefully. And I will show you a great wonder."

"Then I will wait," Gelimer said simply, and seated himself upon a handy rock.

A quarter of an hour later, Gelimer had witnessed the coming and going of the change in the young woman's body. Having seen what he would not otherwise have believed, he tended to believe the rest of the amazing story she had told him.

He had changed his position by the time the story was finished, and was seated upon a different rock, handier to the stream, with Geelong crouching contentedly near his side. Frowning in deep thought, the hermit asked: "Will you describe to me this Cosmo Malolo you say has disappeared? I seldom have any contact with the leaders of the clans, and I have never met any of the younger ones."

When he had heard the mermaid's description of her magician-lover, Gelimer's frown deepened, because now he was sure. The traveler who had called himself Chilperic had given a false name for the man that he was seeking. That man, Gelimer's tragic early visitor, was certainly the same man that this mermaid sought, no doubt with better reason.

Gelimer knew a little more of the truth now, and he knew it was his duty to tell Black Pearl that her lover was certainly dead. But as far as he could see, that truth would be of no benefit to her; it would only deprive her of hope. And if he, Gelimer, were to reveal that he knew where Cosmo lay buried, the mermaid along with other folk would justly suspect that he knew where the Sword was hidden also.

But if he dared not tell the truth to this girl who had appealed to him for help, then what could he do for her?

"I am no magician," he confessed at last. "No real healer, either. If there were any solid help that I could give you, child, I would be glad to do so. But I fear there is nothing."

For several minutes after she heard these words Black Pearl simply sat in the water, staring up at the man she had been thinking of as her last hope. Her very human cheeks had dried in the breeze since she emerged from the water, and they stayed dry; the destruction of hope had been too sudden and complete to result in tears.

The silence stretched on, until at last Gelimer could bear her empty gaze no longer. "I will try," he promised, "to find magical assistance for you somehow."

"Oh sir. Thank you, sir." The words sounded almost devoid of emotion; it was hard for Gelimer to tell if she were only being polite to him in turn, or not. "What can I give you in return?"

Gelimer thought, and sighed. "At the moment, I can think of nothing for you to give me. It may be that I will be able to give you nothing, either. I fear that it very well may be so. And yet I do pledge that I will try."

They exchanged a few more words, and the hermit promised that he would meet the mermaid, at a certain time, at a certain place at the river's edge. Years had passed since he had gone that far down into the gorge, but it was a place he could remember well enough.

Then, after bestowing Ardneh's blessing as best he could, he turned and began climbing wearily back to his house, his watchbeast moving subdued at his side.

With the edge of her despair at least somewhat blunted by the hermit's kindly attention to her troubles, and his conditional promise, Black Pearl pulled herself together as best she could, and started on her way back to the mouth of the stream. The passage downhill, with the swift current's help, was physically much easier than the ascent, and she progressed quickly.

Deep in her own thoughts, she had by now ceased to pay much attention to her surroundings, and she was within thirty meters of the two mercenaries before she saw them.

Calling to her to stop and wait for them, calling to each other to run her down, howling their lust and wonder and delight on finding her almost helpless before them, the two armed and shabby men moved on quick legs to cut her off from the broad river and freedom.

Black Pearl had not seen such men in the valley before, and the strangeness of their appearance only added to her terror. They were dressed unlike any of the native men on either side of the river, wearing scraps of alien-looking armor and green scarves round their throats, and both were well armed.

The men were trying to make their voices soft when they called to her, but the look of their faces belied the softness. In complete panic, her worries about tomorrow swallowed up in immediate terror, Black Pearl turned around and threw her tired body again into the struggle to ascend the stream. One hope, though a feeble one, lay in reaching one of the deeper pools above, where she might possibly lie concealed underwater until the men gave up their efforts and went away. Her only other hope, also a faint one, was that the hermit or the watchbeast might hear the sound of the chase and come to her aid.

At first the two men, being forced to climb or wade among sharp rocks in rushing water, fell behind a little. But then the banks of the stream opened up again, and her pursuers could run, and they gained on her rapidly.

Almost at once a fortunate curve in the stream took her temporarily out of their sight.

Black Pearl plunged into the best available pool, and lay as still as she could on the bottom, suspending her breath in mermaid fashion. She would have no problem remaining so for hours if necessary.

She thought that this was probably the deepest pool she had encountered in her struggle to ascend the stream. Still, the surface of the water was less than a meter above her head. Above her was a small greenish circle of sky; swift fluctuations in the current prevented her seeing more. Distantly she could hear her pursuers, climbing about somewhere on the bank nearby. The water was so clear that she knew she would not be invisible to them if they were to look carefully in the right place; but she would do the best she could. Quietly she turned over, lying face down now, giving them the back of her head to look at, streaming dark hair instead of a pale face.

Hardly had Black Pearl turned over before the faint gleam of something artificial on the stream's bottom caught her eye. Something in the straight and steely look of the thing caught at her memory immediately. Once before, in water vastly deeper and colder than this stream, she had made this same discovery . . .

Moving her fingers with great care in the vicinity of those suggested edges—she had had experience of their unnatural sharpness—Black Pearl brushed away the bottom sand until an ebony handle came into view.

Obviously the Sword had not been dropped here carelessly. Rather it had been buried deliberately, sunk carefully into the bottom under layers of head-sized rocks. And not only buried, but wedged firmly into place in a niche between fixed edges of stone, so that no current in the stream would ever wash it away. But fish, or some other creatures of the stream, must have been nibbling at what had once been a sheath of dark leather, which being only mundane material was almost completely gone by now. The removal of that dark covering allowed a gleam of steel to shine through.

The metal of the Sword itself was just as she remembered it, anything but mundane. There was the white target-symbol on the hilt. The mermaid had a good look at the weapon as she drew it from the hiding place. As she had expected, it showed not the slightest trace of rust or corrosion.

Now feet came stamping nearby, on the bank above her. Black Pearl could hear the voices of the two men almost clearly, and then their shouted triumph at the moment they discovered her in her inadequate hiding place.

"Look here!"

"I'll stir her out!" And a man's hands tossed in a rock that struck the scaly armor of her lower belly, just as she turned face up again; the water cushioned some of the missile's impact.

Black Pearl's head and shoulders came up out of the water, her mouth screaming, the Sword's hilt clutched in both her hands. This was not the first time she had held Farslayer in her hands. But now, for the first time, she could feel the Sword's power come suddenly to life.

The two men were standing on opposite sides of the watercourse, both of them downstream from Black Pearl, one about five meters from her, the other twice as far. When she sat up both mercenaries froze, transfixed momentarily by the impressive sight of the unexpected weapon. Then the hand of the nearer man moved to his waist, and in a moment he had drawn his own short sword.

Black Pearl screamed at him, and willed his death. The black hilt seemed to tear itself free from her clutched fingers, the weapon lunging outward of its own volition. A snarling howl of magic, louder than her own scream, resounded in the little canyon, accompanied by a brief rainbow slash of light that brushed aside the drawn blade in the man's hand. That weapon's owner, his face reflecting surprise, staggered with the Sword of Vengeance stuck clean through him. Then he toppled forward, dead before he splashed into the water.

Yelling in mortal terror, the dead man's companion turned away from the mermaid and took to his heels, bounding in panic down the mountainside.

Black Pearl was already going after the Sword again, struggling to drag her body through the shallows. Despite the thrust of current that now worked in her favor, moving those few meters seemed to take forever. Then, when she had gripped the ebony hilt again, another eternity elapsed in the course of her effort to twist and wrench Farslayer free from the lifeless body of her enemy. The victim's will seemed still alive, embodied in those dead eyes that stared alternately at her and past her with the movement of his head caused by her tugging on the steel between his ribs.

By now the mermaid was sobbing with exertion, hate, and rage. As soon as she had Farslayer free, she threw it forth again, blindly and with all her strength.

"You—you tried to kill me!" she shrieked. The surviving mercenary was probably out of range of her voice; he was already long out of sight, and at the last moment Black Pearl was sure that the effort she was making was hopeless. A reprisal against those who had threatened her was not her only goal. She felt, more strongly than any craving for revenge, the need to keep the power of this Sword for herself, to bargain with.

But the thoughts of that last moment came too late to stop the Sword. For a second time the rainbow blur of power left her hands, again she heard the weapon briefly howling in the air. In the blinking of her eyes it was gone, this time somewhere out of her sight. Though that flight had been hard to follow, she thought the weapon's path had carried it straight downstream.

And again Black Pearl hurled herself splashing and floundering after it, through water too shallow for real swimming. The Sword, as a treasure she might bargain with, represented her only hope. She would go after Farslayer and recover it yet again.

Heedless of minor injuries inflicted by rocks in the shallow current, Black Pearl hurled herself downstream. Luck was with her. The easiest way for a man on foot, running down the slope, was the faint path that almost inevitably followed such a watercourse. In this case the man in his terror-stricken flight had not deviated from the path by more than a stride or two. The mermaid found him lying facedown, Farslayer's hilt and half its blade protruding from his armored back. The Sword had overtaken him from behind. When she turned him over, she looked at his face clearly for the first time, and saw, only now, that he was still a beardless youth.

Again Black Pearl went through the ghastly process of trying to extract Farslayer from a corpse. This time not only bone but armor, a light cuirass, gripped the blade. Her lack of feet and legs with which to brace herself while pulling added considerably to the difficulty of the job; but at least this time the face was turned away.

At last the ugly job was done.

There was nothing Black Pearl could do about concealing this body, or the other one upstream; they would simply have to lie where they had fallen.

The god-forged blade rinsed clean at once in the swift stream. Carrying the Sword ahead of her, gripping the hilt in both hands most of the time, Black Pearl started once more for deep water.

She wondered, now that she had a chance to think again, just how the Sword might have come to be hidden in the stream where she had found it. Might Cosmo himself have brought it there? Or could it have been the hermit's own doing? Had Gelimer known that Farslayer was concealed in the stream she sat in, even while he was talking to her?

In any case, the hermit had offered her little help. But give him credit for honesty at least. It was up to her to help herself. So she was not going to hand this thing of power over to anyone now, except in exchange for the assistance she needed.

Zoltan would be the one to deal with. Bring him the Sword, and let him think that she was madly in love with him, let him believe whatever he already believed. Obviously it was going to take time to conclude any such arrangement. Her immediate need was to hide the

Sword somewhere. Black Pearl proceeded back down-stream, moving carefully. Sometimes she had to use her amulet and murmur the secret words, and stand and walk with the naked Sword held awkwardly before her naked body, both of her smallish hands grasping the black hilt. Walking, she held the weapon very carefully, that she might not fall upon it when the sudden shape change overtook her and she fell.

As she descended the long slope she pondered furious-ly on the question of where to hide the Sword for the time being. Immediately there came to her mind the islands, and the riverbottom. But she did not wish ever to go to Magicians' Island again if she could help it. Unless Cosmo . . .

And Mermaids' Island was generally populated by other mermaids. They, her mermaid sisters, were also forever searching the riverbottom hoping to discover things of value.

Where to hide it, then?

Now Black Pearl remembered passing, on her way uphill, a certain hollow tree, a leaning trunk all twisted and decayed but not yet fallen, that curved almost over this roaring stream down near its mouth. But a moment later she rejected the idea—inside that tree Farslayer would be far more easily accessible to walking people than to her.

When she came to the tree, however, Black Pearl had been able to think of no better place, and changed her mind again. Here the dancing brook that she was following plunged through its own miniature gorge, between high walls of rugged rock. Few people would come walking here, and none could ride.

The spot was almost gloomy even at midday. Yet another struggle was necessary for her to heave her body out of the water, getting the rounded thickness of her fishtail onto a rock, bracing herself there in a sitting position while she lifted the Sword toward the dark cavity of the gnarled bole.

Just as she did so she paused, listening intently. Someone—or something—was approaching. With the sound of a great wind.

TWELVE

W HEN the hermit had concluded his talk with the mermaid, and Black Pearl had begun her struggling return downstream, Gelimer, his forehead set in wrinkles and his mind engaged with problems, trudged back uphill toward his house. The poor ensorcelled lass on her way back to her deepwater home was going to pass right over the place where he'd hidden the Sword. Well, when he'd chosen the place in which to conceal Farslayer, he couldn't possibly have foreseen that mermaids were going to come crawling up the stream bed. This one must have passed over the Sword once already on her way upstream, and without noticing anything. Gelimer considered that he had hidden the Sword well, and he hadn't been back to look at the place since doing so. For anyone to see him taking an interest in that spot now might result in Farslayer's discovery. So, the Sword was going to have to stay where it was.

Ah, but the poor innocent child! What a terrible situation to be in. What could he do for her?

Not until after he had climbed three quarters of the way back to his house, trudging slowly, did it occur to the hermit that he might have escorted Black Pearl back down to the river. Well, too late now to think of that. She had managed the uphill struggle somehow, and doubtless she could manage going down.

Since he was no magician, it appeared to Gelimer that there was not much he could do for the mermaid's benefit, except to offer her some probably foolish hope, and let her know at least that she had a friend in the world.

As he was approaching his door, the hermit felt the demon's presence somewhere in the air, and thought that this time it was passing closer than before.

Gelimer had not been back in his house for more than a quarter of an hour when something occurred that drew him out of doors again.

The hermit had left both the inner and outer doors of his entrance standing open to the mild day, and it was a peculiar wisp of sound that entered through the doorway to draw him out. The sound was almost too faint to be heard at all, but there was a strangeness about it that caught at his attention.

Listening, waiting for the sound to come again, Gelimer stood in the doorway of his small house. He tasted the air, rubbed a hand over his bald head, and scanned the sky. A few times in his life, a very few times and long ago, he had been able to see moving across the firmament some of the powers that served the great magicians. But today he was able to see nothing magical in the sky, nothing at all but a few clouds. He called for Geelong, thinking that if there were strange sounds to be tracked down, the watchbeast would be very useful. But there was no response to the hermit's call.

He was still loitering in his doorway when the strange sound came again, a high-pitched, briefly sustained squealing. Something mechanical, the hermit thought now, a cartwheel needing grease perhaps. Of course that couldn't be right, there were never any carts on these rough trails. But—

His concern, persistent and automatic, for the Sword drew him in the general direction of that weapon's hiding place when he left the house. Gelimer called again for Geelong as he walked, and he continued to listen for the strange noise to come again.

He had not walked forty meters from his door when a shift in the direction of the wind brought the mysterious squealing sound to him more distinctly. It was a high-pitched whining, only superficially mechanical. At bottom it was much more like the cry of some great animal in agony. And at the same time he heard it, the hermit detected a new whiff of the demon's presence, which reached him through none of the usual channels of the senses.

Ignoring the deep command of instinct that urged him to run away from that presence, Gelimer began instead to run toward it. Toward the place from which the sound came also.

A hundred meters of running, moving horizontally along the great slope of the mountain, were enough to bring him to a small patch or grove of stunted thorntrees. Trotting around to the far side of this tall thicket, Gelimer came suddenly in sight of Geelong. The watchbeast had somehow been nightmarishly elevated to twice or three times Gelimer's height above the ground, and all four of his limbs were spread out and pinned on tough thorny branches. Geelong's head was twisted to one side, whether voluntarily or not, so that he looked in the direction from which his master now approached. From the animal's open mouth drooled whitish foam all mixed with blood. The creature's lolling tongue was bitten halfway through. Geelong's eyes were open, and watched Gelimer. His lower belly had been opened also, as if with a dull blade in the beginning of a disembowelment. More blood, much more, dripped from his belly, and a slender rope of gut was hanging halfway to the ground.

Gelimer struggled to find disbelief, but was unable to achieve it. He swayed on his feet, staring helplessly at the horror above him. The noise coming from Geelong's throat swelled up again into a ghastly howl.

At last able to break free of his paralysis, the hermit ran forward. As Gelimer ran he pulled from his belt the hatchet he had lately taken to carrying with him everywhere. If he could only chop free some of those small branches, the ones whose thorns were . . .

A nearby presence, which until now had managed to conceal itself, now swelled up palpably around him. It was a smothering sickness, and a physical force as well. Gelimer's hatchet fell from his hand. He fell staggering back from his first foothold on a tree, to stand choking and almost blinded.

"What do you seek here among the thorntrees, little man?" The voice, sounding like nothing so much as a deafening chorus of insects, came blasting into the hermit's ears. It surrounded him and forced its way into his mind. "You must be careful with that weapon! Otherwise you might do harm to your faithful pet."

And now Gelimer was seized by a presence that seemed to have become as material as his own body, and vastly stronger. Forces grabbed him by an arm, whirled him about effortlessly, and sent him tumbling over rocks and down a slope. Oblivious to minor damage, he stumbled to his feet, and faced uphill again.

Some force like a great wind was shaking the thorntrees now, swaying them out of phase, so that the bloody living body pinned aloft in them was wracked anew. The wound in the belly stretched and oozed and gaped. Once more the horrible noise went up from Geelong's throat, louder than before.

Dazed and blinking, Gelimer looked carefully around him, trying to recognize this world in which he found himself. He turned slowly, making a full circle on uncertain feet, questioning all the corners of the universe as to how such things could be.

He held his fingers in his ears, but that was no more effective than closing his eyes.

"Do you not like the music that your pet makes, little man?" There was no shutting that music out, or the voice of the demon, either. The question was followed by a great hideous rush of what must have been its laughter.

"Do you not like the song?"

Stumbling and choking and weeping, still trying uselessly to shut out the sounds of Geelong's agony, the man went staggering away. Now his feet, without any conscious planning on his part, were bearing him at an angle downhill, toward the place where a month ago he had concealed the Sword.

When Gelimer encountered the rushing mountain stream he tumbled into it, landing on all fours. But he lurched to his feet and went on again at once, following the stream bed downhill, unaware of the cold water and the rocks that hurt him when he fell again.

Something in him knew that the Sword was already gone, even before he looked in the place where he had hidden it. He knew, he felt the truth of the missing Sword at his first sight of the dead man. The corpse, armed and costumed like a poor mercenary, lay some ten meters downstream from the deep pool, crumpled on his side in the shallows, with his body jammed against some rocks by the rush of current.

Something in Gelimer already knew that the Sword was gone. But still he plunged heedlessly into the pool to look for Farslayer, driving his head and shoulders underwater in the deep pool, groping with both hands for the bottom—

A grip that felt like the clawed forepaws of a large dragon seized Gelimer from behind. The man was wrenched from the water, tossed rolling over and over on the hard path along the bank. Even before he stopped rolling, the demon's quasimaterial presence had let him go, had gone plunging past him into the stream. A fountain of water, a geyser of rocks and sand and mud, erupted out of the pool that had been the hiding place. But no Sword. No Sword came flying out, because Farslayer was already gone.

Gelimer was just trying to get back onto his feet when the demon like a foul wind came rushing back to once more give him its full attention. It raged and struck at him, knocked him once more spinning on the ground, so that his head rang with the impact, his arms and legs were newly bruised and bloody.

Its voice of a thousand insects shrieked at him. "What have you done with it, treacherous human? You pretended to have hidden Farslayer in this little pool, pretended to be trying to get it now, but it is not here. What have you really done with it?"

Gelimer was no longer capable of thinking clearly. Even had he wanted to answer the demon's stupid shrieking, he would hardly have been able to speak. He could only cower down and wait for what might happen to him next.

Unexpectedly, the demon-shrieking stopped. There was a silent swelling of the cheated rage surrounding the man. But before the storm of this renewed wrath could break upon him, there came a pause. A break, a distraction, as if the demon's attention had been abruptly drawn from Gelimer to something or someone else.

And in the next moment, the ghastly thing was gone.

Gone completely, to what distance or for what period of time the hermit could not have guessed. He only knew that it had let him go. Sobbing, Gelimer collapsed.

THIRTEEN

O N the day of Black Pearl's visit to Gelimer, and at the very time when she reached a decision on where to hide the Sword, five men were riding in a fishing boat out near the middle of the Tungri. The boat was making progress steadily upstream. The two who worked the oars were fishermen, enlisted today as rowers by the new chief of the manor above their village, Bonar Malolo. That chief, young Bonar himself, was sitting in the stern of the boat, beside his new guest and acquaintance Prince Mark of Tasavalta. Up in the prow perched Zoltan, who talked and sang almost continuously, hoping that his voice would be heard and recognized below the surface, and that he thus would be successful in calling up a certain mermaid from the stream.

Yesterday not much had been accomplished, besides finishing the repair of the hole carved in the manor's wall by Stonecutter. The prince and Ben, weary from a long journey and a night's vigil, had slept and eaten and enjoyed the manor's hospitality.

Today the strong man Ben, along with the magician Gesner, the Lady Yambu, and Bonar's two sisters, had remained in the Malolo manor. It was by no means certain that the mercenaries had departed the area for good; and Mark had wanted to leave someone he trusted in case another winged messenger should seek him there with news.

Bonar had listened doubtfully to the explanation given him early this morning by his powerful guests, as to why it was necessary to come out here and hunt mermaids today, but at last he had accepted it. It was something to do with finding the Sword again, and he was all in favor of that.

A point that had come up for discussion earlier was the question of who was going to get the Sword if and when they did manage to recover it. Prince Mark had already explained that he had a deep interest in retaining possession of Farslayer; in fact, that he had no intention of accepting anything less. Mark's princely rank, his firmness even tempered as it was with courtesy, and the one Sword he already wore combined to give force to his expressed wishes. The effect was augmented by the presence at the prince's side of Ben, who when he chose to do so could look as formidable as a whole squad of mercenaries.

Bonar in fact was overwhelmed by his new allies. He pined in silence to possess the Sword again for himself, but somehow when he opened his mouth he found himself agreeing to the terms which the prince outlined for him—in return for giving up all Malolo claims upon the Sword of Vengeance, he and the remainder of his clan would receive (at some future time) wealth, prestige in the association of his house with that of Tasavalta, and perhaps, at a later date, some military aid as well.

The deal had been effectively concluded on shore some time ago, but still it rankled. Sitting in the boat Bonar took courage and began to murmur: "Still—all that may be very well, but still I think that my family and I ought to rightfully be able to retain *some* rights in that

Sword for ourselves. Even if we allow it to go with you for now. When we have succeeded in finding it, that is.''

Prince Mark only looked at him. But Zoltan was ready to argue the point, and at the same time he was curious.

"Sir—Chief Bonar—when your family had that Sword in their hands before, the result to them, I would say, could hardly be counted as a great benefit. What would you do with Farslayer if you had it in your hands at this moment?''

Bonar frowned at the question. Then his frown cleared up. "You mean what target would I choose? I've thought about that, this past month. I'd pick that cowardly skunk Hissarlik, beyond a doubt. We've heard that he survived the night of killing, and I have no doubt that he's now become the clan chief of the Senones dogs. And I have no doubt that he's killed several of our people. He's probably killed more of us than anyone else who still survives over there.''

"How do you know how many of your people he may have killed, sir? Forgive me, but I'm curious. You mean you have some way of telling, somehow . . . ?''

Bonar was scowling at Zoltan petulantly. "Well, if Hissarlik hasn't killed very many of us yet, he's certainly getting ready to do so. He's a Senones, isn't he?''

Mark was shaking his head lightly at Zoltan, but Zoltan wasn't ready to give up the argument. "All right. Say you did have Farslayer in your hands this very moment, and you killed Hissarlik with it. Zip. Like that. What's the next thing that would happen?''

"The next thing?''

"Well. I mean, someone over there will see Hissarlik fall, or find him dead, and then immediately pick the Sword up and kill *you* with it. Isn't that the way things went a month ago?''

Bonar's eyes lighted up, the eyes of a man who at last

understands a line of questioning, and has an answer
ready. "Ah! Yes, you see, that's where we made our
mistake before. My sisters and I have talked about that.
Next time we'll manage things the clever way. First
decide on a specific target, and then wait for that target
to be in the proper position, or lure him into it if
necessary. By proper position I mean somewhere where
we can get the Sword back quickly after we use it. It
means being patient. Perhaps it means setting ambushes,
which is always difficult. But you're perfectly right,
there's no use in making your enemy the gift of such a
weapon to use against you. Not if you can help it."

Mark smiled faintly. And now Zoltan did give up, at
least for the time being.

But his questioning had prompted Bonar to ask a
question of his own, addressed to Mark.

"Your Majesty—uh, sir . . ."

"Just call me Mark. 'Prince' will do if you really want
to use a title."

"Ah, thank you, ah Mark. If you had the Sword in *your*
hands at this moment, what target would you pick? This
wizard Wood you keep warning us about, I suppose. But
am I not correct? Wouldn't you try to arrange some kind
of ambush first, get the Sword back to use again?"

Mark, shaking his head again, took thought. Then he
answered seriously and courteously. "I certainly
wouldn't hurl any weapon at Wood just now. He is still
in possession of Shieldbreaker, so Farslayer would probably be destroyed. One way to get rid of the damned
thing, I suppose. But certainly it would fail to kill him, as
long as he holds the Sword of Force."

"Is getting rid of Swords such a problem, then?" Now
Bonar was enviously eyeing Stonecutter, which Mark
wore at his side.

"Believe me, there are times when it seems like a good

idea to destroy one, or all of them. Though it's almost impossible. Perhaps that's what your cousin Cosmo had in mind when he rode off with Farslayer."

"Do you think so?" the Chief asked doubtfully. He appeared to be having a hard time digesting that idea.

Mark turned to Zoltan and said: "I mean to have a talk with that hermit you mentioned. We'll take our search for your mermaid out to the islands first if necessary, and then—"

One of the fishermen, rowing industriously, muttered something. From under frowning, shaggy brows he looked up and around the sky.

"What did you say, man?" Mark asked him sharply. "Something about demons?"

The shaggy brows contracted further. "Aye, sir. I'm saying they have been seen in the valley. And that there's a smell in the air just now, this moment, that I don't like."

Bonar started to ask: "Does the Sword you wear, Prince, give you some protection against—"

"Wait!" Mark gestured sharply for silence. Now he too was frowning up at the cloudless sky.

The other men in the boat looked at one another. To all of them, a pall of night and gloom and sickness seemed to be descending upon the sunlit water in the middle of the day.

None of the five men spoke. There was no need. Even those among them who had never before confronted a demon were in no doubt of what this was. One of the rowers, he who had just spoken, now dropped his oar. On trembling legs the man arose, meaning to cast himself overboard. But Zoltan's hand went out and fastened on the fisherman's wrist, and after a moment the terror-stricken one sank back onto his bench.

Zoltan knew something that none of the local people did.

The horror that had just arrived was now sitting, almost fully visible, upon the surface of the water nearby, confronting the five men huddled in the boat. As none of them were any longer using the oars, the boat had now begun to drift.

It was Mark who spoke first, addressing the silent thing that hovered on the water. The confidence in his voice astonished most of his companions.

"Who are you?" he asked boldly.

"I am Rabisu." The voice was a watery gurgling, and somehow it impressed Zoltan's hearing as slime held in his hand would have impressed his sense of touch. "Rabisu. And you must now hand over to me that weapon that hangs at your belt. It will make a good addition to my collection."

"Rabisu." Mark appeared to be meditating upon the name. "I've never heard of you before." So far the prince's hand had made no move toward his Sword. He was squinting into the full horror of the thing that hovered above the water, squinting as if loathsomeness could be as dazzling as brightness.

Meanwhile, in the background, the handful of other fishing boats that had been busy on the visible stretch of the river were all making as rapidly as possible for shore, some heading toward the north bank of the river and others toward the south. The thought crossed Zoltan's mind that under ordinary conditions the fisherfolk of the two enemy camps could evidently share the river in peace.

The presence drifting above the water, just keeping up with the drifting boat, appeared to be hesitating, as if it might have been impressed by the bravery of the man who spoke to it. "You are no magician," it said to Mark at last. The statement was not quite a question.

"That is correct, I am not. Tell me, foul one, which Sword is it that you are seeking?"

On hearing such an insolent response Bonar collapsed completely. He cowered abjectly in the bottom of the boat, as many a strong man might have done in his place. Zoltan was keeping his own head up bravely. It cost him a considerable effort, even though Zoltan knew something about his uncle that the head of the Clan Malolo did not.

"Unbuckle your swordbelt and hand it to me!" roared the demon.

"What if I draw my Sword instead?" And at last Mark's hand went to the black hilt.

And still the demon hesitated to attack. "Before you can draw it, little man, you will be dead!"

"I think that I will not be dead as soon as that. In the Emperor's name, forsake this game, and begone from our sight!"

There was a disturbance above the water, and in the air above the boat, an explosion like the breaking of a knot in which the winds of a hundred storms were all entangled. Such a blast must certainly have swamped the fishing craft, but the disturbance came and went with magical swiftness, before any movement of the water or the air immediately around the boat had time to be effective. This concussion was followed instantly by a roaring bellow, uttered in a voice too loud to be human. It was the voice of the demon, no doubt about that, but in another instant the bellowing had grown faint with distance, and in an instant more it had grown fainter still.

Higher above the world, and fainter.

Gradually, but soon, it was entirely gone.

In less time than it takes to draw a breath the river around the fishing boat was once more silent, sunlit, and serene. There might never have been such things as demons in the world.

Prince Mark sat for a moment with his eyes closed.

Then, leaning forward in his seat, he put a hand on the shoulder of one of the collapsed rowers. Gently he tried to shake the man out of his paralysis. But for the time being, at least, it was no use. The prince sighed, moved himself to the rowers' bench, and reached for an oar.

His nephew Zoltan had already taken the other one. With a couple of good strokes they overcame the boat's drift, and were once more headed upstream toward the islands.

Bonar, looking shamefaced, had by now managed to regain an upright position on his seat. For a time there was silence except for the creak of oarlocks. Then the chief of Clan Malolo, looking about him in all directions, asked softly and wonderingly: "Where is it?"

"The demon is gone," said Mark patiently. "It's all right now."

The young clan leader turned back and forth in his seat, gaping at the Tungri, which ran calm and undisturbed. The day was peaceful. "But gone where? Is it likely to come back?"

"It might very well come back here sometime. But there's no immediate danger. We can go on and talk to the mermaids, visit the islands as we planned."

Hearing calm human conversation around them, both of the original rowers presently revived. Seeing their three passengers serene, and the danger gone, they rather guiltily went back to work, Mark and Zoltan relinquishing their oars.

Bonar was certainly not going to let the matter rest. "But what happened to the demon? It was a real demon, wasn't it?"

Zoltan said: "Oh, it was a demon, all right. As real as they ever get. But my uncle enjoys certain powers over such creatures. Mainly the power to keep them at a distance."

Mark shrugged, under Bonar's awestricken gaze. "It's

true that I'm no wizard. But I do have such a power, from my father, who happens to be the Emperor."

"Ah," said Bonar. But he did not really sound as if he understood, or was convinced of anything. Zoltan could scarcely blame him. Many if not most of the world's people thought of the Emperor as nothing more than some kind of legendary clown.

The clan chief persisted in trying to puzzle it out. "This power over demons that you say you have— indeed, that you have demonstrated. Does it never fail?"

Mark smiled grimly. "It hasn't failed me yet, or I wouldn't be here. Though I must admit I'm never completely sure it's going to work at the moment when I start to use it."

The boat was moving steadily on toward the islands. Now in the forward seat again, Zoltan talked and sang, hoping that his voice would be heard and recognized beneath the water, trying to summon up a very special mermaid.

FOURTEEN

HAVING done the best he could to set the mermaids searching for the Sword, Chilperic was not disposed to dawdle on the riverbank. After making sure that a couple of militiamen remained on the shore to carry news from the fishgirls should there be any, he started back to the manor as soon as possible. He was intent on keeping in close touch with the healer Tigris, and wanted to be first to hear of any change in the condition of her patient.

By the time he and Hissarlik got back to the manor, Chilperic's modest hopes of success for the mermaid project were already fading. He remembered all too well their sullen unwillingness, and he doubted the efficiency of Hissarlik's spell. Chilperic's remaining enthusiasm for that effort diminished steadily as the remaining hours of the afternoon wore on. By sunset he had virtually abandoned hope that the fishgirls were going to prove at all helpful. And he supposed that any program of underwater search they might have begun would have to be abandoned with the onset of darkness, since there was no way to provide the creatures with Old World lights, the only kind that might be used beneath the surface.

Meanwhile, Chilperic was only too well aware that

time was passing and his mission here was no closer to being accomplished. The Ancient Master was not going to be pleased. Soon, Chilperic thought, he was going to have to overcome his reluctance to summon the demon, and order Rabisu to make a direct search for the Sword. There were moments when he wondered uneasily just what the demon might be up to on its own.

Just after sunset, when Chilperic was in his room alone, Tigris the healer came in secrecy to see him. The small blond woman held a finger to her lips for silence as soon as he saw her in his doorway, and she slid quickly past him into his room without waiting to be invited.

"I have news regarding my patient," was her greeting.

"She is—?"

"On the road to recovery."

"Very good!"

"The Lady Megara's conscious now, and in fact ready to have a visitor, if the visitor is careful to treat her gently."

"I certainly shall. But I must ask her some questions. Have you said anything about this recovery to any of the family yet?"

"Of course not." Tigris lifted her pretty chin. "You and I, dear Chilperic, serve the same master, and so my first report must be to you whenever that is possible."

"I should hope so. Tell me, has the woman said anything of importance to you?"

"Not really. She's asked a few questions as to how long she has been ill. I saw no point in lying to her about that."

"No, I suppose not. Anything else?"

"Not that you'd find interesting. Mainly she was curious about my identity. Natural enough. I've already warned her that I might be coming back to the room with a professional colleague, though I haven't actually said you are a physician."

"Better and better." Chilperic smiled briefly, then looked grim again. "Tell me, what exactly was wrong with her? Had it anything to do with her practicing magic?"

"In my opinion—which is valued highly, as you know, in some rather high places—"

"Yes, I concede that."

"In my opinion, the Sorceress Megara's disability was not due so much to magical backlash—though something like that may have contributed—as it was to a mere shock of a much more ordinary kind."

"A mere—?"

"Emotional trauma. Such as might be caused, for example, by the death of someone to whom she was closely attached. They tell me that her father was Farslayer's first victim, on that famous night when the feuding clans all but destroyed each other. And that she was found lying unconscious beside his body. An experience like that would be quite enough to send some people into extended shock. Perhaps to make them lie in a trance for a month." And Tigris smiled a brittle smile.

Chilperic said: "That's right. They were both found out on Magicians' Island. Evidently for some reason he'd gone out there that night to visit her. Or spy on her perhaps."

"So, having her father killed before her eyes could very well have done it. She would be standing there talking with this familiar and dependable figure—then zip! Sudden death comes in the window. Do you have any wine on hand, by any chance? Or maybe a drop of brandy?"

Chilperic had, as a matter of fact. While finding a bottle and a glass, he shook his head. He could not generate any respect for people who allowed themselves to be disabled by things that happened to others. "Well, let's go see her, then. She may know something that will help us find the Sword, and in any case we'll have to deal with her if she resumes some position of leadership here within the family. You say I can talk to her now?"

"If you try not to disturb her too much. Ah, that's very good." And Tigris set down the empty glass.

Chilperic started to open the door to the hall, then stopped in the act of doing so. "I wonder if it would be wise to bring some member of the family along to the lady's room. Naturally they'll want to know of her recovery as soon as possible."

"As you wish. Perhaps that's a good idea. It might be wiser not to confront the lady just now with two relative strangers, and no familiar face in sight."

It was just as well they had made that decision, for as soon as they went out into the corridor they encountered Hissarlik, who, as he said, was on his way to learn the latest on his aunt's condition.

A moment later the three people entered the sickroom, and the servant who had been on watch there bowed and curtsied herself back from the bed.

Aunt Megara looked a different woman from the last time Chilperic had seen her. Although he understood she must be over thirty, she now appeared hardly more than a girl. She was also much more alert than when he had seen her before, and sitting up in bed. The whole sickroom—if you could still call it that—had become a much more cheerful place. Materials used in the treatments Tigris had administered, some of them apparently intended to work on a very high plane of magic, lay scattered about.

"Aunt Meg—how are you? We were all greatly concerned." Hissarlik stepped forward to the bed.

"Better—much better." The voice of the patient still lacked life, but she raised a pale hand, readily enough, to take that of her nephew. "And you," Megara murmured.

"I see that you are still alive, Hissarlik." Perhaps the discovery pleased her, but it was not doing much to cheer her up. Their hands were already separated again.

Chilperic, confident now that he would be interrupting no very fond reunion, took the opportunity of stepping forward. "Do you recognize me, Lady Megara?"

The eyes of the tired and grieving woman turned toward him. "No, I think not. Should I?"

The visitor bowed. "I am Chilperic, an associate of the physician Tigris who has so skillfully restored you. And I too have come here to be of what service to you I may."

The faded eyes fixed on him were more anxious than accusatory. "Why should you wish to do me service? You tell me your name, but who are you?"

Chilperic bowed again. "The master I have the honor to represent—as does Tigris here—wishes to establish an alliance with the worthy house of Senones. His name is Wood, and he is a wizard of some renown."

"Ah." The lady's eyes moved to those of her nephew, and back again to Chilperic.

The latter said smoothly: "You will of course want to have a family discussion about our proposal. There's no hurry. But there is one matter I fear that I must question you about at once—something about which we must be fully informed before your restoration to health can be considered complete."

Tigris was looking at him now, and Hissarlik too, but Chilperic ignored them both. He said: "I am speaking about the Sword of Vengeance, Lady Megara, the weapon that killed your father. Where did that weapon first come from, on that terrible night? Who used it against him? Above all, where is it now? Your own future, and that of your family, depends on that."

Mention of Farslayer brought renewed horror into the

lady's eyes, and there was a pause. At last she shook her
head. "I don't know the answer to either question. I
don't remember much about that night. I was busy,
practicing certain—rituals—in the cave out on Magicians' Island. My father came to visit me—in his youth
he had practiced a great deal of magic himself. And
then—"

"And then?"

"All I know is that the Sword was suddenly there—in
my father's back." The lady closed her eyes. "As if it had
come out of nowhere, through the grotto's wall somehow. And in that instant my father let out a cry, and
fell—of course he was killed instantly."

Lady Megara opened her eyes again and stared at the
wall. When her silence had lasted for a few moments
Chilperic prodded her, gently but insistently: "What
happened next?"

"Next?" Her blank gaze turned on him. "I—I don't
know. I saw Father dead, and after that I can remember
nothing more." Suddenly Megara burst out: "Who else
was slain that night?"

"We've talked about that before, Aunt Meg. Don't you
remember?"

"Not really. Tell me again."

Hissarlik, somewhat reluctantly, began to run through
the roll call of defunct relatives. To Megara, who listened
to the list as if she were mesmerized, the extended roster
of casualties seemed to present a generalized horror,
though for some reason not a particularly acute one.
Chilperic got the impression that she was listening for
some name and had not heard it.

When the listing was over, she commented simply:
"So many on our side were killed, then."

"I fear that is so," said her nephew calmly. Whatever
grief and horror he might have felt on that night had
evidently been exchanged over the past month for fear

and worry. Only his craving for revenge had been retained unaltered.

"And what of the enemy?" Megara's voice grew cold and implacable. "Who among them have we killed?"

Hissarlik, taking turns with Anselm and Alicia who had now come to join the others in the sickroom, recited the names of those they had personally called on Farslayer to strike down, and the other enemy names they had heard called out by relatives who were now dead themselves. The listing sounded quite as long as that of the Senones casualties. When it was over, Megara seemed to relax a bit, apparently slumping back toward unconsciousness.

"Now leave me." It sounded very much like an order, though her voice was weak. "Now I would sleep."

In a moment, Tigris, turned physician again, was ushering Chilperic and the others out.

Chilperic had to admit that he had learned almost nothing of any value in the sickroom. And now there was nothing left for him to do, except to take the decisive step he had been vainly trying to put off. Back in his room alone he went through the few simple steps required to summon the demon.

From an inner pocket of his clothing he drew out the demon's life, caught and trapped in leather by some tricks of wizardry that were as far, or farther, beyond him as the healing skills of the physician. But to use the thing that Wood had given him was simple enough. Stroking the little wallet with his fingers, Chilperic muttered the short formula of summoning.

Then he waited, standing with his eyes almost closed, for the unspeakable presence to approach once more and establish itself inside his room.

He waited, but nothing happened.

The summoning was finished. He was sure that he had

done it properly. Time stretched on, one breath after another, and still the demon did not appear.

Presently Tigris, her healing chores evidently completed for the time being, tapped at his door and came in as silently as she had done before, closing the door immediately behind her. When she saw Chilperic standing with the leather wallet in his hand, she had no need to ask what he was doing.

With Tigris watching him expressionlessly, Chilperic frowned, and rubbed again at his leather wallet, and once more uttered the proper words. He took great care to get the incantation right, rounding each syllable of it distinctly.

But still there came no response from Rabisu.

Something was definitely wrong.

Fortunately for himself, Chilperic was not a man who panicked easily. To the best of his quite limited ability, he scanned the air and earth and water around him, seeking evidence of the demon's presence, or of any interfering magic. He could find neither.

"I sense no opposition," murmured Tigris, who was evidently doing the same thing, at a level of skill doubtless much higher than his.

Chilperic sighed and nodded. So, he thought to himself, what game was this? Perhaps the creature had been called away by some direct command from Wood. Chilperic thought that unlikely, but what other explanation could there be?

In a little while Tigris, having made no comment, left him, saying that she wanted to look in again on her patient. Chilperic was still sitting alone in his room, wondering when to try the summoning again, unable to think of anything else to try, when a servant came to his door bearing a message from Hissarlik.

"My master's compliments, sir, and would you care to

attend him in the great hall? Some men have arrived, claiming to be mercenaries looking for employment, and the Tyrant Hissarlik would like to consult with you on how best to deal with them."

Descending to what was optimistically called the great hall, Chilperic found lamps being lighted against the gathering dusk. Hissarlik was established in a tall chair that evidently served him as a seat of state. Two men, both strangers to Chilperic, were facing the clan chief. One of these visitors, a powerful-looking brute, was standing almost at attention, while the other, taller and much leaner, had seated himself on a table with one foot on the floor, a disrespectful position to say the least. Signs of the military profession were much in evidence in the dress and attitude of both.

The taller stranger stood up from the table when Chilperic entered, and in a moment had introduced himself as Captain Koszalin, commander, as he said, of his own free and honorable company of adventurers. Koszalin was youthful, certainly well under thirty years of age; lean, almost emaciated, with a haggard look as if perhaps he did not sleep well. His stocky comrade was his sergeant.

With Chilperic now standing at the Tyrant's right hand and giving the newcomers a stern look, Hissarlik was ready to speak out boldly from his tall chair.

He addressed Koszalin. "Well then, fellow, what use do you think you can be to us here?"

Chilperic got the impression that the youthful captain was totally unimpressed by this other youth who claimed hereditary power. But Koszalin, who appeared now to be making an effort to be pleasant, scratched his uncombed head and addressed the Tyrant.

"Why, sir, it's like this. I hear that you're on no great

terms of friendship with those people across the water, the ones who call themselves Malolo." When Koszalin shifted his glance to Chilperic, his voice, perhaps unconsciously, grew more respectful. "Nor are you, sir, I suppose."

Chilperic was gradually becoming certain that these were a couple of the same mercenary scoundrels who had been hanging around the Malolo manor intermittently when he had visited there. He had had only the briefest contact with any of them then, but now he could not help wondering whether some of them might recognize him. He would have to make sure of that as soon as possible.

"Ah," said Hissarlik to the captain. "So you've had some contact with the Malolo, have you?"

"Damned unfriendly contact." The commander of the honorable company, wiry muscles working in a hairy forearm, scratched his head again; Chilperic wondered if he was going to have to ask Tigris for a minor spell to repel boarders. Koszalin went on: "Well sir, I'll tell you the exact truth. Their new chief over there, name of Bonar, said that he wanted to hire myself and my men, and then he refused to pay us. Reneged on a deal, he did. Promised pearls and then wouldn't give us nothing. We can't make our living on deals like that. I've got thirty men in my company to look after, men who look up to me like I was their father. You, sir, being a real chief yourself, will understand that kind of responsibility." The last remark was ostensibly addressed to Hissarlik, but with the words the speaker's eyes turned briefly to Chilperic to include him.

Chilperic supposed it was time he took an active part in the questioning. "When was this reneging, as you call it?"

"That's what anyone would call it, sir. It was just a couple of days ago. So, my men and I have decided to see if we can find a better reception on this side of the water."

Chilperic turned his stare briefly on the second mercenary, the powerful sergeant, who straightened up to a position even closer to military attention, but still had nothing to say.

"Well," said Chilperic to Koszalin, "suppose we do hire you. It would have to be on a trial basis. To begin with I'd expect to hear a good deal from you regarding conditions over there in the Malolo camp. We know a good bit already, mind you, and I'd expect what you told us to match in every detail with what we know already. Stand up when you're in this room, I didn't hear anyone offer you a seat."

Koszalin, who had begun to relax himself casually onto the table again, hurriedly straightened up. If he was upset by the sudden order, he gave no sign of it. Yes, undoubtedly a veteran soldier, even if his promotion to captain was quite likely self-awarded. "We could tell you a lot about them, sir. If we can reach a deal, that is, and if you can pay us something adequate on account."

"Very well." Chilperic made a motion with his head. "You and the sergeant wait outside now. We must discuss this matter first."

Koszalin saluted and turned, with his sergeant moving a step behind him.

Chilperic and Hissarlik were left alone. They were on the point of beginning their discussion when Aunt Megara, looking grim and pale, and dressed in a pale robe with a kind of turban wound round her head, surprised them by appearing in a doorway.

"Who were those men?" she demanded, sounding to Chilperic like one who might be ready to assume control.

Hissarlik explained to his aunt. He sounded ready to defend the power he had already taken.

Tigris, who entered close behind her patient, explained in a whisper to Chilperic that Aunt Megara was making good progress though she was still weak, and she had insisted on starting to get about.

"What did those men want?" Tigris added.

Chilperic explained. He was basically in favor of hiring the mercenaries, and told Tigris as much. He added that he privately intended to secure such loyalty as Koszalin and his men might be capable of for the cause of the Dark Master, Wood.

"Of course," Tigris agreed. "They don't appear very effective, but I suppose there's no one better available."

Chilperic nodded. "Soon I'll take Koszalin aside and speak to him."

Hissarlik now joined their conference, apparently without suspicion. He was also in favor of hiring Koszalin and his men, believing rightly or wrongly that they would be tougher and more reliable than his own militia when it came to combat. From what the clan chief said, it was plain that he envisioned another and final assault on the Malolo, with or without the Sword, defeating the ancient enemies of his house once and for all.

The Lady Megara listened to the discussion among the other three, and took some part in it herself. To Chilperic, observing carefully, it seemed that she was not so much interested in the question of hiring the mercenaries as she was in finding an opportunity to talk to them, once she learned they came from the south bank of the river.

FIFTEEN

PRESENTLY the mercenary officer and his sergeant were summoned back into the house. This time Chilperic pointedly invited Koszalin to sit down.

With Chilperic doing most of the talking, Bonar in his tall chair, and Megara standing by, an offer of employment was made to the mercenaries. Modest terms of payment were agreed upon, with the proviso that bonuses would be awarded later in the event actual combat became necessary.

When the agreement had been sealed with a round of handshakes, and the payment of a small handful of coin brought up from some subterranean Senones treasury, the Senones and Chilperic began to question the captain further.

Yes, of course, Koszalin said, everyone over on the Malolo side of the river had been talking about the Sword of great magical powers, with which last month's battle had been fought. And the people over there were all wondering where Farslayer might be. But in fact little effort was actually being made to find it.

"Then," asked Chilperic, "is it possible that the Malolo secretly have Farslayer hidden?"

"It's hard to say that anything's impossible, sir, as you know. But I don't think so."

Koszalin went on to add that the Malolo now generally thought that Farslayer was over here on the Senones side of the river.

"Well, it isn't," said Hissarlik. "And if it's not here and it's not there, where in all the hells is it?"

Naturally no one had an answer for that.

After a time, when odors of food preparation started to waft into the great hall, Hissarlik in a whispered conference with his new vizier asked whether the officer ought perhaps be invited to dine with the family tonight. Chilperic whispered back that he thought not.

Arrangements were made to feed the mercenary captain and his men outside. Before Koszalin and Sergeant Shotoku went out, they were instructed by Chilperic to make their encampment somewhere outside the grounds of Senones manor. They were also ordered sternly to refrain from bothering any of the local people.

In the morning, Chilperic awakened alone in his room, feeling reasonably well rested.

The first order of business was to try the demon-summoning again. The ritual was no more effective than before. Well, there was nothing to be done about it except to try to obtain the Sword without the demon's help; and Chilperic had to admit that he would feel a certain relief if the damned creature was really gone for good.

Descending from his room, he bypassed for the moment the great hall, where something in the way of breakfast would be served, and walked out alone into the misty morning to see how events were progressing in the matter of the mercenaries.

He soon located the small encampment, which had been established near running water as he expected. The captain, up early, came to greet him. Surveying the small handful of tents and shelters, Chilperic remarked to Koszalin: "You said last night that you had thirty men."

The other's mouth changed shape. Perhaps you could have called its new shape a smile. "Some of my men are out on patrol, sir. You see, we're already at work."

"Commendable enthusiasm," Chilperic responded dryly. "Well, until I see them back here, and have a chance to count them for myself, I won't call upon you to do any jobs that might require thirty men."

"Yes sir. That's a good idea."

Chilperic started to say something sharp, then bit the words back. After a moment of thoughtful silence, he extracted a small flask from a pocket, helped himself to a swig, and passed it over without comment.

Koszalin sniffed the flask, and then drank, politely limiting himself to a couple of swallows. "Ah," he said in tones of reverence. "That's something good, I'd say."

"I'd say so, too. Now understand me, Captain. You can tell what stories you want to that boy up in the big house, and his relatives. You can claim to have a hundred heavy cavalry at your command, and they might even believe it. But when you deal with me, I expect to hear the truth, and I can usually tell the difference. Got that?"

"'Sir," acknowledged Koszalin, and passed the flask back with evident reluctance. He belched, almost silently. He looked at Chilperic, evidently reassessing him.

At last he said: "All right, sir. What I've really got is ten men now. Yesterday morning I had twelve, but two of 'em disappeared somewhere."

"Ten men I can believe. Understand me, now. You should do what the Tyrant Hissarlik says, unless I tell you to do something different. But between you and me, I'm the one who's really going to be giving you orders."

Koszalin demurred. "There's a certain matter of

payment, sir. The payment I received did come from the Tyrant, as far as I know."

"You mean that trifle they gave you? I'll double that for you right now." And Chilperic pulled out his purse. After a quick glance around, making sure they were not observed, he handed over a small amount of gold.

Koszalin, expressionless, received the bribe and evaluated it as quickly and neatly as it was given. When it had vanished into one of his inner pockets, he assumed a position of attention. "Standing by for orders, sir," he announced. Suddenly military formality and intelligence had appeared.

"Good. Come, take a little walk with me."

Bawling an order to his sergeant to take charge of the camp for the time being, the captain readily enough joined Chilperic for a stroll through the misty woods, where it seemed probable that they could converse without being heard.

In the course of this talk Chilperic soon heard about the four strange people who had recently arrived at Malolo Manor and established themselves there as unexpected but welcome guests. This was news to Chilperic, and he pricked up his ears at once.

"Two of them are pilgrims, or at least they're wearing gray," Koszalin amplified. "A young man, who's a good shot with a bow, and an old lady. Never heard her name, but she knows how to give orders."

"Oh?" This sounded very much to Chilperic like the pair he had heard described by the hermit. And the time assigned by Koszalin for their arrival at Malolo Manor fit with that identity.

"Then, the next day, or night rather, two more men showed up. I don't know just how they got into the house. I thought we were watching both doors at the time."

"What's that?"

"Yes sir. Two more new arrivals who obviously know the first two. Both of them look like real fighters—probably some kind of officers, I'd say. And, you should know this, one of them is wearing a Sword."

Chilperic, surprised, frowned at the captain. "What do you mean, a sword?"

"What I mean is he's got one of the Twelve strapped on. Trust me, I know what I'm talking about."

"Do you know what you're saying? Which Sword?"

"You can rely on it that I know what I'm saying—sir. I've seen them before. Which Sword this is I don't know, except it can't be Farslayer that everybody's already looking for. Because everybody over there still thinks that one's over here."

Chilperic conversed with the strange young soldier a little longer, then gave him orders to stand by with his men, and turned his own steps back toward the house. Already Chilperic was turning over furiously in his own mind the feasibility of a raid on the Malolo manor— that would at least offer him a chance of getting his hands on this new Sword that seemed to have appeared on the scene. And obtaining that weapon, in turn, might very well placate the dark power that Chilperic served, in the event he failed to find Farslayer.

Before they parted, Koszalin had another suggestion. "The two strange officers who have appeared over there may be scouting in advance of their army. Commanders, high-ranking people, have been known to do such things. But if that's who they are, you can bet that their army, or its advance guard at least, isn't far behind."

When Chilperic returned from his outdoor conference with the mercenary captain, he found the Lady Megara talking with someone in the great hall. Megara was moving about the house slowly and somewhat weakly, not yet ready to go out. But obviously she was no longer going to spend most of her time confined to her room.

Megara turned at Chilperic's entrance, and asked: "Where have you been?" The question was almost a demand.

"Inspecting the defenses, my lady. It's good to see you up and about, and looking well." That was something of an exaggeration. In fact, though she was now more active, the lady indeed looked older than she had when Chilperic had first seen her. He would now estimate her age at about thirty.

"The defenses? You mean those mercenaries we hired last night. I mean to go out and talk to them myself. Later I shall—when I feel stronger."

Chilperic said nothing to discourage this plan, thinking that by doing so he would only guarantee it.

He went on to his breakfast, and managed to enjoy it. Hissarlik did not appear at the table. Soon Chilperic, this time accompanied by both Megara and Tigris was once more closeted in his room, trying again to call his demon.

Again he drew out the leather wallet from his bosom, rubbed it, and carefully recited the words of the incantation.

This time, to his immense relief, Rabisu did respond to his summoning. Not with a physical presence, but at least the insect-chittering of the demonic voice sounded in Chilperic's mind. He thought it could probably be heard in the air around him as well.

The women could indeed hear the voice. Megara appeared largely indifferent, but Tigris frowned at Chilperic, puzzled by what she heard.

Rabisu's first response reached Chilperic in the form

of an extremely attenuated whisper, as if the hideous creature were trying to make contact with him from some enormous distance. Indeed, to begin with the signal was so very faint that Chilperic could not make out what was being said.

But he persisted in his efforts at summoning, and within half an hour the voice of the demon was definitely louder, and marginally more clear. Now and then a word or two came through distinctly, but the man still found it impossible to do more than guess at the meaning of the message as a whole.

Tigris murmured to Lady Megara: "It is almost enough to make one envious, is it not?"

Megara recalled herself from some mental distance. "Envious?"

"Of the power that Wood has granted our friend here. That such a vastly inferior wizard as our friend Chilperic, no wizard at all really, should have such a superior tool as a demon placed at his command."

"I have seen demons," said Megara, still distantly. "I have felt them, too."

"My dear, I suppose we have all seen them at some time—all of us who are acquainted with the art. But to know the luxury of being able to command one . . ." Tigris let her words trail away.

Chilperic naturally had heard the conversation, though he wasn't sure what Tigris was trying to accomplish by it. Now he bowed lightly in Lady Megara's direction. "Should you ever decide to serve my master, lady, I am sure that you would be favored, too."

"Your master? I have little interest in serving any master now."

"When you are fully recovered, my lady, perhaps it will be time to speak of an alliance."

"An alliance? But why—never mind."

Chilperic went back to trying to communicate with his living tool; he was still having only very limited success in that endeavor.

He maintained his calm as well as he was able. But he had to admit to the healer-sorceress Tigris that something was still seriously wrong.

She offered to help.

But Chilperic did not know what the demon was trying to tell him, and thought that the message might well be one he wouldn't want any outsider to hear. He tried to convey this objection to Megara as delicately as possible.

"Of course. I understand perfectly."

Tigris went out with her, for which Chilperic was grateful. He supposed that she would expect a full report later.

Despite the demon's promise of a swift return, many hours had passed and night had fallen before Rabisu's voice was close and clear enough for Chilperic to be able to understand it reasonably well.

But this understanding, when he managed it, did nothing to alleviate Chilperic's growing sense of alarm. Quite the contrary.

Rabisu reported having been forced, by some overwhelming magic, to abandon his place of duty.

"Your place of duty? And where was that? I don't recall assigning you to any particular place."

"I was patrolling in the valley, lord. Trying to look out for your interests as best I could." The demon went on to report that he had been hurled away, to an almost inconceivable distance, by one of a party of men he had discovered in a fishing boat upon the Tungri.

"By a *fisherman?*"

"No, Lord Chilperic, no. Not by a fisherman at all. This man was much more than that."

"I should think he must have been. Proceed with your explanation, then. Tell me what happened."

Rabisu, in a subservient voice, continued his report. The fishing boat had come out, he thought, from the Malolo side of the river, and it had been heading for the islands. The description given by the demon of two of the boat's five passengers matched well with Koszalin's account of two of the impressive visitors who seemed to have attached themselves to the Malolo cause.

And one of these two men had been wearing a Sword. Chilperic sighed deeply. "Was it Farslayer?"

"I do not believe that it was that Sword, sir."

"Then which was it? You are certain it was one of the Twelve?"

"To the second question I answer yes. As for the first, I regret that I do not know."

"Go on."

Rabisu related how he had caused himself to materialize directly in front of the boat, and had challenged those aboard. To his first cursory inspection, none of the men aboard the boat had seemed to be magicians at all—and Chilperic, listening to the story, knew that demons were unlikely to be wrong in such matters. But then, when Rabisu materialized, the man who wore the Sword had answered him with what seemed fearless confidence.

"And then, master, it fell on me as if from nowhere—a stroke that Ardneh himself might have delivered! I could do nothing to resist it, nothing!"

"What kind of a stroke?" Chilperic was still mystified.

"It hurled me to a vast distance. I am at a loss to give any more detailed description."

"Well, can I take it that you are successfully recovering from it now?"

"I am returning to you as fast as I am able, master. As far as I can tell, my powers are unimpaired. If I were to tell you how far that one blow hurled me—if I were to mention to you the orbit of the Moon—then you might accuse me of lying."

If the demon were a man, thought Chilperic, then he might accuse him of being drunk. As matters stood, that suspicion did not apply. He let the point pass for the time being. "And how soon will you be here again, ready to act upon my orders?"

"Within the hour, master. What will my orders be?"

"I'll make a final decision on that when you get here. Let your arrival in my room be as unobtrusive as possible."

Was it possible, Chilperic wondered, that the creature was lying to him? Wood had warned him that insubordination of that kind was a possibility with a demon, no matter what threats or punishment were used.

Probably, thought Chilperic, only Wood himself, or one of his high magical lieutenants, would be able to determine with certainty whether such a creature was telling the truth or not.

Would Tigris qualify? Perhaps.

But suppose that the tale told by the demon, however improbable it sounded, was true. That meant that he, Chilperic, now found himself facing powers that were capable of kicking Rabisu off to the end of the earth, or perhaps farther, like some troublesome puppy. Chilperic knew there were some demons in the world stronger and more powerful than Rabisu. But not very many. So any power that could do that . . .

So Chilperic now felt that whatever Wood might think, he, Chilperic, must decline to enter the lists in such a contest. Unless of course he were given substantial help. It would have to be very substantial indeed.

Frowning thoughtfully, he paced about in his little room until the demon at last arrived.

This time the demonic manifestation was quite modest: only a grinning head that might have belonged to something between a wolf and a snake, which appeared to grow out of the chamber's outer wall.

Speaking forcefully to this apparition, while he held the leather wallet in his hand for it to see, Chilperic gave orders. Rabisu was to fly to Wood, as swiftly as possible, taking word to the master of what had happened to it here. Then it was to return to Chilperic as quickly as it might, bringing whatever orders the master Wood might have for him, as well as whatever help the master might be willing to send.

Chilperic once more closed himself in his room, feeling weary, stretched out on his bed. But before he had gone to sleep, Tigris reappeared, closing the door softly behind her as usual. From the way she smiled at him, this time she was in a seductive mood.

He was not really surprised, and her evident decision to share his bed for the night was welcome, though he thought they had better keep Hissarlik from finding out.

He cautioned his companion on this subject. "The way he looked at you, he's certain to be jealous. And that certainly wouldn't help matters."

Tigris laughed her distinctive laugh. "He is only a boy, and you can manage him without trouble," she assured him.

"No doubt I can."

"Oh, by the way, I thought I should mention to you that I have very recently been in contact with our master."

"Have you indeed? Telling him what?"

"Nothing to your detriment, I assure you, dear Chilperic." Tigris had now begun to undress. "I have described our difficulties to the magnificent Wood, and he assured me that help would soon be on the way."

"Oh, in what form?"

"That he did not specify." She removed the last garment, and bounced cheerfully onto the bed. "And now, dear Chilperic, if you would like to help me with a certain personal problem, kindly place your own clothing on a chair."

On awakening, some hours later, Chilperic found his room still dark, but sensed that Tigris was up and moving about. "What are you doing?"

"I must go and check on my patient again. Go back to sleep."

"Quite a sense of duty you have." Half-consciously he felt in the darkness to make sure that the wallet holding the demon's life, and one or two other things of considerable value, were still where he wanted them to be. Then he let himself drift back to sleep.

Hissarlik, having been awakened by a light tap on his door, felt something in the center of his being hesitate for a beat when he saw the identity of his visitor. Still he was not really surprised. He was the clan leader, was he not? Still a very important person, even in these days when the clan was so sadly diminished.

"Lady Tigris."

"Indeed, it is I, my lord." She smiled at him winsomely. "Aren't you going to invite me in?"

SIXTEEN

MARK and Zoltan's first search for Black Pearl had been brief and unavailing. It was broken off without a landing being made on either of the islands. The small party in their boat observed a gathering of people, including what looked like a small force of militia, on the northern, Senones side of the river. There several comparatively large boats could be seen drawn up on shore in position for launching. When Bonar beheld this demonstration of enemy force he insisted on retreating, and in the circumstances Mark had to agree that might well be the wisest thing to do. Zoltan, worried about Black Pearl, reluctantly went along.

The remainder of the day and the following night passed virtually without incident at Malolo manor. The visitors divided the hours of darkness into shifts among themselves, and with the aid of Bonar and some of his servants, kept watch through the night. But neither the mercenaries nor anyone else appeared to cause trouble.

In the morning, Mark was more determined than ever to locate the mermaid who had said she knew something of the Sword's hiding place; and Zoltan was growing increasingly concerned about Black Pearl. Today therefore a stronger expedition was organized.

This morning the augmented force hiked to the fishing village in the predawn grayness. Shortly after dawn the expedition was ready, and took to the river in two boats. Ben, Lady Yambu, and the magician Gesner accompanied Mark, Zoltan, and Bonar, while Violet and Rose were left in charge of the manor.

Today's boats were larger than yesterday's, and rowed by four men each. These were all armed, so that in all thirteen armed men were taking to the river today, a force everyone agreed was probably substantial enough to face any that the Senones were likely to put in the field.

The sun was still low above the eastern stretch of river, and dew still glittered on the vegetation of Mermaids' Island, when the two boats landed there.

Exploring this scrap of land was the work of a very few minutes. None of the mermaids were to be seen, though their shore living facilities, fireplaces and simple shelters lining one of the convoluted inlets, were available for inspection. The shelters were tiny caves very close to water level, all of them now empty. The inlet was lined with steplike terraces where a mermaid could sit comfortably just in or just out of the water, and have access to the fireplaces on the next level up. Coals glowed brightly in one or two of the small, sheltered fireplaces, and someone had recently been cleaning fish. Near the fireplaces, driftwood had been piled up to dry.

Bonar and Zoltan called, but none of the fishgirls, who had presumably taken to the water nearby, responded. Bonar told his companions that the mermaids who might have been on the island moments ago had doubtless taken alarm at the size and unusual character of this invading force. They would probably be watching from somewhere in the river nearby.

Stubbornly Zoltan roamed the perimeter of the island,

calling Black Pearl's name repeatedly, and waving his arms, hoping to draw the attention of underwater watchers. But he drew no response.

It was also possible to see, on the island, the places of barter where food and other necessities were sometimes left by people coming out from the mainland, in exchange for pearls and other occasional items of value left by the mermaids. Zoltan could see no reason why a direct face-to-face trade could not be conducted— perhaps, he thought, in the early years of the curse mermaids had been considered taboo, or dangerous, and this indirect method had developed.

Whatever had caused the usual inhabitants of Mermaids' Island to absent themselves today, they remained absent, which struck Zoltan as somehow ominous. After pacing from one end of the island to the other, and fruitlessly calling Black Pearl's name a dozen times more, he agreed with the prince his uncle that they had better move on and try to reach the hermit on the south shore. If fishgirls were not to be found, Gelimer seemed to represent the next most likely source of information about the Sword.

Just as they were about to embark again, Mark paused, squinting across the water. "What about Magicians' Island?"

Bonar protested that it was unsafe to visit that place, that mermaids never went there, no one ever did. Gesner, consulted for his professional opinion, admitted that wizards, himself included, visited Magicians' Island from time to time, and that the real danger to anyone had to be considered minimal.

"Then I think we ought to take a look."

The prince as usual had his way. Magicians' Island was not much more than a hundred meters from the shore base of the mermaids. But before the rowers had moved the two boats halfway there, the attention of the entire party was distracted by the sight of someone or something swimming on an interception course toward them, straight from the south.

It was a mermaid, it could be nothing else. A mermaid, just below the surface, coming toward them faster than the boats were moving, approaching at a speed that only a true fish could have matched.

She burst to the surface almost within reach of Zoltan as he crouched in the prow of one of the boats.

"Soft Ripple!" He thought he had recognized the tawny hair even before the mermaid surfaced.

Clinging to the boat, breathless with the speed of her race and with some underlying excitement, Soft Ripple babbled out an incoherent story about Black Pearl's being dead. She added something to the effect that the treacherous Cosmo was to blame.

Gesner and Bonar sat up straight in their boat at the mention of that last name.

But Zoltan had frozen in horror at what he heard.

With the clarity of dazed detachment, he saw that Soft Ripple was holding up something she now wore on a fine chain about her neck. And he could recognize the amulet that Black Pearl had been wearing the last time he saw her.

The mermaid quieted a little when she saw the unfamiliar face of Prince Mark looking over the prow at her.

Lady Yambu, coming up into the prow of the other boat, was sharply soothing, and helped the girl to get herself under control.

"Are you certain Black Pearl is dead? Have you seen her body?" It was Yambu who asked the questions.

"I am certain, lady. I have seen."

"Then show us."

Presently Soft Ripple was swimming again, more slowly this time, leading both boats in the direction of a marshy area along the south bank of the river. This marsh was not far from the outlet of the stream that Black Pearl had ascended, with such difficulty, to visit the hermit.

Before long both boats were sliding and crunching in among the tall green reeds, their rowers swearing at the difficulty, and Bonar muttering his fears of ambush to anyone who would pay attention. No one was paying attention to him for very long.

The mermaid, slithering rapidly through the reedy shallows, and calling back frequently for the boats to follow, remained always a little ahead.

Soon Zoltan saw something floating in the almost stagnant backwater ahead. With a choked cry he leaped from the boat into the waist-deep water, and went thrashing after the pale-skinned, dark-haired floating thing.

When Zoltan came within reach of the body, he felt a rush of relief, intense but brief. This body had two legs, it could not be that of a mermaid. Nor could it be Black Pearl, he thought, perhaps not even a real corpse, though the thing was floating facedown. Whatever had happened to cause death could not have left her looking so shrunken, almost waxlike and inhuman.

"This is no mermaid!"

Soft Ripple looked at him with rage and pity in her face. "It is, it is. We all of us get our legs back when we die. Did you not know that?"

He looked at her, shaking his head. He had never had any suspicion of such a thing.

Ben of Purkinje, leaning from his boat as it drifted nearer, took hold of the body with a huge hand and turned it over gently.

At the first human touch, a little swarm of almost invisible powers, like half-material insects, deserted the corpse and went whining and buzzing their way up into the empyrean.

Ben rumbled: "Aye, this is demon-death if ever I've seen it. Hard to tell how long she's been here, though."

"No!" Zoltan screamed the word. Now he had seen the face. It seemed a modeled parody of Black Pearl's.

Mark put a hand on his nephew's shoulder. Lady Yambu asked Soft Ripple sharply: "Is it really true that your kind always reverts to having legs at death?"

"It is true of all our kind in this river. I have seen it often enough; I ought to know." The bitter hatred in her glared suddenly at Prince Mark, as if he had been Black Pearl's killer. "We are allowed only a few years of life at best."

"I am sorry." Yambu's voice was kind and soft. "How did you come to find the body?"

Coaxed by Lady Yambu, Soft Ripple explained how she had come to make the discovery.

"I have been worried about Pearl for some time, and yesterday I followed her to see where she was going. I saw her start to struggle up the shallow creek here, and I wondered what her goal could possibly be. She was swimming and floundering her way upstream toward the place where the hermit is said to live. I became very worried, and thought of following her even there, but then I gave up that idea, because I thought it was really crazy for a mermaid to try to ascend such a stream.

"So I waited in the river nearby for her to come down again. After a long time, hours, a demon came roaring through the air, and I was terrified. I heard a screaming inhuman sound, and I saw a mysterious and ugly shadow hurtling across the sky. I could see it even from under the water, and I could feel the sickness that the creature brought with it. I wanted to hide, because I thought that the treacherous magician might have called a demon up to kill me—but it wasn't me that the thing was after."

"What treacherous magician?"

The mermaid spat the words. "Cosmo Malolo is the name he's known by in the world."

Bonar, shocked, demanded: "Cosmo is still alive?"

Soft Ripple ignored the clan leader's question. She said: "I didn't dare to come back here until this morning. I hadn't had any contact with Pearl all night, and I was more worried than ever. I looked for her, and I found her here—like this."

Gesner until now had been listening to the mermaid's story in silence. Now he said sharply: "Let me see that amulet that you are wearing."

Soft Ripple raised a pale hand to the chain around her throat. "I took it from Black Pearl's body. What's wrong with that? She was my friend."

Other people in both boats spoke to her more softly and courteously, asking about the amulet. At last she said: "Many of the girls in the river wear ornaments around their necks. Some wear trinkets that they find along the bottom of the river. Some are given baubles by fishermen, because the men hope that the mermaids can send them good luck in return—I don't think it ever really works that way. And some of us are given presents by our families who live on land."

Gesner asked: "But do men ever give you these? I mean, as they might give presents to a girl with legs?"

"Lacking legs and what's between them," the girl said simply, "we have no men. What man would want one who can never truly be a woman? We mermaids have only each other, and our short lives to be endured." She turned to Zoltan and flared up at him: "Why do you weep for her?" It seemed really to puzzle her that a man with legs should do so. "It is we who are still alive who are unlucky. What are you doing? Why do you want to put her body in the boat? Let her go down the river like a dead fish, and be forgotten, the way the rest of us are going."

"The point about the amulet she wears," said Gesner, "is that I can recognize cousin Cosmo's magical sign on it."

Soft Ripple stared at him. When his words had penetrated, she tore the amulet from her neck with fear and loathing, and threw it away into the river. "I never thought that it came from him!" she cried.

Zoltan was sitting now with his head down, not really paying attention to the others.

Mark reached from the boat and caught the raging girl by the hair. "There'll be time later to have a tantrum," he said, in a new and harder voice. "If you can tell me where the Sword is now, do so."

"You are wearing it at your side." But Soft Ripple said this sullenly, not as if she really believed it.

The prince released his grip. "I wear its fellow, which has a different power, and a different mark that Vulcan put on it."

"What power?" It was hard to tell how seriously the question was intended.

"That of cutting stone, swiftly and easily. Ask this Malolo chief here how I cut my way into his stronghold." And the prince's hand touched the hilt of the Sword he wore.

"Indeed." The mermaid flirted for a moment completely beneath the surface, and up again, much as a wholly human swimmer might have done.

Then, facing the prince again, she asked: "You want Farslayer to deal with your enemies, do you?"

"Yes. Especially I want to keep them from getting it.

And they are your enemies as well, whether you know it or not. Chief among them is the wizard who held Black Pearl in thrall when she was far upstream."

"Very well. I know where the Sword Farslayer is now, and I will tell you."

For a moment there was silence, the people in both boats questioning whether they had heard her words aright. Then everyone burst out with questions.

The mermaid hushed them all with a small raised hand. "I know where it is because I saw the demon hide it, yesterday. I think he may have taken it from Black Pearl, though I don't know where she got it—but I did see the demon with a Sword. He hid it hastily. He knew that I was watching him, and he would have killed me, too. Except that there was something else he wanted to do, something he thought even more important than killing me to keep me quiet."

"What else?"

Soft Ripple looked at Prince Mark. "He wanted to go to you. You were sitting in a boat, a boat smaller than either of these, out near the middle of the river, with some of these same people with you. So desperate was the demon to confront you that he would not even pause to kill me first. Someday perhaps he will return and find me and kill me—but I will first tell you where the Sword is hidden."

"Where?"

"Right where he put it. Far underwater, in the deepest channel, not far from Magicians' Island."

"Take me to that Sword now. If you help me to get it, I swear by Ardneh I'll do my best to see that every mermaid in this river is given her legs again. I do not think that is impossible."

Soft Ripple looked at the prince in silence. Then she said, "Follow me," and turned and swam away.

Black Pearl's body had already been hoisted aboard one of the boats, and decently covered with a canvas sail.

Soft Ripple stopped, swimming in place, at a spot where the current was swift, within twenty meters or so of Magicians' Island. The oarsmen in both boats worked steadily to hold their craft beside her.

She said: "The Sword you seek is approximately straight below me. If any of you have the strength of a demon, and can swim like a mermaid, come down with me, and move away the rock the demon placed atop his prize to hold it safe. That rock is more than I, or a hundred like me, could move a centimeter."

Bonar was ready in a moment with the beginning of a plan to move the rock with ropes and many boats, and the help of other mermaids.

Mark instead unsheathed the Sword he was wearing at his belt.

Zoltan had by now recovered a little from the first shock of Black Pearl's death. "Give Stonecutter to me," he told his uncle, "and I'll dive with Soft Ripple, and cut up the rock. I'm a strong swimmer."

Mark, looking at him, thought that Zoltan at this moment was also somewhat reckless of his own life. "No," said Mark.

"Why not? Cutting the stone will be easy."

The mermaid was almost laughing at both of them. "No, you stay in the boat. All of you. Please, or I will have to pull you up out of the water as well. The Sword you want to find lies much too deep, and the current down there is far too swift and cold for anyone with legs to swim in it."

Then she held out her hands to Mark for Stonecutter. "Give me the Sword you wear, and I will dive alone and get the other one for you. If I can chop the boulder into little bits as easily as he says, then the rest will be easy, too."

Mark hesitated just noticeably. But then he handed over the Sword of Siege.

The mermaid smiled at him, and let Stonecutter's weight bear her down below the surface.

Time passed, slowly and intensely. The boats maintained their positions. Mark wished that he had started counting, and wondered if anyone else had. So far, he thought, no more time had passed than a skillful, breathing human diver might require to maintain herself underwater. Or not much more—

Suddenly the water erupted, revealing the head and shoulders and arms of Soft Ripple. She was tailing water strongly in the swift current, keeping herself in position to hold up a naked, gleaming Sword. On her two raised hands the mermaid offered the weapon up to Mark.

He took it from her carefully and turned the hilt to see its symbol. The Sword was Stonecutter.

Soft Ripple said: "The other one is free now. But I can carry only one up to the surface at a time."

With a flick of her tail, she dove again.

Almost absently Mark wiped dry the Sword of Siege upon his sleeve, and slowly he resheathed it. Everyone was watching the water once again, and again some were counting silently.

Ben suddenly snarled out an oath and pointed. The mermaid had reappeared, holding another Sword. But this time she was at the distance of the Isle of Magicians, where she had leaped out of the water almost like a seal, to sit upon a low, wet rock.

She waved across the water with the Sword, offering a mocking greeting to the people in the boats.

"Row! Get us over there!" the prince commanded. Oars clashed and labored. But boats were slow and clumsy, and they were not going to catch a mermaid in the water.

In fact it appeared that they were not going to catch Soft Ripple, even though she was content to remain out of the water for the time being.

"Stop her!"

The mermaid was swinging the heavy Sword slowly, tentatively, awkwardly around her head; the thin muscles of her arms and shoulders stood out with the effort.

Zoltan on hearing that last order from his prince had reached mechanically for his bow, and someone else was reaching for a sling. But both people stayed their hands. If the Sword were to fall into the water from where the mermaid held it now, it would plunge once more into the channel's hopeless depths.

Mark was cursing at the rowers: "Get us over there, quick!"

As fast as the rowers could propel them, the two fishing boats were now approaching Magicians' Island from the south. And still the mermaid, sitting safely out of everyone's reach, twirled the Sword, and still she seemed not quite able to bring herself to let it go. Perhaps for some reason she could not feel Farslayer's power—or perhaps—

Mark issued orders in a low voice: "Ben! Take your boat, land on the far side of the island. I'll take this one to where we can get close enough to argue with her from the water."

It seemed to Zoltan a very long time before the prow of the boat now carrying Ben and himself grated ashore at the nearest feasible landing spot that was just out of sight of Mark's boat, and of the mermaid on her rock.

Ben and Zoltan leaped from their boat and hit the beach running. As they did so, a small horde of minor powers took to the air around them, just as had happened when Black Pearl's body was first disturbed in the water. Zoltan had seen their like on occasion in the past, and more experienced observers than he had never been able to determine whether powerful wizards somehow created such swarming entities, or were only capable of calling them from some other plane of existence. However that might be, Zoltan knew that in a disorganized swarm like this one the miniature entities, for the most part indifferent to human beings, were hardly more dangerous than so many mosquitoes would have been.

Not that danger would have mattered to him just now. He ran forward, hoping to get into position to hurl himself at the mermaid before she threw the Sword, and drag Farslayer somehow from her grip. Still the little powers, doubtless sent here long ago to guard the island from nonmagicians, swarmed about. They were only semisentient at best. One could hear them buzzing faintly in the air, and see them like small ripples of atmospheric heat. Any human with even a minimal sensitivity to the things of magic could feel them in the air as well.

Zoltan had left ponderous Ben some strides behind. Now, approaching the hummock that concealed him from the mermaid, Zoltan slowed and raised his head cautiously over the obstacle. He could see his uncle Mark, standing in the boat, still trying to argue Soft Ripple out of throwing the Sword.

Now he could see the mermaid, too.

Zoltan eased forward, hoping to get close before she saw him. Mark continued his argument. Ben came up silently behind Zoltan, and a little to one side.

But they were all too late, or ineffective.

"If he is still alive, I kill him. If dead, let my hate follow him to hell!"

With a last hideous, obscene malediction against Cosmo Malolo, the mermaid let the bright blade fly.

SEVENTEEN

GELIMER had just finished the painful task of burying his faithful Geelong in the cemetery grove, when the Sword of Vengeance entered his life again.

It had taken the hermit a long struggle to get the beast's mangled body down from the thorntrees, and Geelong had died well before the process could be completed; had died—for which Gelimer was thankful —even before the hermit could get into position to administer the mercy stroke himself.

After that it had been a struggle for the hermit, himself wracked by physical as well as mental pain, to get the animal's body uphill to his house. His arms and legs were bruised and every muscle in his body ached, making it a slow and painful process for him to do anything. All through the following night Gelimer, lying beside his pet's blanket-wrapped body, had tried to rest, tried to recover from the injuries caused by the demon's manhandling.

And in the morning, for the first time, he thought he knew what it felt like to be old. Moving as in a dream of pain and suffering, he had lifted the rude bundle containing his companion's mangled body, placed it on a kind of travois, and had urged his own battered body to pull the contrivance in the direction of the cemetery.

He could not have said how much time was taken by the work of pulling, selecting a gravesite, and digging. He had just finished his prayers to Ardneh over the refilled grave, had turned and started for home, when the Sword came.

Gelimer first saw the rainbow streak moving across the distant sky, coming from the north and angling to the west. Then the bright track curved, until it appeared to be coming directly at him. And now he heard and felt the all-too-familiar onrush of its approaching magic.

For just a brief moment Gelimer believed that Farslayer was coming for him, and he stood motionless and unalarmed while something in him responded with eagerness to the thought of death. But the Sword rushed by overhead. The truth was that nobody hated him, no one was his enemy, no one any longer even knew him well enough to want to waste a Sword-blow on him.

The Sword of Vengeance had not been sent to strike the hermit's heart. The rainbow streak of the Sword, swifter than any arrow Gelimer had ever seen in flight, arced close over his head, coming down directly into the cemetery grove he had just left. There, somewhere under those tall trees, it struck home with an earthen impact, dull and loud as a blow from a god's hammer.

Gelimer dropped the handle of the empty travois he had been dragging, and with his shovel still clutched in one hand hurried back under the trees. The spot of impact was impossible to miss. Something had cratered the black dirt and the spring flowers, sending earthy debris far and wide. The flying Sword had landed directly on the site of the last grave but one that he had dug.

The hermit ran forward. Regardless of the slippery

mud, regardless of the protests of his own painful body, he plunged his shovel into the cratered ground and began to dig again.

Presently the smell of old death, as if at some opening of hell, came surging up to meet him. He choked on it, but persisted.

In a few moments he was sure of what had happened. He could see now that the body of Cosmo Malolo, which had been decomposing for the past month inside its crude blanket-shroud, had for a second time been pierced through the heart by the Sword of the Gods.

Gelimer threw down his shovel. His muddy fingers, trembling, closed upon that black, mud-spattered hilt. With that contact his fingers ceased to tremble. Muttering half-finished prayers of gratitude to Ardneh, and perhaps to other, darker gods as well, the hermit carried the Sword up out of the shallow, blasted pit.

Exactly who had thrown the Sword this time, and why vengeance had been wasted upon a victim already dead, were questions that did not now even cross his mind.

The grove around him was as silent and tranquil as ever. Though the day was bright, here under the trees it was almost dim with their heavy shading. Standing erect, Gelimer saluted the grave of Geelong with the Sword. Then, gripping the knurled hilt in both hands, the hermit began a ponderous, spinning dance—

His dance was carrying him, step by step, out of the grove and into the open air, where you could see for kilometers in all directions except that of the mountain whose shoulder he was standing on. He had not whirled thrice beyond the trees before there appeared to him, standing only forty or fifty meters away in sunlight, the image of the demon Rabisu. The demon came in the guise of an armored man, tall as a house, half transparent but immense, who ran forward threateningly, raising some blurred weapon—

Gelimer saw the approaching shape, and uttered a hoarse cry. In the next instant he felt the Sword fly free, tearing itself by its own power out of his grip, an instant before he would have let it go.

The blade passed straight through the demon's image as through a mirage, seeming to do no harm. Then, like an intelligent arrow, Farslayer curved its own pathway in mid-flight. But not back toward the apparition. Instead the Sword went down on the north side of the river, somewhere over the Senones stronghold.

The figure of the demon had stopped in its tracks, and turned to watch that darting descent. Now it turned back to confront Gelimer. Rabisu's assumed countenance, which had been recognizable as the semblance of a human face, was now chaotic, indescribable. The apparition stood as if paralyzed, and from its demonic throat there issued a last cry, a great howl that went on and on.

That outcry lingered in the air even after the image of the demon had disappeared.

The mermaid, Soft Ripple, had plunged into the river immediately after she threw the Sword. But she surfaced again very quickly, risking retaliation by the angry men around her, unable to resist the attraction of watching the weapon in flight. Not that there was much to see, a mere rainbow flicker toward the slope of the mountain to the south.

A moment of silence hung over the boats and the island. It was broken by another loud outcry, near at hand.

This scream had come from the throat of a woman Zoltan had never seen before. Her thin figure, wrapped in the robes of a sorceress, came tottering forward from a recess among the rocks of Magicians' Island. Facing the mermaid, this apparition halted, and uttered another hoarse scream. "Not Cosmo! No! You shall not kill him!"

Bonar raised a hand and pointed. "That is the Lady Megara Senones, the bitch-sorceress. We must take her prisoner. Gesner, can you deal with her magic?"

Gesner opened his mouth and closed it again, making no promises, not even of effort.

But Prince Mark was paying little attention to his immediate companions. "My lady," he called to the figure on the rock. "Are you in need of help?"

The woman Bonar had called Megara, the supposed sorceress, turned a distracted gaze in Mark's direction. And Zoltan, as he got his first full look at her face, took her for an old woman, even older than Yambu perhaps. At a second look he was not so sure of her age, but certain that she had been through terrible things.

Soft Ripple, thrashing in the water nearby, shrilled at her: "I know who you are, old woman. Your Cosmo is dead now! Even for you there can be no stopping that Sword. Not even you damned arrogant magicians can manage that!"

Slowly, in small jerky movements and little slumps, Megara standing on her rock relaxed from a posture of rage and anger into one of weariness and despair.

When she spoke again, she glanced toward the mermaid, and her voice was very tired. "I fear that you are right, fishgirl. If Cosmo was not dead before this . . ." Then she saw Bonar glaring at her in something like triumph. She cried to her hereditary enemy: "Will you kill me, then? Strike, if you will, there is nothing to prevent you now!"

Ben edged a little nearer Bonar, ready to restrain him from accepting this invitation.

Mark, still speaking calmly, told the lady: "We are going to the south shore, after the Sword. Come with us, if you will."

"It no longer matters to me where I go," the sorceress said after a pause. "What magic I can attempt no longer works. Except my little boat . . . yes. I accept. I'll go with you. If I could even see his body there—it would be better if I could know with certainty that he is dead."

"Cosmo Malolo?"

"Of course. He and I are lovers." The claim was made proudly but it seemed grotesque.

"Ah," said Yambu, who until now had been attending silently. "And that night, on this island, where the killing started—the two of you were discovered by your father?"

"Yes. That is what happened. And Cosmo killed him, with the Sword."

Mark had by now gone to the lady's side, and was offering her his arm, while Bonar seethed in not-quite-silent protest. His protests had no effect. Both boats were shortly under way again, Megara riding with Prince Mark aboard the one that did not hold the clan chief of the Malolo. Soft Ripple followed swimming, staying within easy earshot.

The young mermaid had more that she wanted to tell Megara about Cosmo.

"I knew what you were doing, the two of you, meeting on the island. I watched your two boats coming and going. And I knew what he did to my friend Black Pearl. Did you know that your marvelous Cosmo screwed around with mermaids?"

Megara was sitting straight in her seat, looking straight ahead, as if she could not hear.

"Tell us about it later," Ben grumbled at the mermaid in a low voice.

"No," said the prince. "No, I think that we should hear Soft Ripple's story now."

The oarsmen worked, the two boats moved steadily

toward the south shore of the river. Soft Ripple kept on talking.

"I knew Black Pearl was up to something," the mermaid said. "Finally I followed her, and I found out that she made many visits to Magicians' Island. Eventually I found an underwater tunnel there."

Soft Ripple went on to relate how she had discovered that a Malolo boat, the same one, was invariably tied up in one of the island's concealed coves when Black Pearl paid her secret visits there. Later on she became aware of another boat, one that came out to Magicians' Island from the Senones side of the river, propelled by sail and with a single occupant. It was a small craft, and Soft Ripple thought that perhaps it was partly propelled by magic. Certainly magic had somewhat protected it from observation. It had invariably come out to the island when Cosmo's craft was also there. On the first occasion this might have happened by accident, but on later occasions their meetings had obviously been planned.

Soft Ripple had at length grown curious enough to risk the secret underwater passage for herself, choosing a time when the island was otherwise deserted. Overcome by curiosity, and perhaps by jealousy, she had forced herself to go on, despite the buzzing of minor powers that generally frightened away her mermaid sisters as well as the fisherfolk of both clans.

Later, her curiosity grew so great that she even dared the passage when she knew that Meg and Cosmo were in the grotto, and she had spied on them, unsuspected, as they lay together.

"We can sometimes see quite well from underwater, did you know that? And we can hear. I saw and heard the two of you, holding up the Sword and talking about it."

Lady Megara turned finally. She changed her position so that she was looking down at the creature swimming in the water beside the boat.

Soft Ripple's eyes were glittering as she spoke. "Then, later, I spied on Black Pearl and Cosmo. He was magician enough to fix it so she grew legs, if only for a little while. Did you know that? Legs, and what's between them, too. That's what he wanted from her. That's what men always want. Yours wasn't enough for him."

"Fables and fairy stories," said Lady Megara instantly. Her voice was as soft and certain as any that Zoltan had ever heard. "Cosmo told me about you. And about the other one, Black Pearl or whatever her name was. How he had been trying to help you, out of the goodness of his heart. How you became impatient and angry when he couldn't cure you immediately, how you were starting to make up lies about him. Yes, yes indeed, he told me." And the lady in the boat nodded and smiled, almost sweetly, at the accursed creature in the water.

"Oh no. Oh no. It's you who lie." The mermaid, swimming on her back, gazed up at the people in the boat, gazed at the Lady Megara in particular. It was as if the enormity of what the lady was saying held her hypnotized. "I talked to Cosmo, yes. Why shouldn't I? I told him that I wanted legs, too. And he—he said he'd kill me if I tried to make trouble. But if I waited, and was patient, and said nothing to anyone, then maybe it would be my turn next. I knew what he meant, he meant after he was through with Black Pearl. Then he would see to it that I got legs. But I would only have had them for a few minutes at a time. Now I know he never really meant to help any of us . . ."

Lady Megara had long since ceased to listen. She said, to Mark and the others in the boats: "Cosmo showed me the Sword that he had hidden. He told me what it was going to mean for our future. Our families were both hopeless, lost in feuding. But that was not for us . . . the two of us were going to run away, taking the Sword with

us. We would sell Farslayer in some great city, and that
would give us the money we needed for the future.

The lady had grown animated in telling her story. "Let
our families feud and kill each other if that was what
they wanted. We would get away, and live our own lives,
lives of peace and decency, somewhere else."

"Of course"—and her animation fled—"we would
have to avoid my father at all costs."

"And then," said Lady Yambu, "one night your father
caught up with you."

The two boats still made progress toward the south
shore, while the mermaid continued to swim beside
them. Now, reviving from the near silence of pain and
despair, she once again shrieked curses against Megara
and her beloved Cosmo.

Lady Meg continued to ignore her. But Zoltan, listening to Soft Ripple, believed what she said, or most of it,
and thought that most of the other people in the boats
believed her also. Zoltan wondered if Megara had ever
suspected that her lover had been given to seducing
mermaids. If so, Megara had put the idea firmly from
her, and was not going to entertain it now.

Judging by Megara's expression, she was still refusing
to credit such outrageous allegations, or even to think
about them. Refusing to admit that such creatures as
lowly fishgirls could have any important role to play in
anything. That anything about them could be of any
importance to the important people of the world.

But the lady in the boat was more than willing to
converse with Mark, the prince who would accept her
and listen to her as an equal. "I loved him," she repeated
brightly, proudly, confidingly, as if she and Mark were
the only people on the river. "We met on the island—the
first time quite by accident. We loved each other from
the first."

Again the mermaid screamed something foul.

The lady ignored the fishgirl. "And then, Cosmo showed me the marvelous Sword that he had hidden here."

At last, with an appearance of confidence, she deigned to answer the one who taunted from the water. "Yes, Cosmo told me that sometimes he caught mermaids. He was a kindhearted man, and he wanted to do something for the poor creatures. So sometimes he took them in one of his magical nets, for purposes of experimentation. It was all for their benefit. Of course I never asked their names. As for the idea that he might have had affairs with them . . ." That was obviously too absurd to deserve denial.

"He had Black Pearl. And he was going to have me next, I tell you!" Soft Ripple shrieked, her voice almost unintelligible now. Her small pale hands were pounding water into foam.

"But he never did, did he? I'm sorry for you, my dear."

"He had Black Pearl, and—and—"

Soft Ripple's voice broke, then collapsed completely in grotesque hatred, jealousy, suffering, and rage. And then suddenly she was only a young girl, weeping, drifting almost inertly beside the boat.

Mark asked the Lady Megara: "If I may, my lady, go back to the Sword for a moment. Where did Cosmo first obtain it? Did he ever tell you that?"

"He told me, freely, that he traded with a mermaid for it. And he had begun to fear that some of the creatures were developing their—their own grotesque feelings for him. That they were making up fantasies. I only know that he never . . ."

Lady Megara talked on, and now it was the mermaid's turn not to listen. Soft Ripple had fallen quite silent, gliding on her back, looking up expressionlessly at the sky. But still she swam beside the boats, as if secured to them by some invisible chain.

The woman in the boat continued speaking. "But my father grew suspicious. He must have followed me, secretly, that night. It may be that some of my magical powers were beginning to fade, because I was no longer a virgin." The Lady Megara made the declaration proudly.

"He came upon us as we lay together. He stood over us, hand on the hilt of his sword, thundering judgment, consigning us to our fates. I, the faithless, treacherous daughter, was going to spend the rest of my life in a White Temple. As for Cosmo, the Malolo seducer, a hideous death awaited him.

"But for once the judge was not allowed to enforce his sentence. He turned his back on us, and I suppose he was about to call out to his men to come in. But as soon as he did so, Cosmo pulled the great and beautiful Sword out of its hiding place, and stabbed him through the back.

"I had risen to my knees, about to try to plead with my father. When I saw Cosmo strike him, I could neither speak nor move. My father never uttered a sound. He turned partway around, with the Sword still in him, and looked at me with a great and terrible surprise; it was as if he thought that I had been the one to strike him. And in a way I had."

"Now, for once, I saw him as someone who could be hurt, someone who could need my help. He tried to speak again, but he could not.

"And then, a moment later, he fell dead."

Lady Yambu said something, so low that Zoltan could not make it out. Still the oarsmen rowed stolidly, and the boats advanced.

"Cosmo must have tried to talk to me after that. But I was paralyzed in shock.

"Perhaps I said something to him then, something terrible that made him leave me and run away. I don't remember. I don't remember. All I know is that I loved him, and I love him still."

Megara suddenly slumped over in her seat, swaying as if she might be on the brink of complete collapse. Yambu soothed her, stoically and almost silently, with memories in her own mind of some similar experience herself.

Eventually Megara raised her head and spoke again. "The next thing I remember is that my father's men had rushed into the grotto, and were trying to revive me. His body still lay there on the couch, or just beside it. Someone had already pulled out the Sword that had killed him, and I suppose had already used it again. When the men saw that my father had been struck down by Farslayer, they naturally assumed that it had come magically into the grotto from a distance—and that one of the Malolo must have thrown it. Of course none of them blamed Cosmo, or even thought of him, I suppose. If they ever thought of him at all, he was not considered dangerous.

"And so began our night of the great slaughter—but I knew no more about it. I knew nothing else very clearly for about a month."

Soft Ripple, abstracted now, continued to swim silently beside the boat.

And Bonar, riding in the other boat from Megara, confirmed how, on that night of terror, Cosmo had returned from one of his magical night outings, at about the time of the first (as the Malolo thought) Sword-death.

It had been a night of vile weather, of sleet and wind and snow. As a result, almost all members of both rival families had been gathered around their respective hearths.

There had been quite a number of eager, excitable

young Malolo men on hand that night, the flower of the family youth. The same thing across the river. And the leaders on both sides had been killed quite early that night.

Cosmo on coming home that night had of course said nothing about his having been on Magicians' Island, or about the patriarch of their enemies having died there at his hand.

But Bonar could say something now about his cousin having gone to that island frequently.

He added that, on that night, Cosmo had tried to get the others to interrupt the cycle of killing. But as usual no one had paid him much attention. Cosmo had been no more highly respected by his own family than he was by their enemies. He was looked on as a failed magician, who had not been very good at anything else, either. His pleas and warnings on the night of killing had been scorned and disregarded.

Then the Sword had struck again—for what was to seem to others the last time that night—coming in through the stone walls of the Malolo manor and killing someone.

This time Cosmo had been first on the scene and had drawn the weapon from the corpse. But instead of striking back in his turn, like a true Malolo, he had seized Farslayer and run out into the night with it.

Soon the remaining family members, few, bereaved, and bewildered, discovered that he'd reclaimed the mount he'd recently left in the stables, and galloped off, the gods knew where.

Before leaving he'd said something, a few words to a stablehand, that indicated he felt responsible for some reason for the slaughter that had now overtaken his own family.

"We cannot be sure what he was thinking. But it seems

that he meant to take the Sword somewhere where it could do no harm."

"A goal with which I can feel some sympathy," said Prince Mark. "In fact I can remember trying to do something like that once myself. When I was very young."

The two boats moved on steadily toward the south shore, where Mark and his friends were determined to find the hermit Gelimer.

EIGHTEEN

HISSARLIK, sitting on his high chair in his great hall and enjoying a solitary meal, suddenly gave a great shriek, and tumbled writhing to the floor.

Three servants, who were the only people in the room with the clan chief at the moment, became aware at that same moment of the return of a terrible visitor: the same Sword that a month ago had well-nigh depopulated the house of its owners and masters.

This time the onlookers' first glimpse of the weapon came as it fell clashing on the floor beside their wounded Tyrant. Hissarlik's clothes and the floor around him were being drenched in a steady outpouring of his blood.

Two of the servants rushed immediately to the assistance of the Tyrant. In moving the Sword out of the way, they saw that it held, impaled near its tip, a rather peculiar-looking leather wallet. The wallet was heavily spattered with Hissarlik's blood; and it was not immediately recognizable as leather, having curled up into a dry and lifeless-looking scrap of what looked like parchment.

Hissarlik was not yet dead. In fact he was not even completely disabled, though his side had been deeply gashed and blood poured from his wound. Ashen-faced, he demanded to be helped to rise. With a servant's help he got himself up on his shaky knees, and then by dint of grasping another servant's arm, hauled himself to his feet. Then, almost falling again, he bent over with difficulty to grasp the deadly Sword by its black hilt and pick it up.

The third of the servants present, who for some days now had been secretly in the pay of Tigris, had already dashed out of the room to tell her newest employer what had happened.

Meanwhile, Hissarlik, even though his eyes were glazing, had shaken free of the arms that supported him. He was holding the Sword's hilt with two hands now, and doing his staggering best to spin around.

He muttered a name, and threw the Sword, which vanished in a flash through the stone walls of the room, as magically as it had come in through them. A moment later, the latest wielder of the Sword of Vengeance had fallen again, to lie at full length on the floor. Hissarlik's eyes were glazing more rapidly now.

A door banged open. Tigris, who had been unable to stay with him at every moment, came rushing in angrily from two rooms away. She was moments too late to witness Farslayer's latest departure.

"Where is the Sword? What have you done with it? You fool, you've thrown it away, haven't you!" In a controlled rage, she knelt beside the fallen man. "Did I hear you cry out a name? That of the target, it must have been!"

The dying Hissarlik, his side still spouting blood, was trying to focus his eyes on the face of Tigris as she bent over him. He was trying to tell her something that seemed to him to be of great importance.

But she gave no indication that she was interested, or that she was about to practice any of her healing arts on him. "What's this? The demon's life, well skewered, just as I thought it might be!" In her rage she hurled the scrap of leather down. Then she gripped the dying Tyrant, and shook him angrily. "I thought the Sword might be coming to you—but why did you throw it away? Why? I needed that Sword, you fool!"

But she received no answer.

Chilperic had left the Senones manor surreptitiously before dawn, and made his way quietly to the camp of Koszalin's mercenaries. He found the captain and his men ready and waiting. Chilperic's objective today was to lead this small force against the Malolo stronghold in what he hoped was going to be a surprise attack.

They managed to cross the river under cover of darkness, but experienced some trouble with the boats, which the mercenaries handled awkwardly. As a result, the expedition landed on the south shore a great deal farther downstream than its leader had planned, and the day was well advanced before they got back within striking distance of the place he wanted to attack.

Koszalin and Chilperic had some desultory conversation en route, not all of it acrimonious. Chilperic at least felt that they had come to understand each other on several levels. But there were still problems between them.

Chilperic, checking the leather wallet in his inner pocket at frequent intervals, thought that the ten men he was leading, with a demon to back them up, had every chance of seizing the undermanned enemy fortress in a surprise attack.

Koszalin also discounted the Malolo defenses, except for those that the strange visitors might be able to provide, as consisting of no more than a handful of frightened servants.

Having seen something of the Malolo manor and its defenders firsthand, Chilperic was inclined to agree with this assessment—but not to trust it with his life.

At last, wanting to make sure that Rabisu was going to be available this time when he was needed, Chilperic overcame his distaste for the creature and tried to call it up.

As on the previous day, his first attempt got no response at all.

Chilperic muttered to himself: "What now, has the damned thing got itself banished to the orbit of the Moon again?"

But this time things were subtly worse than yesterday. Today there was not even the proper feeling of power in the leather wallet when he stroked it.

Looking carefully at the mottled, folded leather, he realized that though it was as glossy and rich-looking as usual, it was not the same wallet he had been carrying yesterday. There were subtle differences in appearance.

Looking back across the river, he swore, viciously and quietly.

He could remember all too well his nighttime visit from the damned enchantress Tigris.

Swapping passengers from one boat to another in midstream was a little chancy, but Bonar and Gesner insisted on taking over one of the boats for family affairs as soon as they had convinced themselves in discussion that the Sword had again begun to bear the deadly traffic of the feud. The mermaid had thrown it against Cosmo, alive or dead, and it had whirred off somewhere.

Just where, was a question. Mark and Ben, who had had some previous experience with the Sword of Vengeance, were not surprised that it was difficult to gauge the point of impact from a glimpse of the Sword in flight. But Cosmo alive or dead had probably not been very far away, and Farslayer would most likely be picked up again by someone involved in the affairs of the valley.

Bonar in particular was determined to reach the

stronghold of his family manor as rapidly as possible, now that Farslayer had begun to fly again.

"If it is my fate now to be struck down by Farslayer," said Bonar with considerable dignity, "then I must fall where someone of my own house will be on hand to avenge me."

Mark had no wish to argue with him. But he detailed Ben of Purkinje to accompany the head of the clan and his magician back to the manor. Mark himself, with Zoltan and Yambu accompanying him, still intended to find the hermit Gelimer and search the upland where the hermit lived. That seemed to them to be the area in which the Sword had most recently come down.

The boat carrying Ben, Bonar, and Gesner pulled away, riding swiftly downstream with the current augmenting the rowers' efforts. The remaining craft, on the prince's orders, pulled straight toward the south shore. On landing, Mark detailed the four armed oarsmen to guard the boat, while Mark, Zoltan, and Yambu started uphill intending to find Gelimer.

Lady Megara climbed along with them, saying that she wished to confirm Cosmo's death and see his body. It seemed that a spot of uncertainty regarding his fate still lingered in her mind.

Aging and tired as she looked, she somehow found the energy to keep up with the other three, and the ascent went fairly swiftly. The four had not spent much time on the trail paralleling the little watercourse before they came upon the hermit.

It was Zoltan, climbing in the lead, who saw and recognized Gelimer first. The hermit was crouched over two dead bodies, one dripping wet, that were laid out side by side on the bank of the stream. When the young man got a little closer he could see that the dead men were armed and had probably been mercenaries; judging by the green scarves they both wore, they had been members of the same company that had invested Malolo manor.

Zoltan halted on the path, while Prince Mark came up silently behind his nephew and stood looking over his shoulder.

"Gelimer," Zoltan whispered.

"I surmised as much," Mark said in a low voice. "But how do two of Koszalin's people come to be lying here?"

The hermit, at last becoming aware that he had company, raised his head and stared at his visitors. Gelimer looked worn out, thought Zoltan, and perhaps a little mad. As the company of four once more approached him, he stared at them without seeming to notice whether they were friends or strangers.

"The Sword again," said Gelimer in a cracked voice. "It kills and kills, you see. You can see its mark on each of these. How many more funerals," he asked the world in general, "am I going to be required to conduct?"

"I cannot tell you that, old man," said the prince. And indeed Gelimer did seem to have aged considerably since Zoltan had seen him last.

The hermit, for his part, now at last indicated that he recognized Zoltan and Yambu as the two pilgrims who had dropped in on him only a few days ago.

The hermit was introduced to Mark and Lady Megara. It was impossible to tell from Gelimer's demeanor whether he had ever heard of the Prince of Tasavalta, or whether Megara's name meant anything to him or not.

"I suppose that you are after it, too," he said to the prince.

No need to ask the old man what he was talking about. "I admit that I am," said Mark. "I want it for a good reason."

"It was here, you know. Only a little while ago. I held

it in these hands." And Gelimer spread his work-worn hands and held them out for inspection, as if they might be considered trustworthy evidence.

"Where is it now?"

"Gone again. Across the river—I think that's where it went. I sent it after the life of the demon, and now I think that creature will trouble the world no more." The hermit spoke with a kind of dreamy satisfaction.

"Where was the demon's life concealed, good hermit?" Mark had to take the old man by the arm and shake him gently before he would respond.

Gelimer blinked at him sadly. "Where was its life hidden? I don't know. I don't understand demons. But I expect we can be sure of one thing, that one's now dead. As dead as my Geelong."

"Geelong? Who's that?"

Yambu said: "That was the name of his pet watchbeast, I believe."

Megara, looking physically frail again after the burst of energy that had let her climb, was growing impatient with all this talk of demons. "Old man," she demanded. "What can you tell me of Cosmo Malolo?"

She had to repeat the question before Gelimer truly heard it. Then he said: "Cosmo Malolo? I am sorry, my lady, but that man is dead."

"Dead?" Megara smiled gently. Zoltan, watching, thought that in the space of a few moments the lady came to look older than the hermit. "Yes. Yes, I thought that he was dead."

Prince Mark persisted in coming back to the subject of Rabisu. "Tell me about the demon, Gelimer. I wonder where his life was hidden?" He gazed intently at the hermit. "Did you say that the Sword went across the river?"

Gelimer looked toward the north side of the river and gestured vaguely. "It went through him, right through him. And then, yes—it came down somewhere over there."

Mark muttered: "It can dart back and forth across the river faster than we can ever hope to follow it. And it probably will, assuming that the feud's still on."

Lady Yambu nodded. "I think we must assume that."

Zoltan said: "Then, if Farslayer last came down somewhere in Senones-land, the chances are its *next* target will be somewhere on this bank."

"In or near the Malolo manor," Yambu added.

"That seems likely to me," said Mark. "Well, our quickest way of getting downstream will be by boat."

"You are returning to the river?" asked the hermit. It seemed that for the moment he had forgotten completely about the two dead bodies at his feet. "I shall come down to the bank with you, if I may. I want to talk to a mermaid, you see. Black Pearl is her name."

The other two men were already moving down the trail again, and neither turned back to answer him. Yambu, falling into step beside Gelimer, explained to him that Black Pearl was dead. He heard the news without any real surprise.

While the five people were descending the hill, Gelimer told his companions a more detailed story of what Cosmo had done, and what had happened to Cosmo, on that night of many killings about a month ago.

The Lady Megara listened carefully to the story of that strange visitor, his stranger death, his burial, and his bizarre second "killing" today, by the same Sword; but it was as if these events had happened to someone she did not know.

When the party had regained the riverbank, they found the boat, which Mark had feared might be gone, still waiting for them. The oarsmen, thought Zoltan, had probably not yet had quite enough time to convince themselves that they had better desert their clients and return to their own village.

Soft Ripple was nearby in the water, and swam closer to shore at once when Gelimer began to talk to her. In turn, Gelimer heard from her the details of Black Pearl's death, and saw the mermaid's body, which was still aboard the boat.

Soft Ripple listened quietly when she was told that Cosmo had been already a month dead when she had thrown the Sword at him. Her only comment was: "I wish it could have followed him into hell!"

If Lady Megara heard this, she had nothing to say in reply. She had reached a state of imperturbable calm, and the additional confirmation of her lover's death meant nothing.

Eventually Yambu asked her friends: "But who killed Cosmo? Who actually used the Sword on him the first time? He wouldn't have carried it all the way over here from the manor, simply to throw it at one of the Senones. And even if he had, why would the Senones finally decide at that point to kill Cosmo, after having ignored him all night?"

Gelimer nodded sadly. "I have thought much about those questions. And it seems to me that that sad young man must have killed himself."

"No," said Lady Megara, softly but decisively. She had, it seemed, been listening after all.

Mark scowled. "He stabbed himself in the back, with a weapon more than a meter long? That would take some doing."

"No, he did not stab himself. I think he went outside my house, where there was more room to dance and spin. And he hurled the blade, willing his own death— vengeance on himself, for the disaster he had caused that night, including his treacherous killing of the Lady Megara's father."

And Gelimer went on to expound further on the behavior of Cosmo Malolo on that last night of his life. "Things might have gone differently, had he not fallen from his riding-beast and injured his head. Or the outcome might have been the same—who can say, now?"

"I still think," said Mark, "that Cosmo's goal when he left his manor that night must have been simply to take the Sword of Vengeance out into an empty land somewhere—such as these mountains might provide—and lose it there."

"Or perhaps," said Yambu, "to kill himself with it out there, where neither his body nor the Sword might ever be discovered."

"We'll never know."

"What's that?"

Gelimer was pointing up into the sky.

The others squinted, shading their eyes against the sun and peering.

"Some truly giant bird."

"No. No, surely that's a griffin, carrying someone."

Wood was known for using griffins. And now one of the bizarre creatures, bearing on its back a single human figure, was swiftly crossing the river from north to south, heading in the direction of Malolo manor.

NINETEEN

MARK and his companions embarked again, leaving Gelimer and Lady Megara behind them on the bank. At the last moment the hermit had asked to be allowed to bury Black Pearl's body. This wish was readily granted, and the body unloaded from the boat. Zoltan made no protest; with every minute that passed, the horrible thing under the wet canvas seemed to have less and less connection with the girl he had begun to know three years ago. And in any case, he felt that duty now compelled him to go on with his uncle Mark without delay.

Lady Megara, though saying very little, had conveyed to the others that she wanted to stay with Gelimer, and to climb with him to the cemetery where Cosmo lay.

The remainder of the party got into the boat and pushed off. The prince, seated amidships, urged on his four rowers in a princely way. And those men, finding themselves now on a direct course for home, complied to the best of their ability. The boat sped downstream, headed straight for the fishing village in which Yambu and Zoltan had spent their first night in this country.

Soft Ripple, as Zoltan observed without being able to understand the fact, was still accompanying the boat. It occurred to him to wonder whether the village ahead had once been her home—and possibly Black Pearl's also.

"Are you armed?" Mark asked Yambu, when they had been under way for a minute in silence.

"Only with my wits," she answered calmly. "In this most recent epoch of my life I have forsworn the use of steel. Except of course in dire emergencies."

"Then probably you are better armed than I, my lady," Mark admitted. "Still there are times when steel has its uses."

"And such a time, you think, lies close ahead of us. I think it quite likely you are right."

Mark looked at his nephew. "If the Sword comes within reach of anyone in Malolo manor, they are likely to dispute its ownership with us. Especially if Bonar is still alive."

Zoltan nodded, and made sure that his own short sword and his knife were ready. Then he squinted ahead, looking along a western reach of river. The other boat, the one that had preceded them carrying Ben, Bonar, and Gesner, must by now be very far ahead—indeed, Zoltan, shading his eyes, was unable to see it on the river at all.

"Quite likely," said Mark, as if reading his nephew's mind, "they've already landed."

Ben, Bonar, and Gesner had indeed docked and come ashore at the fishing village. There their oarsmen had vanished at once among the huts, pausing only long enough to tie up their boat. The other inhabitants of the village, Ben noticed, were keeping out of sight also, as if perhaps they expected trouble.

Gesner, Ben, and Bonar, the latter looking around him in vague apprehension, at once started walking inland from the village, along the road that led toward Malolo manor.

Ben's presence put an obvious damper on conversation, a fact which did not bother him in the least. The three had traversed perhaps half the distance to the manor in near silence, when Gesner suddenly held up a hand, and said something to stop his companions.

Now Ben too was aware of a foretaste of magic in the air. He turned, looking high, and then he saw the rainbow flicker coming toward them.

Bonar, looking in the wrong direction, was just starting to ask a question.

Meanwhile, Chilperic and his crew of mercenaries, who had finished making their way back upstream along the southern bank, had begun to move cautiously into position for an assault. With the demon still missing—today Rabisu's absence had a kind of finality about it—Chilperic had just about abandoned the idea of attacking the manor directly, at least by daylight. Instead he hoped to be able to catch some of the enemy out in the open, or, failing that, to gain at least a good idea of the lie of the land before nightfall.

Koszalin, on Chilperic's orders, had deployed his ten men in something like a line of battle. They were combing a half-wooded area between the manor and the village. Thus Chilperic and those with him were also in position to see the Sword as it came hurtling down from the sky to land—somewhere nearby.

Chilperic cursed, knowing how difficult it was to predict, from such a brief glimpse, exactly when the Sword was going to strike its blow, what roundabout path it might follow on its way to the chosen target, or exactly who or where that target was.

Bonar was lying on his left side in the middle of the path, his arms outflung. His fingers twitched, but he was stone-dead, with Farslayer run clear through his pudgy body from front to rear. The youth had been taken unawares, cut off in mid-sentence. Actually his mouth was still open and he looked surprised. He had managed to get within a few minutes of his home before Hissarlik's dying throw reached him and struck him down.

Gesner, who had been walking close beside the youth, bent over his dead body and reached for the black hilt.

"Don't touch it, wizard."

Stopping his fingers before they reached their goal, Gesner looked over his shoulder to see Ben standing very close to him, his own utilitarian blade already drawn.

The huge man went on: "I warn you, wizard—if you really deserve that name—the Sword is mine."

Gesner, without saying anything, straightened up and moved away from his fallen leader. The magician's hands were empty—or were they? Now they appeared to be slowly curving into a gesture aimed at Ben.

Ben did not appear to be impressed. He advanced on the other man, his own drawn sword still leveled. "I've seen too much of you to have much respect for your magic at this late hour—now stand back. I mean you no harm, man."

Gesner the failed magician, now failed again, dropped his hands and stood back for the moment.

Ben had just sheathed his own sword, and started to reach for the black hilt, when Gesner's hands swept up again, and a jet of something as colorless as heat seemed to flow from his extended fingertips. Something that brought pain and tingling—

The big man had not been taken unawares, and his reaction was instantaneous and strong. He moved one long stride to Gesner, and a backhanded blow from his huge right fist knocked the small man sprawling. The slow-developing spell was broken before it could reach anything like full power.

Ben needed only a moment to twist the Sword of Vengeance free of Bonar's ribs and backbone. Then, with Farslayer in hand, he was standing over Gesner, somewhat surprised to see that the single bare-handed blow had killed him. Gesner's head was twisted to one side in a way that indicated his neck was broken, and his eyes looked unseeingly across the litter of the forest floor.

Well, no more problems there. Ben straightened up, looking about him in the scrubby forest. He had the Sword, for Mark. Now all he had to do was get away with it.

Faint noises indicated that a number of people were coming in his direction from the west. It sounded almost like an advancing line of infantry, clumsily trying to be quiet.

Ben drew his own sword again, and dropped Farslayer into the sheath at his side. While the Sword rode there it would be impossible for him to drop and lose it; and his own blade, good weapon that it was, would serve him as well in a fight. Holding it drawn and ready, he got himself moving, away from the two fallen men, and back in the general direction of the fishing village. He knew that Mark, coming after him, would probably land there first.

Back in the great room of Malolo manor, the sisters Rose and Violet had been arguing, and had at length managed to agree that they ought to order out some of their retainers to await their brother, in case he needed aid. Now a panicked servant came running into the house, saying that he had seen the mercenary force trying to encircle the manor.

Tough, fanatical Violet was stimulated by this news, and announced that she was ready to lead a motley force of servants—if she could raise one—into the field herself. Meanwhile Rose, more resigned than frightened, threw up her hands and retired to her room.

And at the same time Chilperic, Koszalin, and their men, alerted by certain sounds indicating a brief scuffle not far ahead, changed the course of their advance. Not realizing it at first, they were starting to close in on Ben.

On first sighting the huge man, they were spurred into action at the sight of the unmistakable black hilt that rode above the scabbard at his side. They were running, spreading out to encircle him, when Tigris hurtled into view, low in the sky, riding the griffin on which she had come to Senones manor.

She skimmed close above Chilperic while he ducked and yelled threats at her, then circled him and his small force higher aloft.

"Who has it now?" she shouted down to him.

"Bitch! Treacherous bitch! Where is my demon's life? What have you done with it?"

"The life of your precious demon has been ended by the Sword—as Hissarlik's was cut short, as your own life would have been, had you still been wearing Rabisu's next to your ribs. I saved you by taking it away, you fool!"

Chilperic snarled something incoherent at her.

The griffin's beating wings hurled the air of its passage into his face. Its rider turned her head and shouted down at him: "I have authority from Wood to take command here when I see fit. And I am exercising that authority now. Do you understand me?"

Meanwhile Koszalin had been standing nearby, looking keenly from one of the disputants to the other.

"Orders, sir?" he now asked of Chilperic, calmly enough.

Chilperic in rage pointed at the woman in the air. "Bring her down from that beast!" he bellowed. "Kill her, if need be!"

Koszalin shouted and gestured to his men. A ragged volley of stones and arrows combed the air around the griffin; it was hit, and perhaps hurt—Chilperic knew that the creatures were not invulnerable, though neither were they easily killed.

The rider appeared to escape injury. Spurring her flying mount into a burst of speed, Tigris escaped for the moment beyond the range of missiles.

Mark, Zoltan, and Yambu, landed at last and moving inland toward the manor, heard military-sounding voices somewhere ahead of them, and saw a griffin flying low.

After a brief conference with Mark, Yambu chose not to run into a fight, but rather to make her way around it. She would seek to reach Malolo manor and try to exert some favorable influence upon events there.

Uncle and nephew, with their weapons drawn and ready, ran on into the area where Koszalin's men had just beaten off the griffin. Mark was wielding Stonecutter—like most of the Twelve it was an impressive physical weapon, even with all magical considerations left aside.

Ben had moved a little distance toward the fishing village when he was ambushed.

Movement in a nearby thicket drew his attention and he looked closely, to behold a familiar face, altered by death. Gesner's face. Head twisted to one side, cheeks pale, eyes fixed and staring. It was a shock to see. Then the pale hands of the standing corpse curved and moved, and a wave of heat, or something akin to heat, came washing out at Ben . . .

Not to be beaten that easily, he grunted and thrust into the thicket with his sword. Gesner toppled out. Evidently there was one trick that the little wizard could do properly, and it had not worked for him.

Ben thrust again, and once more, into the body at his feet, making as sure as possible that he was going to leave Gesner dead for certain this time.

Ben had caught one glimpse of Chilperic's people already, and he was sure that they were still after him, and were likely to catch up with him again. To gain support from his friends, Ben thought he had better continue to make his way back in the direction of the river, reasoning that Mark ought soon to be approaching from that way.

If he, Ben, could establish himself near the fishing village, find a hiding place from which he could watch the path or road leading from the village to Malolo manor, he thought he would be in good shape.

He would have to be careful about his route; the open road would not do. If matters ever came to a chase in the open, he was lost; he knew he would never be able to outrun a swift pursuer. On the other hand, few if any of these ragtag mercenaries, even if they were better armed, would be anxious to challenge him one-on-one.

Yambu, meanwhile, had reached the manor, where she was recognized and admitted. Next she exchanged a few words with the sisters there, who were anxious to get her report of events on the outside.

It had proven impossible for them to get any kind of a force together to go out in aid of Bonar. All of their able-bodied servants had disappeared.

The women talked and waited. Yambu was satisfied in

her own mind that for the moment there was nothing better for her to do.

As it happened, some of Koszalin's men caught up with Ben again before Mark came into sight.

Fortunately Ben had thus far sustained no wounds. Still, he had no hope of being able to outrun the enemy, much less their missiles; the only way to protect himself from their stones and arrows was by getting deep into the densest thicket he could find, which involved doing himself some damage on thorntrees.

When his breathing had quieted somewhat, Ben was able to hear his enemies on all sides of him again. Now that he was sure they knew where he was, he gave out a loud rallying cry. He had nothing to lose now by being heard.

Ben had to call three times, before he heard a distant but very welcome answer.

Zoltan and Mark, now running forward yelling, trying to sound like a whole squad of infantry, had to drive away one or two people before they came within sight of Ben.

Ben, at the moment his friends sighted him, was engaged in a one-on-one struggle, near the edge of the thicket, with powerful Sergeant Shotoku. The sergeant, a young man looking for a challenge, was the only one of the mercenaries who had been eager to go into the tangle of thorny brush after Ben.

Resistance from two or three other mercenaries prevented Mark and Zoltan from actually reaching Ben's side, and they were still some thirty or forty meters away from his position in the thicket, and only able to catch an occasional glimpse of him.

The captain himself was coming to join this skirmish.

* * *

Several of Koszalin's men had deserted him as soon as the fighting actually started. Only five or six were still obeying his orders. But these remaining men were fighters, and they still outnumbered the opposition.

Tigris chose this moment to reenter the action, daringly hovering on her griffin.

This time she chose to approach Koszalin, arguing with him, trying to get him to ally with her instead of Chilperic. She complained that the thornbushes were protecting Ben too well from above, for her to be able to fly at him with her griffin.

"What gain is there to me, sorceress, if I do switch my allegiance to your cause?"

"Name your price, soldier, if you can get me Farslayer."

Koszalin shook his head. "I think you would not pay it."

"Between my master Wood and myself we can pay much. And we will, if you bring me the Sword."

"Yonder prince has one of the Twelve, too. What about that one instead?"

"The same pay for that. And my help to you against whatever others are here. My spells are weak, now that blades are out and blood has flowed. But this is a fighting creature that I ride."

There came another small volley of missiles aimed at the griffin, on the orders of Chilperic.

Tigris's next move was a counterattack on her former partner who was trying to kill her now. First an approach as if to parley again, then a charge, striking him down, using her griffin's powerful, lionlike forepaws as her directed weapons.

Chilperic, too crafty ever to be taken by surprise, got home on the griffin with a good swordsman's thrust in the instant before he perished.

The beast reeled in midair, and almost plunged to earth; Tigris wondered if Chilperic's own sword might have had some touch of magic in its steel, to let him strike like that at a creature of such magic.

But the griffin bore the victorious Tigris up again, just before they would have crashed into a tree. Certainly, at least, something of speed and maneuverability had been lost.

In another moment or two Tigris had to admit that the situation was worse than that. The animal was going to have to land somewhere, at least until she was able to work some of her healing arts upon it. Gently she urged it down, at the same time muttering curses upon Chilperic's magically poisoned steel.

During this part of the fighting, Mark was beset by two or three opponents, and he fell, dazed by a slung stone. One of the mercenaries closed in for the kill.

Zoltan was near his uncle, but fully occupied at the moment in his own fight, unable to come to Mark's assistance.

Ben, near the edge of the thicket thirty or forty meters distant, had just overcome Sergeant Shotoku with a stranglehold. Now Ben had to throw the Sword of Vengeance at the mercenary threatening Mark if the life of the fallen prince was to be saved.

The flying Sword skewered the mercenary and knocked him down.

Koszalin bravely charged in Mark's direction.

But not to strike the helpless prince. Instead the captain seized the Sword, wrenching it free from the torso of its latest victim. Then Koszalin ran off, dodging among bushes, to get the few moments of privacy he needed.

Tigris, still on the ground tending to her griffin, was unable to keep the captain from doing what he wanted with Farslayer in the next few moments, though she probably saw him take the Sword, and guessed, and feared what he was about to do.

Some of Koszalin's men, having overheard the lady's dazzling promise of riches and other rewards, were quite ready to dispute this point with him; and Koszalin needed to kill one of them with the Sword, never letting go of its black hilt, to make his own point perfectly clear.

Koszalin was ignoring the fact that the griffin and rider had managed to become airborne again. He was ignoring his other opponents, including some who had been his own men. All of them were coming to kill him now in an effort to get Farslayer for themselves. But they were all going to be too late. The captain spun around and chanted, and launched the Sword of Vengeance on a new mission.

The recovering Mark, and others closing in on Koszalin, were able to obtain only a brief glimpse of the Sword's trajectory on this occasion. From what they could see, the indication was that the Sword of Vengeance was departing on a very long flight, headed somewhere in the general direction of the southern horizon.

Exactly who or what had been Koszalin's target was something that no one else present then understood. If any of them had heard the captain's last shouted word, which might be assumed to be the name of his chosen victim, that name had meant nothing at all to them.

But Koszalin, dying after being cut down—too late to stop the Sword's departure—was heard by several people to mutter something about a promise at last fulfilled.

Sergeant Shotoku, having survived the stranglehold, and coming to make sure that the fight was really over, had a comment to the effect that now at last his captain would be able to sleep. And indeed there was a look of peace upon Koszalin's face.

TWENTY

THE fighting and dying in the thickets and on the hillside along the road to Malolo manor had come to an end in early afternoon. Now, just a few hours later, all was quiet in the valley of the Tungri just below the Second Cataract.

With Bonar and Gesner dead, Prince Mark and his companions had no desire to try what sort of welcome they might receive from the two sisters who still occupied the manor. Lady Yambu, coming out from that house before anyone could begin to worry about her, advised against it. So when the last live mercenary had disappeared from the scene of fighting, the four instead made their way warily back to the fishing village, with whose inhabitants they considered themselves likely to be still on good terms.

At the village they were received cautiously but without open hostility. And they found Soft Ripple there, drifting in the water beside a dock, talking to some on the land who had once been her own people. Several other mermaids were gathered not far offshore, holding position effortlessly there against the current, as if they might be waiting to hear news of the day's events.

Lady Megara was nowhere to be seen, and Zoltan

supposed it likely that she was still upstream somewhere with the hermit, perhaps beside Cosmo's grave.

Zoltan, feeling exhausted, stood on the bank, looking across the river to the north. What might be going on now over there, in and around the stronghold of the doomed and decimated Senones clan, was impossible to tell from this distance. But, to most of the people who were still alive on the south bank, that no longer mattered.

Yambu came up beside him. "If you wish," she said, "I will release you from any pledge of service you have made to me."

Zoltan picked up a pebble and threw it into the river. "Are you still going on downstream as a pilgrim, my lady?"

"I am. If I can find a way."

"Then I'll go with you, if you'll have me."

"Indeed, I'll have you with me, Zoltan, if I can."

"That's good, Lady Yambu. I feel an urge to see the place where this great river pours into the sea. Also I think my uncle will not mind my scouting the land downstream, and bringing him a report someday in Tasavalta."

It was the hour before sunset. Zoltan and Yambu, being still minded to continue their pilgrimage, were trying to negotiate a boat ride downstream in the morning, when a small winged messenger arrived, spiraling down out of the northern sky. The creature bore a communication for Mark, for it was able to recognize the prince among others, and settled on a branch beside him.

After exchanging greetings with the creature, the prince carefully lifted off the message pouch it had been carrying. He opened the pouch, and from among the few small items inside took out a rolled-up strip of thin and almost weightless paper.

Unrolling the message, Mark read the fine printing that it bore. Zoltan could see but not interpret the change in his uncle's weary face.

"From the Emperor?" asked Zoltan at last, unwilling to be patient.

"No, not this time. This is from home." The prince handed the parchment over to Ben, whose heavy-featured face remained expressionless while he studied the message.

"A day or two ago," said Mark, "being concerned about mermaids and what might be done to help them, I sent a message off to old Karel." That was the name of Tasavalta's wisest wizard, and a relative of Princess Kristin and family counselor as well. "Now Karel has replied, with commendable promptness. From what he has to say, it seems that mermaidism produced by magic ought to be a very easy thing to cure."

Ben suddenly began to read aloud: " 'Indeed', says Karel, 'the problem would seem to me to lie rather in sustaining such a spell than in curing it. Surely any wizard of even moderate competence ought to be able to effect a permanent cure in a reasonably short time.' Bah." And Ben, after passing the message on to Lady Yambu, turned his head away from the others and spat.

"Then," said Zoltan, woodenly, "Cosmo could have cured them all, permanently. If he had really been trying to do so."

"Or Megara could have," said his princely uncle. "Or any of the magicians in either clan, down through the years. At any time. If any of them had ever really tried."

No one said anything for a time.

"Where has Soft Ripple gone?" Mark asked at last. "Karel encloses in this pouch certain magical materials that he says ought to do the job quickly and easily."

But Zoltan was now looking at the note, where Karel had also written: "I should think that achieving a temporary cure would be actually harder than finding a permanent one." He crumpled up the note unconsciously, and let it fall from his hand. He wondered if Black Pearl's body was under the earth yet. He hoped it was. He wanted to think of her resting high on a hill and far from water.

"Where is Soft Ripple?" the prince repeated. "She must know about this. And these things must be given to the mermaids."

"She's there in the water," said Yambu. She sighed. "Give me the things, and I will talk to her. To all of them."

There was a distraction. Violet, the tough one of the Malolo sisters, with a very modest armed escort—actually it consisted of no more than one very nervous footman—came exploring, or perhaps wandering, down to the village from the manor to talk to the victors and to see what was going on.

Tough Violet did her best to put in a last claim for the Sword, saying that no agreement made with Bonar was any longer valid. She would not believe that the Sword of Vengeance was gone.

"Believe it or not, then," said Prince Mark. "As you choose."

Zoltan tried to imagine what the future would be like, here. Each of the two rival clans had now been reduced to a minimum of survivors. Perhaps the older sister was now going to inherit the manor after all, but perhaps she, Rose, still had no wish to own it. Perhaps there was no longer really anything to inherit.

Violet complained: "Anselm and Alicia are still alive over there. And they will still want to kill us."

To Zoltan it now seemed certain that at least one

person, on each side, was going to try to go on with the feud, as best he or she could.

Violet had plans for the future, too. She said something about young children, distant relatives now living in distant places, who could be brought here and prepared to carry on the feud when the present generation had been totally exhausted.

Zoltan did not wish to hear any more, and walked away.

People still scanned the sky from time to time, but Tigris and her griffin were no longer to be seen. They had departed shortly after Farslayer's final disappearance. Whether Wood's lovely sorceress had gone in direct pursuit of the Sword or not was hard to say, but there seemed reason to hope that she knew no more than anyone else here of its latest destination.

At dusk, Zoltan, having heard what words of comfort could be offered him by Lady Yambu and others, went to lie down in the bachelor's quarters again, where he tried to get some rest.

Soft Ripple came to visit him one more time, and this time he did not recognize her at first. She entered the building from the land side, walking on two well-formed legs and decently clad; she startled Zoltan as he lay there, half waiting for an eruption from the water that never came.

The young woman and the young man had both, in their separate ways, loved Black Pearl; and the two of them thus had something in common.

As dusk fell, Prince Mark was still sitting outside, his bandaged face lifted to scan the dimming sky, waiting for his next message from the Emperor. Nearby, Ben, his right hand near the hilt of his sword, sat slumped over, gently snoring.